The Noble Profession of Leaf Chasing

— A Novel —

Mitchell J. Rycus

iUniverse, Inc.
New York Bloomington

The Noble Profession of Leaf Chasing
A Novel

iUniverse books may be ordered through booksellers or by contacting:

iUniverse
1663 Liberty Drive
Bloomington, IN 47403
www.iuniverse.com
1-800-Authors (1-800-288-4677)

ISBN: 978-1-4401-9695-9 (pbk)
ISBN: 978-1-4401-9696-6 (ebook)

Printed in the United States of America

iUniverse rev. date: 1/14/10

In memory of my dog Sonni, the very first professional Leaf Chaser

Lovingly dedicated to my wife, Carole, who said to me one day,
"Why don't you just make it up?" … and so I did.

The author may have an idea that he can put down on paper, but it takes an editor to make it a story. I would like to acknowledge my editors Lorna Lynch and Shellie Hurrle for doing just that—taking my words and making them into an interesting and compelling story.

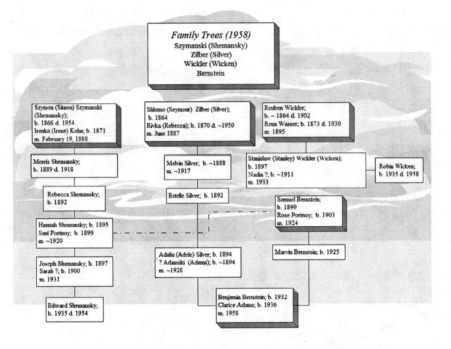

Family Trees (1958)
Szymanski (Shemansky)
Zilber (Silver)
Wickler (Wicken)
Bernstein

Szymon (Simon) Szymanski (Shemansky);
b. 1866 d. 1954
Irenka (Irene) Kohn; b. 1871
m. February 19, 1888

Shlomo (Seymour) Zilber (Silver);
b. 1864
Rivka (Rebecca); b. 1870 d. ~1950
m. June 1887

Reuben Wickler;
b. ~ 1864 d. 1902
Rena Wasser; b. 1873 d. 1930
m. 1895

Morris Shemansky;
b. 1889 d. 1918

Melvin Silver; b. ~1888
m. ~1917

Stanislaw (Stanley) Wickler (Wicken);
b. 1897
Nadia ?; b. ~1911
m. 1933

Robin Wicken;
b. 1935 d. 1958

Rebecca Shemansky;
b. 1892

Estelle Silver; b. 1892

Samuel Bernstein;
b. 1899
Rose Portnoy; b. 1903
m. 1924

Hannah Shemansky; b. 1895
Saul Portnoy; b. 1899
m. ~1920

Joseph Shemansky; b. 1897
Sarah ?; b. 1900
m. 1931

Adalia (Adele) Silver; b. 1894
? Adamski (Adams); b. ~1894
m. ~1928

Marvin Bernstein; b. 1925

Edward Shemansky;
b. 1935 d. 1954

Benjamin Bernstein; b. 1932
Clarice Adams; b. 1936
m. 1958

PROLOGUE: *Stormy*

Ben never forget how he looked when he first caught his eye—a fluffy bundle of apricot and white fur. He probably weighed less than three pounds, his little tush wouldn't stop shaking, and his stubby little tail never stopped wagging. He followed close on Ben's heels wherever Ben went, and when Ben looked at him, he'd roll over to have his belly rubbed or just sit there to have his ears and head scratched. Like the man who sold him to Ben's family, the Bernsteins, said, "It's really the puppy that chooses the family, not the other way 'round."

The Bernsteins were in the man's backyard for less than five minutes when they knew this little guy was the one. But they looked at all the other pups anyway, just to be sure the fluffy one was truly meant for them. As it turned out, it was no contest. The owner of the pups had a large hand-painted wooden sign out in the front yard: MIXED-BREED PUPS $5—so Ben's dad paid the man his asking price, and with great anticipation, and a little trepidation, they took him home.

As soon as they walked into their house, the little fluff ball ran from room to room, stumbling over his own fuzzy little paws and banging into doors and walls in all his enthusiasm.

"He's like a hurricane or a little tornado—look how he's running all over the place," Mr. Bernstein said with a big grin. The little guy was grabbing anything he could fit in his mouth and stopping to sniff everything else he couldn't carry away. Ben and his father were laughing hysterically at the puppy's antics, while Mrs. Bernstein was chasing after him with newspaper, afraid he'd poop or pee someplace.

"Let's call him Stormy 'cause he's just like a storm," Ben said. And so they did, and Ben loved him—and he loved Ben—right from the beginning.

When they got Stormy in 1947, Ben was fifteen, and it was his job to take care of him. It was right after the war, and times were getting better financially for the Bernsteins, so his parents said it would be a good idea for Ben to take on the responsibility of caring for a dog. They said it would help Ben grow up and make him more conscientious about school too. And they were right.

Ben loved Stormy more than anything in the world. Stormy was Ben's only real friend. He could tell Stormy anything he wanted, and Stormy would listen to him and then lick Ben's nose to tell him everything was all right. They spent hours together, doing homework (it was Ben's first year in Central High School), listening to the radio, and going for walks. People would remark, "What a cute dog! What kind of a dog is he? He's so friendly ... Yes, yes, little fella ..." Stormy would lick their noses, wiggle, and roll over, and the people would just love it.

"He's a mix of spitz and some other small breed. At least that's what the man who sold him to us said," Ben would answer. They would continue to rub his tummy and say how friendly and playful he was. And he was playful, if nothing else.

Stormy's favorite game was chasing the dead leaves when the wind blew stronger during the late fall and early winter. When a bunch of leaves were stirred up, Stormy stiffened up, his tail upright and ears alert, and then he chased after them. He'd get one leaf in his mouth and then go after another ... and another ... until he had to choose between the ones he had in his mouth and the one he just caught.

Ben never fully understood Stormy's selection process, but the puppy seemed to know what he was doing. Ben took great pleasure in watching Stormy's leaf chasing. He looked so serious, as if the world depended upon his capturing those dead leaves and breaking them up into smaller pieces. If the wind was light and only a couple of leaves would be blowing around, Stormy would catch one, hold on to it, and carry it back to the house; then he would try to bring it inside the house, which Mrs. Bernstein didn't allow.

Because of his job as Leaf Chaser, Stormy became Ben's philosophy teacher. As Ben watched how serious he got during his leaf-chasing activities, how he carried his small frame so gallantly erect, and how he looked so important during the pursuit, Ben couldn't help but wonder what was going through his little head while he was working. Did Stormy truly *think* that what he was doing was going to make this a better world for everyone? He certainly looked as if he did. Ben, and whoever else watched him chase leaves, could only smile and think how cute it was. But if he was as serious as Ben suspected he was, then maybe Ben shouldn't have laughed and smiled.

And then the analogy hit Ben: suppose God and his heavenly entourage of angels and other immortals were watching us while we worked away, trying to make a peaceful and a democratically organized society for the betterment of the entire world. Suppose God was saying, "Look how cute they are—they actually think that what they're doing is important!"

And the angels would all laugh, smile, and say something like, "Yes, they certainly are cute. Oh, look at those mortals over there working on something called the United Nations—isn't that a stitch?"

At fifteen, that was a rather heavy bit of philosophy for Ben, even though he had been a yeshiva *bucher*—a rabbinical student—up until he started high school that year.

Ben would then fantasize that there might be metagods watching our God and his immortals, saying the same kinds of things: "Look how cute *Hashem* is playing with his creation. He thinks they did something grand." And the metagods would laugh and smile, carrying on for those meta-metagods that might be watching them.

Living in an urban environment in those days meant that having a dog was, at best, a relatively short-term affair. If one of the various worms didn't kill him, then the traffic would. A car killed Stormy when he went chasing after a leaf shortly after Ben's sixteenth birthday in the summer of 1948. In his deepest sadness, Ben found a little comfort in the fact that Stormy died doing what he really enjoyed … his very important job—leaf chasing.

In the fall of 1954, Ben entered the University of Michigan as a freshman after completing a four-year tour of duty in the navy. It was time he started off on his own leaf-chasing career.

Part I

ONE: *In the beginning ...*
—Genesis 1:1

Professor Szymon Szymanski had just walked into the observatory to conduct some late-night observations. He was tired and concerned about the growing political unrest against the Jews in Europe at the end of the nineteenth century, so he wasn't concentrating when he entered the building.

Professor Reuben Wickler, his colleague who had earlier converted to Christianity, was there waiting for him, and he immediately pounced on him with his usual incoherent invective.

"You did it ... you did it, you and your Kabbalist sorcery. You cheater, you liar, you dirty Jew ... That's what you are, a dirty Jew!" Reuben screamed.

Szymon was not in any mood to contend with Reuben that night. He gave him a scornful look and said, "Reuben, if you weren't so insane, I would teach you a lesson for trying to besmirch my name, my work, and my heritage. Now get out of my way before I really get angry."

He was shaking as he turned around and walked out of the observatory, heading toward the Grunwaldzki Bridge. Now he was no longer in the mood for making any observations. Looking into the heavens after hearing Reuben's rants did not appeal to him. Reuben quickly caught up to him, still ranting and raving, although he sounded amazingly in control of his thoughts, even in his drunken stupor. Once again, he started hollering. "Liar! Cheat! Why don't you confess? Tell everyone the truth about your famous dissertation. Tell them how you cheated, how you lied!"

"Why do you say I'm a cheat and a liar? What are you talking about?" Szymon asked, mustering as much composure as he possibly could under the circumstances.

"You were worried about people finding you out, weren't you?" Reuben sneered. "Now I know I was right all along—you are a liar and a cheat like all the other Jews. If it weren't for *kishufim*, you would have nothing. How we Christians put up with your type I'll never understand."

Reuben continued making outrageous allegations, while Szymon tried to explain each ridiculous complaint rationally, but Reuben would have none of it. Unable to take much more of the maniacal accusations about witchcraft, Szymon continued to cross the bridge. He was no more than one hundred meters from the end, just past the middle of the bridge, when he had to ask Reuben, "And what *kishuf*—what spell—are you talking about? You keep saying *kishufim*. This completely befuddles me; in fact, you befuddle me. I don't know why I'm even bothering with you."

As Reuben continued his alcoholic rant, he frequently stumbled on his words. "Yes, and I suppose you forgot that too, or do you have another clever answer for your involvement with the Kabbalists? I know, as do—eh ... does—everyone else at Charles that last night you got your final observations. You claimed that in the old cemetery, the Maharal's dybbuk left his grave and entered you! You had everyone believing that you could bring the golem in the shul's attic back to life again. You had them terrified you were going to have the Maharal's golem kill all the Christians if they threatened you. You are an evil Kabbalist sorcerer! You are ..." Suddenly, Reuben charged at Szymon, fists raised and flailing in the air.

Szymon was so flabbergasted by what he had just heard that he simply put out his long, powerful arm and pushed the crazed Reuben Wickler to one side. Reuben ran headlong into the low railing, clearly about to go over. Szymon saw that he was about to fall and could have reached out with one arm and grabbed him, but he didn't. Szymon watched as Reuben went into the Wisla.

* * *

In 1866, in the Jewish quarter of Warsaw, Szymon Szymanski was born to a middle-class Orthodox Jewish family. At that time, the area of Europe that was enclosed by an almost circular ellipse, starting around Paris and ending in Lviv in the Ukraine, was the scientific and cultural center of the world. The area included the Austro-Hungarian Empire and most of Germany. The ellipse also included many major European cities like Leipzig, Prague, Vienna, Budapest, Kraków, Warsaw, and Bratislava. Szymon was educated in the European tradition as well as in the heder—Hebrew school—of the Orthodox Jewish community. His knowledge of science, especially astronomy, amazed his teachers, and he was encouraged to pursue an advanced education in the sciences. That was what Szymon truly wanted to do, even though his father would have preferred that he become a rabbi.

Szymon's father owned a jewelry store in Warsaw, with a large Christian clientele, and he could well afford to send Szymon to the best private academies, which is where Szymon received his early science education. After Szymon finished at European Gymnasium, an elite preparatory school, at eighteen, his father, on the advice of his teachers, was preparing to send him to Prague to study astronomy, hopefully under the famous scientist Avraham Seydler—Szymon's hero—at Charles University. But to ensure that he would still practice his orthodox religion, his father had asked Rabbi Schmuel-Mordecai ben Yitzhak—their synagogue's chief rabbi—to write a letter to Rabbi Yehuda Halevi ben Meisel at the Staronová synagogue in Prague, near Charles University, asking him to look after Szymon's religious education.

"Well, my son, you're off on an adventure," Szymon's father had said. "Hopefully, you'll learn a lot more about science, but you'll also have a good teacher in Rabbi Yehuda so listen to him and take his counsel seriously. You know we love you and wish you only the best … so write often or your mother will be crying on me. Don't make me hear your mother's tears, my son." With that bit of final advice from his father, Szymon boarded the train for Prague. He was too excited to be sad, yet a little nervous about being out there on his own.

Arriving in Prague, Szymon left the train station and caught a hansom cab to the rabbi's house in Josephov, the Jewish section of Prague. He noticed that the afternoon shadows were already lengthening as fall approached. It was a beautiful September 1884 day in Prague. The sun was shining, the sky was blue, and the temperature was in the seventies. Still, the late summer sun was not as white as a midsummer one, and the leaves on the trees looked tired and eager to change color.

The cab took Szymon to the heder in the rabbi's house at Brehva 1, near the Staronová synagogue, where he was to meet with Rabbi Yehuda.

Arriving there, Szymon was taken to the study, where Rabbi Yehuda was expecting him. The rabbi motioned for Szymon to sit down, but Szymon was anxious and immediately handed him a letter. Speaking in Yiddish, he said, "I have my letter of introduction from my rabbi in Warsaw. I know he already sent you a letter asking if you would serve as my religious advisor and counselor. Also, Rabbi, I have no place to live right now and was wondering if you could find me a place to stay while I complete my studies at the university."

Szymon spoke rapidly in a self-assured yet still youthfully stilted voice that showed intelligence and maturity—as well as a touch of self-importance. At eighteen, Szymon was a tall young man with a square face and huge arms. He was not handsome in the usual sense, but he had a gentle, sweet face; however, his beard and size made him look much older than the young schoolboy he actually was.

"Well, let us see this introduction of yours," the rabbi said, taking it from Szymon and quickly reading it. "Oh, yes, it's from my good friend Schmuel-Mordecai, and yes, a few weeks ago, I did get his letter about your coming to study in Prague. From all that I've heard about you, I was wondering why you aren't going to study at our yeshiva. I understand that you are a quick learner and a true scholar. You know, we have an arrangement with other universities and scientists here in Josephov so you can study physics and math while studying for your rabbinical certification. Do you think that would work out for you?" he asked in a gentle but anxious way, for rabbinical scholars in the sciences were getting rarer to come by. Rabbi Yehuda had hoped that his orthodox congregation would expand its worldliness, and thereby its congregation, by getting more men of science, as it had in years past, into the congregation and on the bema.

"I have honestly thought about that as an option for my life's work, but I have concluded that the amount of time—especially the amount of nighttime viewing—I would be putting into astronomical observations would not possibly allow me to prepare for two professions." Szymon was able to answer with self-confidence because he had given it some thought. Religious mysticism had occupied a significant portion of Szymon's intellectual pursuits since his bar mitzvah five years ago, and he did feel conflicted about the possibility of having to leave those studies behind.

"It appears that you have already considered my offer, even before I made it, which is good. That means that there is still the chance that we can convince you to study for two professions—if you decide later that you may want to do that." The rabbi smiled affectionately and pressed him no further. "Now come meet my family. You will have dinner here and stay with us tonight, and I will have someone escort you to Charles University tomorrow so you can get started on your program. It's not a long walk from here. I have already asked Frau Zofie Kohn if she could board you in her house at Maiselov 3, here in Josephov, and she is looking forward to having you stay with her."

They were walking into the rabbi's living quarters as he continued. "She is the widow of Reb Mirek Kohn, and she has a daughter, Irenka, who helps her out in her boardinghouse, where two other students—both Jewish, of course—are in residence. I know you'll like it there." The rabbi didn't tell him that the other two students were yeshiva *buchers*. He thought it best to let young Szymon find that out for himself because he did not want Szymon to feel that he was trying to pressure him into rabbinical studies.

* * *

Early the next day, a young yeshiva student took Szymon to the Charles University Astronomical Institute and showed him where the rector's office was located. On the way to the university, he also showed him where Frau Kohn's boardinghouse was, telling him to go there when he was finished interviewing and settled into his program. He said his luggage—both his suitcases and his toiletry bag—would be with Frau Kohn when he came back.

Szymon was pleased, even though he was still a little nervous being away from home and having to communicate in a different language. But so far, his German and Czech were going smoothly for him. As any good citizen of the Austrian Empire, Szymon spoke a number of languages, including Russian, Polish, and other Slavic languages, as well as German and English, and he was, of course, fluent in Yiddish and Hebrew. He could also read and understand Italian, Greek, and Latin, and his French and Romanian were passable, even if his heavy accent was not nearly as romantic as the French would have liked. That was quite an accomplishment for an eighteen-year-old, but not that unusual for a well-educated person born Jewish and middle-class in that part of eastern Europe.

Szymon carried his papers with him in a well-organized portfolio. He kept his correspondence with the rector, Professor Karel Prazsky of the Astronomical Institute, in his portfolio, along with his diploma from the preparatory school in Warsaw and his letters of recommendation from his instructors. He had already received confirmation of his provisional admittance, so today's meeting would hopefully be a mere formality. Szymon was hoping to get Professor Seydler as his mentor because he wanted to do his doctoral research in astronomy with Seydler as his dissertation chairman. While he waited on a bench outside the rector's office, Szymon checked and rechecked his portfolio, making sure all his papers were in order.

"Szymon Szymanski?" the rector said when he came out of his office. "Do come in, please." Szymon was scheduled to meet with the rector, Herr Doktor Professor Karel Prazsky, and be interviewed by him, but the rector had already reviewed Szymon's admission request and the requisite materials and decided he wanted to have him at Charles. His decision was more difficult than usual since Szymon was an Orthodox Jew, and the Jewish quota at Charles was almost met. Jews were probably freer to go about their business in Prague than anywhere else in Europe, but Europe was still a collection of Christian monarchies like the Austro-Hungarian Empire, and anti-Semitism still prevailed in many of the European countries. For the most part, Jews were restricted to separate enclaves or ghettos. However, in many modern cities like Prague and Kraków, Jews could live anywhere. At Charles, there was a good mix of Jewish scholars, but the administration was definitely Christian, and they only wanted Jews who were presentable—that is, Jews who looked and talked like them.

"Are you going to continue wearing that beard while studying here?" the rector asked.

Szymon had not expected that question, and he was a little taken aback by it. Even at eighteen, he was not so naive as not to know that the question was a direct affront to his religion. "If the rabbi of my congregation will permit us to shave on weekdays, I will probably shave it off; otherwise, I shall want to wear it," he answered in a respectful but forceful manner. "But it would be neat and trimmed at all times, even on the Sabbath."

The rector smiled, impressed that this young man was not cowed by him and had religious convictions that he would live by. "Fine," he said, "that sounds fair enough. We have no dress code here, or preferred manner of personal hygiene, but we do expect our faculty and students to behave and look in a manner acceptable to the social customs of the Prague scientific community; you understand that, of course." He then went on to say, "I've already reviewed your credentials, and they are outstanding, as I'm sure you know. I am indeed impressed by your language skills and your excellent mastery of modern science—in particular, the newer astronomy as opposed to the older astrology. We still teach some astrology, but it would seem that most of our younger faculty and students at the institute want only the more scientific astronomy topics, which is fine with me. Have you thought of whom you might want to be your mentor—you know about mentoring, don't you?"

"Yes, I do, and I would be very happy to have Professor Avraham Seydler mentor me through the program. I've read his papers, and I feel I would be a worthy student of his," Szymon said enthusiastically, but he stopped there, not wanting to sound too excited.

Postgraduate education was different in the nineteenth century; there weren't any standardized programs of study, but each advanced program was uniquely modeled for the student by his mentor or thesis advisor. A student could pretty much take any course that his advisor thought he should, and that he was prepared to take, while directing him along his path to graduation. As the student progressed, he did most of his work independently, working with his mentor.

"Well, that was no surprise after reading your letter of intent. It was obvious to me that you'd feel Professor Seydler would be the one best suited for you. But I'm going to take the liberty of changing that, assigning you instead to Professor Tadeas Wazewski. The reason I'm doing this is because Professor Wazewski is younger and more knowledgeable in the latest advances in the field of mathematical astronomy. Also, I think Professor Wazewski has more in common with you, and that the two of you will make a fine team."

The rector noticed that Szymon looked about ready to cry. "Now don't fret over this. I can tell you're disappointed, but give it a while, and if you don't think your mentoring is working out, come see me … and I promise we'll change it for you." And with that, he signed some papers, put Szymon's documents in a file, and handed him a note. "Here, if you go to room 2333 at the observatory in Letenské sady, you'll find Professor Wazewski. You can take the newer electric trolley over the river to the entrance of the institute's villa. Give him this note, and then the two of you should get acquainted. He'll explain how things work here, but I expect you already know all about us. Well, good luck in your studies—we expect great things from you." He stood up and extended his hand, which Szymon shook firmly, as he'd been taught, while thanking him for his time and concern with his education.

To say Szymon was disappointed would be an understatement. He had been so certain that Professor Avraham Seydler was going to be his mentor that he had already mentally laid out his entire academic plan. He wanted to cry, but he wouldn't; he was much too stoic for that. Besides, he knew that a man of his size would look like a silly fool if seen crying. So he slowly walked back to the trolley stop, took the next one over Čechův most, and got off on Quai Edvarda Benes. Szymon could not help but notice the world-famous Prague Castle as they were crossing the Vltava River. He wondered if he would be able to visit St. Vitus's Cathedral, which was on the castle compound. He could see the church towers overlooking the castle, and he'd heard that it was not to be missed. However, as an Orthodox Jew, he had never stepped foot in a Christian cathedral, and he was uncertain as to what would happen if his rabbi found out.

As he walked into the observatory on the institute's villa, he looked around a little just to get used to the facility and compose himself. He wanted to see the telescope—one of the finest, albeit an older one, in Europe—and the newer electric labs with all the latest technology in astronomy. School was not officially in session yet, so there were few students around, but those who were there were cordial and spoke to him in German when he asked for directions or for information about the equipment they used. Szymon was comfortable speaking German. He went to the second floor, where most of the offices were located along a round corridor that housed the dome. He found room 2333, with the name Professor Tadeas Wazewski painted on the door. Szymon knocked forcefully—but just twice, as he was taught—and heard a voice say, "Do come in, Szymon."

* * *

Professor Tadeas Wazewski was a young man, not yet thirty, with dark hair and deep brown eyes. He was clean-shaven and nicely dressed in a tan summer suit, white shirt, and brown tie. His hair was tousled, but Szymon soon noticed that it was that way because he frequently rubbed his hands back and forth through it as he talked or thought about something. It was a disarming gesture, and it made Szymon smile.

"So you met our rector, the very noble Herr Doktor Professor Karel Prazsky," Professor Wazewski said with mock pretension. "Actually, he's really a very nice man and not at all pompous, and he's quite intelligent. But there are times when he can appear to be a bit harsh, like I'm sure he was when he told you that I would be your mentor and not Avraham. But whether you know it or not, the entire institute's faculty, not just the rector, determines the student's mentor. The decision was not just his to make. We all had a say in it," he explained. "Now, let us get acquainted and see if it is a good idea for me to be your mentor."

The two men sat and talked for over three hours about all the new and modern mathematical theories, and how physics was leaving the old world of mechanics and coming into the newer world of electricity and magnetism. "So you've learned Maxwell's equations and know how to do matrix algebra," Tadeas said.

"Yes, we covered Maxwell's work, but I must admit that I have lots more to learn. As for mathematical methods, I've already had advanced calculus and matrices and vector spaces, but I just know how to do the various operations. I'm not fluent in the theory," Szymon said, afraid that he might be given more credit than he deserved for knowing all these advanced topics.

"Not to worry—you've got the hard part done, and from here on, I'll help you, and you'll help me as we work on getting you a doctorate ... and the two of us becoming famous astronomers!" Professor Wazewski said with an affected pumped-up chest and a broad grin. He continued a little more seriously. "I think we'll have great fun together. Look, it's getting on in the afternoon, and I'm sure you haven't eaten a thing all day. Let's stroll over to that outdoor café on the quai and grab something to eat and drink; what do you say? Oh, and by the way, please call me Theo unless we are in a formal setting. Then you should call me Professor Wazewski—yes, yes, I'm a Polish Jew like you, only with a Czech first name that I'll explain later—and I will call you Sy informally and Herr Szymanski when we are in a formal setting. Are you all right with that?"

Szymon was more than all right with it; he was thrilled with his mentor. He would be working with a fellow Jew in an egalitarian environment, and since Theo was older and wiser, then the relatively informal collegial environment would make it so much easier for Szymon to communicate and learn from his mentor.

The two young men walked out to the Café Rusin on the Quai Edvarda Benese. Their table was right on the riverfront, and they could easily see the cathedral towers from their location. They continued to talk as they ate and drank, their conversation getting more animated all the time.

"I was really hoping to do work on stellar chemical abundances using the new spectroscopes you have here in Prague," Szymon explained. "But if you feel that there is something more demanding, or more interesting to you, that I should be working on, then I'll do that too."

"Stellar spectroscopy could turn out to be very fruitful for our research since there've been so few newer instruments developed," Theo said, rubbing his hair. "You'll need more chemistry than you've had, both qualitative and quantitative analysis, and a thermodynamics course as well."

After their light meal, Theo said, "But enough academia for today; let us just enjoy this beautiful late afternoon, and when we've finished here, I'll help you move into your new quarters. Where did you say you were staying again? Oh, by the way, I was born in a shtetl to the south and east of Warsaw—Luboml, have you heard of it?—and was educated much as you were. But my mother was Czech and that's how Teodozja became Tadeas, but of course I'm Theo to all my friends."

"Yes, I think I have heard of Luboml … I know it has a large Jewish population, right?"

The small talk continued for another half an hour while they finished their wine. The two of them then walked south into Josephov and then down to Frau Kohn's on Maiselov Street.

They entered the house through the open front door, and although it appeared modest on the outside, it was quite grand on the inside. There was a large entranceway with an ornate oak staircase going up to the second floor. The front room was large and furnished in an eclectic mix of older rococo and modern neoclassical styles. There were many chairs and sofas—it appeared to be twenty or more—that could seat a rather large number of people. The parlor, they noticed, was behind a nearly closed door on the left, but they imagined it was just as uniquely furnished. The door was slightly ajar, and they could see that there was a stylish piano in the parlor, where someone looked as if she was about to start playing. From the front room, they could see the dining room, with the table set for five people, although it could easily seat ten or even more. Two doors on the left side probably led to the kitchen, where, no doubt, Frau Kohn spent much of her time.

When they walked in, talking somewhat loudly and a little tipsy from the beer and wine they'd had, Frau Kohn must have heard them, and she came out of the dining room toward the entrance to greet them.

"Hello, Szymon," she said as she approached the young bearded Szymanski. "I've been so looking forward to meeting you. And who is this gentleman you've brought with you?" she asked with an enchanting smile.

"Frau Kohn, my pleasure, I'm sure. This is Professor Tadeas Wazewski, my mentor from the Astronomical Institute of Charles University. He has offered to help me settle in today. I hope that is all right with you, of course." Szymon spoke as if he had been in the country for months instead of just one day.

"Oh, it certainly is. You are lucky, for not many students at Charles would have their mentors help them move in. Will you stay for supper, Professor Wazewski?" Her voice was delightfully melodic, and you could see that she was quite at ease having Theo there.

"I would be most honored to have supper with you and your other houseguests tonight," he said. "I made no other plans for today because I knew that Sy would be coming in, and I planned on spending the day with him, so supper here would be most welcome."

Just then, piano music drifted in from the parlor; it was a modern romantic music piece probably written by the young Czech Dvorak, but Theo could tell it was written for a lesson.

"That's my daughter, Irenka," Zofie said. "She's taking lessons, and it's her practice time. I hope it won't disturb you. She's only thirteen, but she plays like an adult. Let me show you your room, Szymon, and you can settle in. Supper will be at six thirty tonight—will that be all right with you and Professor Wazewski?"

"Please call me Theo; Professor Wazewski sounds so old, and I'm really not that old," Theo said, smiling and rubbing his hair. You could tell he was quite taken by Frau Kohn.

Frau Zofie Kohn was a delicate woman, still in her twenties, who looked like the young wife of a doctor or other professional, rather than someone who managed a residence quarters for students. Her husband, Reb Mirek Kohn, had died of a heart attack two years earlier, when he was only thirty-two years old. Reb Kohn was the only son of a wealthy banker, and he was working for his father. Everyone told Zofie to sell the house and take Irenka, who was eleven at the time, and retire to a smaller place. There was more than enough money to take care of them, and Reb Kohn's father had agreed to support them, until either Zofie remarried or Irenka left home. After that, Zofie would still have most of her inheritance and a small but comfortable pension until she died.

But Zofie refused the kind offer. She inherited the house debt free, and with her monetary inheritance, she felt she and Irenka would be fine if she could rent out two or three rooms to Jewish students either attending Rabbi Yehuda's yeshiva or Charles University. The rent money would go for a lot of the house's upkeep, which included a cook, two maids, and a part-time handyman, and all her other needs would be covered from the interest on her inheritance. But, because of the relatively high upkeep, her student boarders would have to have wealthy parents, like Szymon's, to pay the rent that Frau Kohn would be asking.

"I have two other boarders who are here from Rabbi Yehuda's yeshiva. They should be returning after *Mincha* services—they will have time to eat and then return for *Ma'ariv* services later. It still stays light out well past suppertime," she explained as they followed her upstairs to the rooms.

The upstairs living quarters were as elegantly carpeted and furnished as the downstairs. At first, it appeared that there were a large number of rooms upstairs because of the long corridor and the distance between the doors, but when Szymon mentally counted the doors, there were only seven. He surmised that three were for the boarders' rooms, one was for Frau Kohn, one for Irenka, and two were lavatories—one for the family and one for boarders. His room was the third one down and second to last on the left side. It was nicely decorated for a student, with a desk, bookcase, wardrobe, single bed, two comfortable chairs, and a divan that would seat two cozily. His suitcases were on the floor, but his clothes had been carefully removed and placed neatly in the wardrobe. His toilet bag was not opened and was left on the bed. Clean towels were also left on the bed. Frau Kohn showed him the guest lavatory, which was right next to his room, and explained how the water system for bathing, washing, and the toilet worked.

"I'm sure you are familiar with all these modern appliances," she said, "but if you need any help, just let me know." She then left the two men, saying, "I'll see you gentlemen around six thirty in the dining room. We don't dress formally for weeknight supper so please be casual."

After looking around his room and putting some of his books and writing paraphernalia in the bookcase and on the desk, and slightly rearranging the wardrobe, he sat down with Theo and quietly smiled at the comfort of it all, the location and the room. It was past five, and his window was facing west, toward the setting sun. *It's nearing the end of a perfect day,* he thought. *If life is like this while I study in Prague, then all will be marvelous.*

Szymon was somewhat surprised that since both of the other boarders were from the yeshiva, Rabbi Yehuda hadn't said anything about them. Maybe he didn't want Szymon to feel he was being pressured into studying with the rabbi. In any case, Szymon was pleased that the two rabbinical students were here because he had earnestly wanted to continue with his religious education. He was especially interested in studying Kabbalah with them since they were just beginning to cover the Kabbalah service and the *Mishnah* at his Hebrew school in Warsaw. Szymon was anxious to meet his fellow boarders because now it was with them that he planned to continue—in an independent manner— his religious studies. He knew that religious discussions went better with three participants than with only two because of the questioning process they followed in Talmudic learning.

Szymon and Theo rested in the room, reading and just relaxing for an hour or so before washing up for supper. As they went downstairs, Szymon thought of how much he looked forward to the years he would be spending here in Prague, and of the people he would be involved with. He was thrilled to be away from home, meeting with such intelligent, cultured, and well-spoken people. What a difference from how he'd first felt when finding out that Avraham Seydler wouldn't be his mentor.

TWO: *Now the Lord had said unto Abram: "Get thee out of thy country."*
—Genesis 12:1

They were all quickly introduced as they sat down to supper with Frau Kohn and her daughter, Irenka. It was still warm on that late summer evening in September of 1884, and with the windows open, they could hear the activities on the street: children playing, women gossiping, dogs barking—all good sounds of a city full of life and activity. Irenka, at thirteen, was just beginning to blossom into womanhood, and she looked as if she would be as beautiful as her mother. Frau Kohn was charming and delightful trying to entertain her boarders, be cordial to her guest, Professor Wazewski, and still be mistress of her house by overseeing the cook and serving maid.

"Do you live in Josephov with your family, Professor Wazewski?" she asked.

"No, I live by myself—I'm not married, so it's just me—in a flat near the park Letenské sady. My parents, as well as the rest of my family, still live in Luboml, in Poland. I spend most of my time at the observatory, especially on good seeing nights—that's astronomer's jargon for essentially clear nights. It's nice to be able to walk home and back as I please." Theo paused briefly and then continued. "My work keeps me very busy, as it will, I'm afraid, for our friend here, Herr Szymanski." Theo was smiling while he ate, but when he talked, he couldn't keep his hands from rubbing his hair. He also could not keep his admiration for Frau Kohn from showing through all his gestures.

Szymon broke into the conversation. "I enjoyed your piano playing today, Dívka Kohn; I hope I'll have the opportunity to hear more of it." You could tell he was just trying to make polite conversation and act more like an adult. But it was also genuine, and so it did not seem to bother Irenka, who just smiled and blushed a little at his compliment and kept on eating.

"So tell me, Reb Zlatnik, how long have you been studying with Rabbi Yehuda?" Szymon asked.

"Gabi and I both started lessons with him before our bar mitzvahs and have been doing our rabbinical studies here at the yeshiva since we were sixteen." Looking up at Szymon, he said, "I understand that you, too, were on a rabbinical track when you decided that science and astronomy were more to your calling, Herr Szymanski. Is that correct? And please call me Meir since we'll probably be seeing each other every day."

The boys all agreed that first names would be more appropriate, and so did Irenka, who didn't like the title dívka, or miss, because it sounded too patronizing. However, Frau Kohn and Professor Wazewski, both being older, continued to be addressed by their proper titles at the dinner table. The six of them sitting there chatting, at times very excitedly—about religion, science, music—looked like a typical middle-class family at supper.

* * *

Over the next two years, Szymon took the requisite courses in math, physics, astronomy, and chemistry to be able to start developing his own theories on the universe along with Theo. Stellar spectroscopy was all the rage in mathematics and astronomy since Fraunhofer's midcentury technical inventions and spectral analysis theories. Though Szymon wanted to continue with spectroscopy, Theo felt the field might be saturated by then, and nothing earthshaking could be done anymore. "All that's left are just a bunch of relatively routine and probably boring measurements to look at and analyze on some large-sized, low-magnitude stars," Theo said.

But Szymon did not believe this. "Theo, I'm telling you there is more to spectroscopy. I feel that the main problem is bad seeing—that there are not enough good seeing nights for us to truly be able to understand what it is we have seen, and how we can analyze it. We need a telescope in space, above our atmosphere ... but that isn't going to happen, so let's see what we can do from here."

Szymon was referring to the fact that the earth's atmosphere caused stars and other objects to appear to wiggle around; and the more distant and smaller, or dimmer, the bodies were, the more they wiggled. That wiggling was called *bad seeing*. *Good seeing* was when the objects wiggled less, and it usually occurred on cold, clear winter nights with no moon or other bright objects near the observed objects.

"So you still think you can do something with a grating and possibly map the heavens in ways that have never been imagined before?" Theo said. "That would be a dissertation worthy of your effort. If you come up with any ideas, let me know and I'll try my best to work with you on it, all right?"

In December of 1886, Szymon did come up with something. He found that by mounting a ten-centimeter-long-by-five-centimeter-square rectangular block of optical glass on a six-volt electric motor and rotating the glass on its long axis at about 150 revolutions per minute, the image of a wiggling star, when passed through the rotating glass, appeared to stabilize. The image wouldn't be a clear, perfect shape anymore, but it would stay steady—and that's what Szymon wanted. He called the rotating glass device a "noise suppresser" because it quieted the image down for observation. Now he could take the smallest object visible through their aging seventy-five-centimeter refractor and analyze its spectrum without having the image bouncing all over the viewing screen. Most important, he could now analyze distant galaxies and various star clusters that nobody fully understood. He couldn't wait to show Theo.

"Look, look—do you see how the image of Iota Tauri there, near M45, has stabilized? And now I'll pass it through the scope, and there's its spectrogram!" Szymon was talking about a five-magnitude star in the constellation Taurus, near the Pleiades. He was beaming, especially when he watched how Theo was just incredulous at the projected image. "Look how clearly we can distinguish the red shift when all the various series of absorption lines are lined up with that shift. Isn't that grand? Did you ever think you would see that type of imagery from such a dim star?"

"My God," Theo gasped. "That is truly unbelievable! With that kind of imagery obtainable, even on bad seeing nights we should be able to discern star patterns that have never been known before—we can ..." Theo paused. "No ... *you* can develop a whole new theory of cosmological dynamics, and *that* would be some dissertation. Now get started—and let me know what you need and where I can help."

Szymon was so excited by Theo's reaction that he could not stop giggling like a schoolboy for a long time. The two scientists talked on for another two or three hours, true colleagues now—no longer as student and mentor.

* * *

A lot had happened since Szymon arrived in Prague a little over two years earlier. Theo had courted and married the widow Kohn and was now living in the same house at Maisclov 3 with Szymon, while Szymon and Irenka, who was now fifteen and a full-grown woman, were definitely becoming interested in each other.

It was time for Irenka to be considering marriage, and Szymon knew that he too would someday wed ... and why shouldn't it be Irenka? She was intelligent, gifted, and beautiful to look at. In some ways, she was like a little sister to Szymon, and in other ways, she was his passionate tormentor. Hormones and youth can be extremely confusing, and Szymon, who was barely twenty years old, had both in abundance. A little comment from Irenka on how Szymon looked, or how his words fascinated her, could make his stomach tingle in ways he never fully understood or had felt before.

Szymon had shaved off his beard a year earlier as Rabbi Yehuda's congregation became a larger mixture of orthodox and other more liberal congregants. The rabbi had no problem with shaved faces as long as the men didn't shave on Shabbos. Szymon wore his beard for that first year, and without making an issue of it, he just shaved it off one day.

Of the two yeshiva *buchers*—who were also still living in the boardinghouse—Meir shaved his beard, while Gabi left his intact.

Both Szymon and Meir looked significantly younger than Gabi, who, with his full black beard, appeared to be the old man of the group.

Irenka was so surprised and pleased the first time she saw Szymon without his beard. "Sy, you've shaved your beard off! You look so much younger now," she said, beaming. "And you look so much closer to boys my age than you did with that old man's hairy face. I really like it ..."

Szymon was thrilled but tried not to show it. "Well, yes, yes ...," he stammered, a little shaken by her initial reaction. "It's much more in keeping with these modern times, you know. Most of the faculty shaves, and I thought ... Well, I thought that maybe I should be more like them. I mean, look more like them ... Well, you know what I mean ..."

And that was the start of their romance. He taught her math and science, and she taught him about the arts and music.

When she asked him about his work, he tried to explain. "In doing spectroscopic analysis, the researcher—that's me—has to hold the observed object steady in the instrument's aperture—that's a narrow slit. From the slit, the image passes through a prism and other optics, and then it's projected on a viewing screen, where I can analyze it." He watched her expression. She seemed to be interested, so he continued. "When seeing is bad, the image can't be analyzed. Stellar spectroscopy works best with larger, bright objects during times of good seeing. The final analysis can tell me what the physical makeup, or chemical abundances, of the objects are. I know that the temperature of the object and relative speed and distance of the object from the observer can also be calculated using Fraunhofer's newer diffraction grating rather than a prism, but this is just a theory and still needs to be demonstrated."

With that last statement Szymon knew he lost her. "Szymon, you're so smart; I can listen to you all day, but it's time for my practice. Come sit with me," Irenka said, and the two went into the parlor.

Szymon and Irenka became inseparable, always involved in deep conversations or just sitting quietly together while Szymon worked on his dissertation or when Irenka was reading. They went on picnics and other outings with some of Szymon's fellow students, and on many warm evenings, they would be alone, locked in romantic bliss as they discovered love and each other under starry skies. That thrill of a kiss, and then a deeper one as lightly clothed bodies rubbed together, was a ritual they looked forward to every chance they got. But because of their sense of morality, or their youth, they never went any further than heavy petting and kissing.

* * *

But the heavenly feelings of romance and courting soon dulled due to the rigors of academia. The next year, 1887, was the most brutal year of Szymon's young life. He and Theo had published a couple of short papers on their work; actually, the papers were teasers in order to feel out the scientific community on how their analyses might play out. The response was amazing:

> *Wazewski and Szymanski's two papers on cosmological dynamics would have us believe that their results were based mostly on observations of magnitude-six and higher objects, and that they had made many of these observations in a few short months. I don't challenge them on this, but I also do not think it is humanly possible to have gotten that many observations of such large-magnitude objects over such a short time, much of which was not in winter, using only the physical equipment at Charles.*

An eminent scholar had written that critique in a prestigious journal. The larger the magnitude of a stellar object, the dimmer it appeared to the naked eye. In fact, a magnitude-six object was about the dimmest object one could see unaided. But nobody challenged the resultant theory that they laid out about the cosmos, just the accuracy of their data.

They had not divulged Szymon's noise suppresser but merely indicated that a "device" had been utilized to help stabilize the images. Most of the responses were about the device, asking how it was constructed, and what the theory behind its operation was. Theo was a little taken aback by all the fuss, but it was clear that until Szymon could defend his dissertation, they had to buy time to let him develop his theory in greater depth. As much as Theo wanted to tell everyone about Szymon's instrument, he knew that once everyone had a noise suppresser (they were remarkably easy to make), the resultant observations from all the senior astronomers in the field could easily cloud Szymon's originality, which might make it impossible for him to defend his research.

"Sy, you'd better get started writing as soon as you can. The longer you wait, the more likely your noise suppresser will be discovered, and the field will be overwhelmed with contrasting or similar theories," he said, rubbing his hair furiously. "You only have this fall and the early winter period to do it all … and still have time left to transfer over to Jagiellonian University in Kraków for your defense next year. Do you think you can do that?"

"I'll just have to," Sy said. But a chill ran down his spine as he thought about all the work he had done up to now possibly going up in smoke.

Szymon was transferring to Jagiellonian University for two reasons. In those days, defending one's dissertation was truly a public affair, and if you were well known, many people would show up and have the right to question you on your work. The process could take hours and create difficulties for the examining committee in deciding on a favorable judgment. Szymon and his work were well known by now, and there would be many people coming to his dissertation defense to hassle him. The second reason was that Theo had arranged for Szymon to get an appointment as a junior faculty member at Jagiellonian University, starting in 1889. The transfer would give him a good opportunity to learn about Jagiellonian before joining the faculty.

Over the next few months, Szymon had to write up his theories in a clear, concise, mathematically logical, and validated format. Getting those theories in place would be the most tedious part, and then validating his results with his new observations would be the next hardest task. In addition, there was all the paperwork and preparation for going to Kraków.

Szymon and Irenka would also be getting married before leaving for Kraków, and the wedding arrangements frequently became a diversion, taking time away from his work. Irenka was driving him crazy with talk about her dress, whom to invite (his parents were coming down from Warsaw), and all the horrors and terrors that young women suffer when they are about to wed. The young man, barely out of his teens, also had to decide if he was more inclined toward the newer, more liberal model of Judaism than the traditional orthodox doctrine that he was raised in. This decision was important because it would determine which synagogue he and his family would become members of.

No wonder Szymon had chills running down his back.

* * *

The weather in Prague was exceptionally mild during the fall of 1887. It had stayed unusually warm into November, so most people celebrated the good weather and hoped it would last forever. But Szymon needed to make more observations, and good seeing would help considerably. It was true that his noise suppresser would help him, but only to a point. If the seeing was terrible—if the sky was cloudy or hazy, along with a turbulent atmosphere—even the reduced noise wouldn't help much. Bad seeing was disconcerting enough for Szymon, but he was also involved with Meir and Gabi in heavy discussions about mysticism. Meir was leaning toward the liberal movement, while Gabi, a traditionalist, remained strictly orthodox.

On one warm late October evening, the three of them were out in the yard, discussing religion. "As a scientist, I just find it hard to believe that we as a rational people could still believe in things like the golem," Szymon said. "Tell me why it's not just a silly myth, as are so many of the stories in the Torah." It was interesting that Szymon referred to himself as a scientist already, even though he hadn't finished his degree. Some may think it was a bit arrogant on Szymon's part, but those who knew Szymon knew it was just his way of expressing his scientific passion.

"The Torah is not mythology," Gabi said emphatically. "Those stories and events are true. All the rabbis and scholars—and many were scientists, I might add—have historically supported their validity."

"No, they haven't," Meir said. "The scholars frequently pointed out that many of the stories in the Torah, as elaborated on in the *Mishnah* and the *Zohar*, were parables, or metaphors. Like the golem, which is a metaphor for an army. Since the Diaspora, we Jews never had an army, so the golem was more or less our army. It was supposedly created out of clay, like my childhood toy soldiers, and it did only what it was told to do, which, for the most part, was kill enemies. And if the golem's creator wasn't careful, it would kill him. What better definition of an army is there?"

Gabi replied, "Then why do they say Rabbi Judah Loew—one of our shul's founders and a scientist who worked with Johannes Kepler and Tycho Brahe here in Prague—created a golem almost three hundred years ago? I've been told that it's still up in the shul's *genizah* with other sacred objects and holy books waiting to be buried." Gabi was looking right at Szymon when he mentioned Kepler and Brahe.

"Because we need the goyim to believe the golem is real—he's our army!" Meir said. "If they remain afraid of him, then maybe they won't bother us as much as they have over the last two thousand years. It's as simple as that."

"Are you saying that the mysticism we get from the Kabbalah is simply metaphor? Or made up to scare the goyim into leaving us alone?" Szymon asked Meir with some incredulity. "Well, then, what metaphor, or symbol, does a dybbuk respond to?"

"There's nothing to explain," Meir said. "All religions and even paganisms have some creature or nonliving spirit in their folklore. Call it a ghost, a specter, or lost soul—whatever is needed for them to believe that something like a life after death exists; otherwise what's life all about? Why do we bother to suffer if there is no 'heavenly reward,' as the Christians would say? The dybbuk in Kabbalah mysticism is simply just that, but notice that the dybbuk is never a good spirit ... only a bad one. That's to discourage suicide, lest you want to come back as a dybbuk."

"They're not always the spirits of suicide victims," Gabi interjected. "They could be from anyone whose life was not fulfilled, even Rabbi Judah Loew the Maharal. He was said to have died too young—when he was eighty-four years old—and had lots left to do here on Earth before *Hashem* took him. But I do agree on that one: a dybbuk is not unique to Jewish tradition."

"Enough of this," Szymon said. "I have too many other things to worry about now. Whether I remain an Orthodox Jew or move on to a more liberal Jewish congregation will have to wait. Ask Rabbi Yehuda if he will take us up to the *genizah* in the attic to see the golem, then maybe my decision will not be so hard," Szymon joked.

"You're like so many other supposedly educated rational people who say they must see the face of *Hashem* before they'll believe he's there," Gabi said gravely. "Well, my Polish cousin, I'm afraid that's not going to happen in your lifetime, no matter how much science you throw at it. The scientific method may be your method of inquiry for seeking truth, but my method of inquiry is based on faith."

"I must admit that at times my newer liberal viewpoint does not always get me to where Gabi is, but I still think it's the way to go," Meir said, a tender smile on his face for his old friend and colleague.

Szymon noticed for the first time that it appeared that the two lifelong friends were drifting apart; he could imagine that in a few years, each would be teaching his own brand of Judaism in heders and yeshivas somewhere else in Europe, or even the rest of the world. He wondered if he would run across them where he was going, and what form his own religious pursuits might take. But that was something else to worry about later. Right now, he had to finish his dissertation, and that meant getting observations.

* * *

It was now mid-December, and Szymon still did not have all his observations for validating his theory. He waited until around eleven o'clock on the night of Wednesday, December 14, before going up to Letenské sady for his scheduled time on the telescope. It had finally become colder, and that night looked like it might be a good one for getting his last observations.

He had been working on the theoretical elements of his dissertation, and one element—a lemma that he had postulated for one of his three theorems—was causing him trouble. The lemma was an integral part of this third theorem, which dealt with star clusters, and it was presented more as a conjecture. He had roughed out a possible proof for it, but he wasn't totally comfortable with the way it was written. He knew it was right, but he hadn't teased it out to a point where he felt others might be comfortable with it, and he still wasn't quite sure how to prove it himself.

He felt a little feverish and was not paying attention as he walked north to the bridge. It was less than a kilometer to the observatory, and as he walked up Maiselov from the boardinghouse, he passed the

Staronová synagogue on Cervena. There were no lights on at the yeshiva. It was very cold now—below freezing—and everyone had gone to bed to keep warm for the night. Szymon came to the end of Maiselov, and instead of going right on Brehova, he unintentionally turned left.

The main reason for his mistake was that the wind coming down from the north had picked up over the Vltava River, and a mist had developed because the water was still quite warm. The wind intensified, and the mist turned into a snow squall—that small hard snow that stings when it hits your face.

All of a sudden, he realized he was next to the old cemetery, which was so full of graves that it had been closed for almost a hundred years. He knew that Rabbi Loew the Maharal was buried there, and as he became aware of where he was, an off-season flash of lightning lit up the cemetery. He could see the outlines of gravestones and was certain that someone, or something, was moving in there. When the thunder hit, it almost shook him out of his boots. Something strange had happened: his skin crawled and he felt his hair standing on end. He was both freezing cold and feverishly hot at the same time, and the sky had never looked blacker. For a second or an hour—he knew not which—he stood locked in that spot. He then quickly ran up Listopadu to Parizska, then over Čechův most to the observatory.

It was only a little after eleven at night, which surprised Szymon, when he stumbled into the telescope users' waiting room and rechecked his scheduled time. He had the scope from eleven fifteen until four fifteen in the morning to do his work; five hours should be more than enough. "Is Ludwik still using the scope?" he asked one of the other graduate students.

"Yes, but he should be out soon. He knew you were coming," the grad student said. "Here, Szymon, sit and warm up for a while. It's really cold in there today. You look like you've been up for days. Are you all right?"

"Did you see that unusual lightning strike a little while ago?" Szymon sat down and loosened his outer coat and boots. "And thunder … wow! I thought the sky was falling," Szymon remarked in mock fright.

"I didn't see any lightning, but the wind did pick up a little while ago, and the temperature dropped dramatically," his fellow grad student said. "It should be good seeing tonight for your final observations. Boy, is your face ever red; are you sure you're not sick?"

Szymon felt as if he were on fire. He was dizzy and knew something was wrong, but no matter what, he was determined to finish his observations that night.

When Ludwik came out a little before eleven fifteen, he saw Szymon sitting there. "Hey, Sy, it's all yours if you want it now—I'm through. It's still a little rough seeing out there, but it should quiet down in an hour or so. Hope you have good seeing. Is your equipment ready or do you need help?"

"Thanks, Ludy," Szymon said to his fellow Pole, "but I think I can manage to be set up in an hour or so."

"You don't look good, Sy," Ludwik said with some concern. Grad students, especially doctoral students, form a tight bond. They usually help one another because they all know how much suffering they have to go through during the entire painful process. "Are you sure you don't want me to hang around and help out tonight? I know how important this is for you."

"Thanks, my friend, but this should be easy tonight. You're right. I don't feel 100 percent, but I'm sure it's just a cold, or maybe total exhaustion," Szymon joked. "In any case, I'm almost done, God willing, and I feel well enough to get it done tonight."

Szymon went into the unheated workroom under the dome and started setting up his noise suppresser and the spectroscope, and then he adjusted the sidereal mounting of the seventy-five-centimeter refractor for the right coordinates he needed for his last observations—a magnitude-eight star in Orion the Hunter. He was working with stars in Orion, hunting for data to fit his theory, and hoping his own hunter's skill would find the stars to help finalize his theoretical validation. *How fitting*, Szymon thought.

Later in the month, when Szymon was reducing the new data he'd gathered on that cold night in December, everything started to fall into place. It was as if someone had taken over his pen and was writing for him. The model became so clear in his mind, and the data was so relevant to the theory, that his dissertation seemed to write itself. For a while, Szymon actually thought that someone had taken over his soul … but how could that be?

* * *

By late January of 1888, Szymon felt he had a good solid draft of his dissertation and enough data to validate his basic hypothesis. He had developed three new theorems—one was jointly developed by him and Theo, but the other two were strictly his. These theorems led to a new model of cosmological dynamics that could predict the relative location of all stellar objects over time, with respect to each other, and could possibly explain the origins of the universe. It was a historic and heroic piece of work. He had over fifty pages of data generated from his model, and when he compared it with actual observations, he found that the observed and theoretical data matched well within the expected error. Szymon was feeling good. He was finally over the flu, or whatever it was he'd caught in early December, and he was strong enough to start helping Irenka and Zofie with the wedding plans for next month.

"So what do you think, Theo?" Szymon asked his stepfather-in-law to be. "Is it enough for my doctorate, or do I have to do more?"

"Remember, Gauss's dissertation was only six pages long—but then again, you're not Gauss," Theo teased. "Don't worry so much; it's a fine dissertation."

* * *

Szymon and Irenka's wedding went off like clockwork on Sunday, February 19, 1888. His parents and an aunt and uncle came in from Warsaw, and the few relatives Zofie still had in Prague were also there. There were also many of Szymon and Theo's friends from the university and the yeshiva. On that bright, sunny, and relatively warm day, Rabbi Yehuda performed the service in the parlor of Zofie's house. Early the next morning, the honeymooners would leave by train to Vienna.

They had known each other for almost four years by then, and living in the same house, they were comfortable with each other's company. But aside from some heavy petting when no one was looking, or those late evening outings, they didn't have any intense sexual experiences together. But during the cold night of their wedding—the last night Irenka would sleep in her mother's house—the young couple, snuggling in bed together to stay warm, did briefly and excitedly finally attempt that most intimate process. The experiment ended in partial failure:

Szymon was finished in a matter of seconds, and poor Irenka was left feeling frustrated and inadequate. After a while, they good-naturedly promised each other that in Vienna they would practice everything until they got it right.

They spent two wonderful weeks in Vienna, going to operas, shows, museums, marvelous dinners—and learning how to make love properly. Irenka was a little homesick a couple of the days, but she pulled through like a seasoned traveler. They were not planning to return to Prague but were going straight on to Kraków on Sunday, March 4. All the arrangements in Kraków had been completed, including an apartment for them at 110 Jakuba Street Kazimierz District, right across the street from the Remuh Shul on Szeroka Street. Their old friend Rabbi Yehuda had written to Rabbi Mojzesz ben Yisrael Zalman of the Remuh Shul and asked him to find an apartment in Kazimierz for the newlyweds.

"I understand that Jews are now free to live anywhere in the city," Szymon told Irenka on the train to Kraków. "I heard that many Jewish families were leaving Kazimierz and becoming assimilated with the Christians. But I'll be more comfortable with other Jewish families."

The predominately Jewish Kazimierz District was going through a cultural and social change as more middle-class Jews left the community and poorer non-Jewish immigrants from eastern Europe moved in. The Kazimierz district, like Josephov, was close to the university's observatory; at less than two kilometers, it was still basically within walking distance, and Szymon was pleased at the convenience of having his work so close to his home, just as he had in Prague.

Relieved of the tensions associated with getting married, and the fact that his dissertation was now done, all Szymon needed to accomplish was his oral defense for the final validation for all his hard work. Szymon still felt stressed and somewhat incomplete as they left Vienna for his native country. He seemed melancholy on the train ride to Kraków, but Irenka tried cheering him up, telling him, "Smile, my sweet husband—we are starting a new life, and for me, I'm going to a new country. Don't spoil it by being moody now."

Szymon did smile, but somehow he couldn't lose that feeling of insecurity he got when he thought about leaving Charles University; all his friends and colleagues; and especially his two religious mentors, Meir and Gabi. For some reason, he felt that he may never get over this loss. But he hoped that someday he might return to beautiful Prague and settle down where he felt safe: in Frau Kohn's—now Frau Wazewski's—house.

THREE: *Thou shalt not commit adultery.*
—Exodus 20:14

When they arrived in Kraków on that Sunday evening after a five-hour train ride from Vienna, they were immediately impressed by the streets all lit up with gaslights. They had gaslights in Prague, but Kraków's lights were older, more ornate, and closer together, making the streets appear brighter. With centralized electricity and modern sewerage, Kraków was truly an advanced city.

Szymon and Irenka had most of their belongings sent ahead and stored in their apartment. However, Szymon carried enough copies of his dissertation for his entire committee with him at all times like any good doctoral candidate would. He also left copies in Prague and a copy with his parents in Warsaw—the typical paranoid behavior of a doctoral student about to defend his thesis.

Rabbi Mojzesz had asked a young couple from the congregation to set a fire in the fireplace for them and wait there to greet them. The couple also prepared a small supper for the Szymanskis because it was still winter, and with snow on the ground, they knew it would be difficult for them to find a place to eat when they arrived. Reb Shlomo ben Yitzhak Zilber and his wife, Rivka, opened the door for them when the cab arrived. After some brief introductions and a quick tour of the modest apartment, they sat down for a supper of pickled fish, potatoes, beans, and a tomato salad washed down with hot Russian tea. The salad was a real treat for that time of year.

"So how long have you two been married?" Szymon asked, happy to be speaking Polish again.

"Only eight months—we were married last June," Shlomo said. "I'm still working on my doctorate in mathematics at Jagiellonian University, but I hope to be done by next year. I understand that you will be teaching here next year after you defend your thesis and complete a postdoc. We've heard all about your work in cosmology, and I would love to see your equations of motion for the entire universe." Shlomo spoke with great enthusiasm.

"I will be delighted to share my work with you," Szymon said, pleased to find a kindred spirit.

Rivka was less than three months pregnant with their first child, and they were extremely excited to share the news with somebody. The Zilbers lived only a few doors down, and it looked like they would become good neighbors and fast friends, with the Zilbers helping the Szymanskis blend into a Jewish congregation at the shul and the academic community at the university.

* * *

In May of 1888, Theo took the overnight train from Prague to Kraków to cochair Szymon's defense. Herr Doktor Professor Paul von Stoepel was Theo's friend in the Physics, Astronomy, and Mathematics Department at Jagiellonian University, and he agreed to cochair Szymon's dissertation with Theo.

The room was packed with graduate students, faculty, townspeople, and even Rabbi Mojzesz and Szymon's new friend and neighbor Reb Zilber. Szymon was feeling anxious but sure of himself when he made the obligatory twenty-minute opening presentation summarizing his work. He stated his findings, discussing what was unique about his model as opposed to similar representations of celestial mechanics.

As is the custom, the committee went first, asking Szymon specific questions about certain areas of the dissertation: "Why couldn't you use previously gathered data to test your theory?" "What impact do you see your theories having on new research?" "Have you patented your famous noise suppresser?"

Szymon answered all the questions without any hesitation and with the self-confidence of a seasoned scholar, until Professor Stoepel asked, "Herr Szymanski, can you show me how the lemma you state on page ... uh ... where is that ... page sixty-six? Yes, page sixty-six ... that lemma, equation thirty-seven ... yes, yes ... tell me, why is that so important to your overall results?"

Szymon felt sweat under his arms and on his forehead. He was never thrilled with his proof, but he was sure the lemma was correct. He always wondered why, during the writing up of his dissertation, that mystical feeling of clarity he sensed for everything else was not forthcoming for his proof of that damn lemma.

"Yes, Professor Stoepel, that lemma is needed for me to prove my third theorem, which, along with theorems one and two, forms the basis for my model." Szymon had answered truthfully but skirted the proof issue. The committee asked no further questions about the lemma. Szymon felt some relief that maybe they accepted it as a conjecture.

Then the rest joined in on the fun. "Szymon, will your new theory prove or disprove God's design for the universe?" a theologian asked.

"My model has nothing to do with religion," Szymon responded politely. "It merely explains, or rather describes, how celestial bodies move around. It doesn't at all deal with how they got there or who put them there." He knew that anytime new astronomical theories came out, Jewish and Christian theologians worried that their teachings of God's creation would come under question. So Szymon was careful not to sound too pedantic or all-knowing.

"How far into space could you see more clearly with your noise suppresser?" a doctoral student that Szymon had met recently, and become friends with, asked.

"Well, we don't really see any clearer with it so much as we see the image steadier, making it easier for us to analyze its state," Szymon replied. "As for how far away we can see, it's more a matter of how far into the past we're looking. When examining celestial objects, we know we are looking into the past since it takes time for the light of the object to reach us. Fizeau had shown—almost fifty years ago—that light travels at around three hundred thousand kilometers per second. Given the distances of some of the dim objects that we have analyzed, the light we were actually observing had left them literally millions of years ago."

"Did you see the beginning of time? What did it look like?" his friend good-naturedly asked with a broad smile.

"I'm not sure I saw the beginning of time, but if I had, the one good thing about it is that I wouldn't have had to look at your homely face," Szymon retorted with a big grin. The crowd laughed, and the light-hearted atmosphere was enough to allow the committee to close the questioning period. The good-natured chiding was all part of the pageant. It was, as they usually are, set up by a fellow graduate student, and indicated to the committee that the serious questions had been posed and answered. It also signaled that it was time to stop the public questioning and finish the process.

The committee adjourned to a small anteroom to deliberate, and Szymon felt good about it; his anxiety had waned, and he was sure he had passed. His friends, colleagues, and acquaintances got up and wandered over to congratulate him. Their joking and upbeat conversation continued for a while, until they noticed that some time had passed since the committee adjourned. Many people left, and only his close associates and some other faculty remained.

The room was quiet when the committee returned, looking a little grave. Szymon's heart began to pound as Theo read from a prepared statement. "The dissertation committee of Herr Szymon Szymanski has concluded the following after hearing his oral defense: One, the dissertation is thorough enough to cover the topic. Two, the dissertation demonstrates knowledge of previous work on the topic. Three, the dissertation demonstrates new and original research that leads to new and demonstrable results. Four, however, the committee feels that a part of his research—as described below—is inadequate and needs further development before his degree can be granted."

Theo took a deep breath and then said more informally, "Szymon, I suspect you might have guessed what it is we need from you. We need a better proof of that lemma on page sixty-six. The committee agrees that it probably can be done in a few short months. We suggest that you spend your postdoc here, resolving that issue. Also, they feel there is no need for them to meet again, and upon the satisfactory completion of your proof to Professor Stoepel, he will simply sign off for the entire committee, and your degree will be awarded."

Although Szymon was disappointed, he understood the issue and would have done the same in their shoes. He also knew that with time to do nothing but work on the proof, he would get it done. The committee congratulated him and talked about how they looked forward to him teaching next January. They said they enjoyed his presentation and repartee with the questioners, showing courtesy and respect when called for, and good humor and wit when it was appropriate. There were handshakes all around as the committee left. Then only Theo, Professor Stoepel, and Szymon remained in the room.

Professor Stoepel, who was responsible for the final decision, said, "Szymon, I have no doubt that you could deliver a better proof than the hand waving you had written in your dissertation. I, as well as you, realize the importance of that lemma and its need for your theorem to be valid, so we don't want anything left undone that might cloud your marvelous work."

There were no hard feelings; the prevalent attitude was simply *Let's get the job done so we can all be proud of this achievement.*

There was a party at Szymon's apartment afterward, with much celebration. Theo told Szymon, "Well, it's all over now … except for that little polishing up. You have nothing else to do—no more data gathering, no more looking for distant stars—so just work on your proof. And the best part is that you'll be paid for it!" He raised his glass. "So let's enjoy the party tonight. I have to take the train back tomorrow, but I leave you in good hands with Paul, who has promised to look after you and see that you do finish." Theo spoke in a calm, relaxed way that let Szymon finally start coming down from his all-time high and just dwell on his future as a teacher, scholar, husband, congregant, and who knows, maybe even a father someday.

* * *

Szymon finished the proof of his lemma by the middle of the summer, and Professor Stoepel was more than pleased. "Now that's what I consider a sophisticated proof. You know, Szymon, that lemma could almost be a standalone theorem in its own right. But enough—let's move on. So, what are your summer plans?"

"Irenka and I were hoping to travel a little before the fall term to visit with our relatives. I'll start teaching my own new courses in

January, so I'll have the entire fall term to develop them. And I would like to sit in on some of the other advanced classes that I feel I should also be familiar with. What do you think, Professor?"

"Please call me Paul now. After all, we are colleagues; once I sign this document and send it in, you should be called Doktor Szymanski, so start getting used to that," Paul teased. "Yes, I think it's a good plan. Knowing what your colleagues teach is important for two reasons: you won't duplicate their efforts in your teaching, and you'll see who you might want to collaborate with on future research."

After a summer of traveling and relaxing with friends and relatives, Szymon—now Doktor Szymon Szymanski—sat in on some of his colleagues' courses that fall. They were the more advanced courses that would follow the basic courses that Szymon would be teaching. Also, watching the senior faculty teach gave Szymon more insight into how he might want to design and teach his courses. He did not find anyone in particular that he would like to collaborate with on research, so he continued developing his own research agenda. However, he did share his work with his friend and neighbor, Shlomo Zilber, who later became his colleague in the department.

In January 1889, Szymon started his teaching career at Jagiellonian, teaching undergraduate math and physics courses and one graduate seminar on cosmological dynamics. Zilber finished his degree that year and was given a teaching position in the applied math program starting in 1890.

* * *

Over the next ten years or so, Shlomo and Szymon would collaborate on many papers and research projects, as well as share a number of graduate students that they jointly mentored. Shlomo was Szymon's most prodigious colleague. Separately, the two were like two good musicians, but when they played together, they became one great performer.

Szymon's religious training at Frau Kohn's boardinghouse was based on questioning, and he transferred that process over easily to cosmology, always asking *why*? On the other hand, Shlomo's ability to follow up by mathematically demonstrating what it was that Szymon was asking was brilliant, and the two of them worked amazingly well together. Shlomo loved his role as Szymon's mathematician, and when the two of them worked on a project—developing some new theory or correcting an old one, often without sleep or food—it was magical to watch them. Szymon wrote the music, but Shlomo wrote the words, and the two prospered greatly from their collaboration.

The combination of Szymanski and Zilber as authors, coauthors, or collaborators with other well-known scientists at Jagiellonian dominated the astrophysical and applied math journals of the day.

"Does anybody else at Jagiellonian do any publishing?" someone asked them at a physics conference at the University of Leipzig. "All I see are your two names in the literature. Are the two of you trying to take Leibniz's place?" he said, making a joke about Gottfried Leibniz, the famous seventeenth-century German scientist, mathematician, and philosopher.

"No, no, no … many of our colleagues are as productive as we are. It's just that our work is about cosmology—something everyone is in love with now," Szymon said.

"Yes, who knows what other fad the public may grab onto next?" Shlomo added in his self-deprecating way. "You know, this new genre of literature called 'scientific romance' has captured the public's imagination. That Frenchman Jules Verne has noticeably impacted that genre, and that's probably what's driving all the interest."

Their work was known all over the world, but Szymon's work in astronomy, especially after the publication of his dissertation, was groundbreaking, and he became an icon in the field of astral spectroscopy.

During the 1890s—with the advent of larger telescopes, especially the large reflectors, and advancing photochemical technology in general—astrophysical research became ubiquitous at all institutions of higher learning. The refinement of spectroscopic analyses using much more sophisticated noise averagers than Szymon's original noise suppresser certainly helped in the advancement of new technology. Szymon's theoretical model was now referred to as Szymanski's law of cosmological motion, or simply the Szymanski model.

The two friends and colleagues not only worked together, but they also attended shul together with their families. The Zilber and Szymanski families had grown by three children each; Mordechai ben

Shlomo Zilber was born in the fall of 1888. Estella came along in 1892, and Adalia was the last, born in 1894. Rivka had problems giving birth and would have no more children after Adalia. Szymon and Irenka were just as prolific. Moishe ben Shimon Szymanski was born in 1889, followed by Rivka—named after Irenka's aunt—in 1892. Channa—a lovely, well-behaved child—was born in 1895.

Both families had drifted from the orthodox congregation toward the so-called "reformed" congregation at the Remuh Shul, which was under the leadership of Rabbi Mojzesz. Even more liberal reformed congregations were growing in the city proper. They called them temples; and the services were not conducted in the traditional ancient Hebrew, but in Polish or German. These synagogues were built for those Jews who had left the Kazimierz District and wanted to be assimilated into the larger Polish community, but who still felt the need to be identified as Jews.

"I'm all for reform," Szymon said. "But not wearing a yarmulke or tallis at services would make me feel very uncomfortable." Shlomo felt the same way about not wearing a head covering or not wearing his nice blue and white silk Ashkenazi tallis. Breaking that tradition was definitely out of the question. "These customs have been followed by Jewish men at prayer for centuries, and I feel that it would be totally disrespectful to my forefathers to disregard them now," Szymon told Shlomo.

"You're right, and I'm not about to give up my traditions either. I feel it is imperative that I let non-Jews know who we are, and how much we respect our heritage," Shlomo answered with feeling and a sense of awe for his own passion, even though he was not as religious as Szymon, nor as learned in Judaism.

* * *

The Szymanski and Zilber families became so close that they moved in together—into a large, two-story house at Jakuba 3 in 1895. They thought that their families were finished growing by then, so they had the house divided into two separate living spaces. The new house was even closer to the shul, and they could still get to it easily by walking through the old graveyard.

As for getting to work, it was only a walk of a kilometer and a half to the research observatory on Barska, crossing over the Grunwaldzki Bridge. The university's main optical observatory was on the edge of the city on Orla Street, but Szymon did most of his research at the spectroscopic lab on Barska. He spent most of his teaching time at the university's facility on Krupnicza, where Shlomo also spent the major portion of his time. It was so much like Prague—living in a Jewish district, crossing a bridge over a river into the city, and entering the observatory—that Szymon had to remark once, "My working life has not seemed to change since I was eighteen years old."

Well-known in the astrophysical community, Szymon was always asked to be a panel moderator or session leader for the many professional organizations he belonged to. He was expected to attend every conference related to his work. He was also expected to present a publishable paper, or other research-related project that he and his students might be working on. That included math conferences with Shlomo, as well as physics conferences with other colleagues. But he attended most astronomical conferences by himself.

All that travel, research, and preparation during the school year had made his home life less than ideal. His children were growing up, and he was missing the opportunity to spend more time with them. His oldest child, Moishe, was eight years old and enrolled in both a heder and a traditional European school. Rivka, at five, was just starting school, and Channa, who was only two, was more than a handful for Irenka.

All three children seemed to have violated Mendel's laws of genetics. It appeared that all three of them inherited Szymon's large, square frame and masculine face. On the other hand, they all inherited their mother's sensitivity for the arts. Szymon's son, Moishe, was not really interested in science (other than photochemistry) or math but was drawn more to music and the graphic arts. And although he was a good student, he was definitely not the star that Szymon had hoped for. Irenka loved her kids and cherished their artistic sensitivity, but she was disappointed for Szymon that none of them would follow his lead in the sciences.

But the most disturbing aspect of their lifestyle for Irenka was the fact that Szymon was always too busy, too tired, or just not interested (or rarely interested) in having sex with her. She knew that she had changed. Her figure was not as svelte as it was when they were first married, and her soft, clear complexion had suffered as well in Kraków's urban-industrial environment. Her skin was darker and slightly blemished now. But she did miss the camaraderie and touching, if not the physical act of sex itself.

* * *

In mid-March of 1897, Szymon was attending an astrophysical conference in Prague. He had left on Monday; it was now Wednesday, and Szymon was due to return the next day, Thursday, March 18. Irenka was up later than usual for a winter day. The weather had turned mild, and she wanted to make sure the house was in order when Szymon returned the next day. After cleaning up the place and bathing the children and then herself, she put on her nightclothes and was quietly reading in the kitchen at around ten thirty that night.

At the same time, Shlomo was coming home from a long and tedious faculty meeting that he had to chair. As he approached the house at 3 Jakuba Street, he couldn't help but notice that while his side of the house was dark, a light was on in the Szymanskis' kitchen. He had told Rivka not to wait up for him because it would be a long meeting, and he wouldn't be home until well after ten. He also knew that Rivka wouldn't wait up for him anyway—she was always in bed before Shlomo, pretending to be fast asleep when he came to bed, no matter how early or late it was.

Shlomo started to enter his side of the house, but something told him to see if everything was all right at the Szymanskis', as he knew that Szymon was away at a conference. He quietly knocked on the side door, which was near the kitchen, and Irenka came to investigate.

Opening the door she said, "Shlomo, is that you?" She recognized his distinct figure even in the poor visibility on the side porch.

"Yes, it's just me," Shlomo replied. "I saw your light and was wondering if everything is all right. I know Szymon's not due back till tomorrow, so I was a little concerned. Is everything all right?"

Even though Irenka was only wearing her nightgown, albeit a winter one, she wasn't really embarrassed. The two families had been living so close for the last two years, like one big family, and Shlomo had seen her in worse.

"Quick, come in before the neighbors start to wonder what's happening out here," Irenka told Shlomo.

As Shlomo came into the house, the light in the kitchen illuminated Irenka so that the outline of her naked body could easily be seen through her gown. As she turned and walked to the kitchen, her still very attractive silhouette made Shlomo's desire for her painfully obvious. He felt that tingle in his stomach that he hadn't felt in years; and when she brushed by him, the light touch of her body almost made him dizzy. He knew this shouldn't be happening, and he knew he should leave immediately … but he also knew that he was not going to leave.

"What keeps you out so late tonight, Shlomo?" Irenka asked.

Shlomo sat down at the kitchen table and said, maybe a little too dramatically, "Oh, those damn long faculty meetings—they drive me crazy!"

Irenka just smiled, took his hand, and asked, "Would you like some tea, my poor overworked and under-appreciated Shlomo?"

Her touch, her softness, and even her silly teasing drove him incoherent with desire. "Tea is good," he mumbled. "I would prefer some stronger stuff … uh … you know, maybe schnapps or whatever."

"Shlomo, you hardly ever drink—why now?" Irenka asked with a little concern, but she was still smiling, detecting his sexual discomfort, and she too was getting a little excited. Men hadn't paid her much attention recently, and she was enjoying flirting with Shlomo. "Does my nightgown bother you? If so, I'll be glad to change into something that would make you more comfortable," she teased.

That's all it took for Shlomo to simply take her and firmly put her on his lap, where she felt that marvelous erection she had noticed earlier. They were both excited now, and Shlomo, making sure there was no real resistance, pulled her to him and kissed her fervently. He held her on his lap, rubbing her back from her shoulders down to the top of her buttocks. Then he lowered his head and kissed her breasts through her nightclothes. She held his head tight against her breasts, whispering, "Shlomo, Shlomo … you know we shouldn't be doing this. Why are we doing this?" And then she moaned deeply, "Oh my God."

Irenka slowly got up, took Shlomo's hand, and led him into the living room, where the two of them fell into one of the deep, soft couches. There in the dark, with the only light coming in from the kitchen, the two of them undressed and made love as if it were the first time for either of them.

For Shlomo, it had been a long time because Rivka had stopped having sex with him shortly after their third child was born. Shlomo kept busy with work, and Rivka had the kids and her social life. He had always been a little attracted to Irenka, and she'd felt the same for him.

They lay together now, talking and comparing notes about each other's partners. Shlomo explained why he and Rivka didn't have sex anymore. "She's literally terrified of becoming pregnant again. I've told her there are things we can do to prevent it, but she doesn't seem to want to try them."

"You know, it's much the same with me and Szymon—he's always so busy now that we never have time to make love." She then added coquettishly, "Also, Shlomo, I've always thought you were just a little too handsome to ignore." She never raised the issue about becoming pregnant, but now the thought began to bother her.

Even though each of them felt it was primarily his or her spouse's fault that their encounter occurred, they agreed that it would never happen again. They kissed, embraced, and had sex one more time before getting dressed. It was well after eleven—they had talked and made love for over an hour—when Shlomo went through the kitchen doorway to his half of the house and crawled into bed with Rivka, who was sound asleep.

Irenka stayed downstairs for a while longer, cleaning Shlomo from her body and straightening up the living room. When she went up to bed, Irenka felt quite contented with herself, but she still had a little longing for more romance. She did feel a little guilty, but that feeling of guilt actually soon turned into a feeling of desire for making love to Shlomo again. She was sorry now that she promised not to make love with him again, but then again, that could change if need be … or so she thought.

* * *

When Szymon came back Thursday afternoon, he had no plans to go to work on Friday. He was relaxed and pleased about the way the conference went and how well his paper, coauthored with one of his students, was received. Irenka was all happiness and joy, and she had prepared a marvelous dinner, even though they would have a big Shabbos dinner Friday evening. She was so pleased at how relaxed he was that she went out of her way to please him, make him comfortable, and make herself desirable. They went to bed early that night, and with surprisingly little encouragement, Szymon was more than receptive to having sex. They even engaged in some foreplay. She rubbed his penis while Szymon played gently with her breasts.

Szymon was careful to make certain that he completely satisfied his wife before letting himself go. He was a little surprised at how quickly Irenka became aroused, and how quickly she climaxed—twice, then three, then four, and finally a fifth time. With such a love-thirsty wife, it was most rewarding for Szymon to reach a climax himself.

When they lay there cooling off, Szymon said, "We have to do this more often," and he giggled like a schoolboy. Irenka had a little smile, almost a smirk, on her face as she agreed with him, for little did he know what, or rather *whom*, she was thinking about the whole time they were having sex.

It didn't take long for Irenka to figure out that those two nights of blissful sex had caused her to become pregnant again ... only whose child was it? Realistically, there would be no way she'd ever know—both men had the same color hair and eyes; Szymon was a large man, but Shlomo was more delicate, like Irenka. No matter what Irenka might imagine, she would always have to assume that Szymon—who would love, feed, clothe, and care for the child—was the biological father.

Later that year, on a snowy Tuesday, almost exactly nine months later, on December 14, 1897, Jozef was born. They had to expand the Szymanski side of the house to accommodate the new arrival. It was hard to tell at birth, but it would appear over time that he inherited his mother's delicate good looks; and later they would find that he had inherited his father's math and science capabilities. Finally, Szymon had a son that would follow his vocation and go on to be an even greater scientist and mathematician than he himself was.

* * *

By the turn of the century, the two Polish academics had seven children between them—three Zilbers and four Szymanskis. Szymon's youngest, Jozef, was the last one born in his family, whereas Shlomo's youngest, Adalia, had been born three years earlier, in 1894. Irenka and Shlomo never did get together again, but their lives did seem to improve, not because of their affair but in spite of it. That is, until another faculty member got involved with Szymon and changed his life as no one could ever have predicted.

FOUR: *Thou shalt not kill.*
—Exodus 20:13

Reuben Wickler received his undergraduate education in Luboml, Poland, at the Humboldt Gymnasium. He was not an outstanding student, but he did well enough to get a recommendation from his teacher in 1891 to attend the Astronomical Institute at Charles University in Prague to study cosmology. He was good with numbers and enjoyed observing the night sky; and although he attended a heder as a boy, neither he nor his family was particularly religious.

He had heard of Professor Tadeas Wazewski, who was also originally from Luboml. However, Reuben thought that Tadeas was a Czech, because of his first name, and he considered him lower class and maybe someone he could push around a little. From the time he arrived in Prague, he had heard about Szymon Szymanski and his famous cosmological model, and he knew that Wazewski had been his mentor.

When he met with the rector for the first time, Reuben, in his typical acquiescent manner, told him, "I would very much like to have Professor Tadeas Wazewski for my mentor if that is at all possible." Theo was mentoring a large number of students at that time, and the faculty decided that Wickler would be a little too much for Theo to handle, so they assigned Reuben to someone else. Wickler always felt slighted by not getting Theo as his mentor, not knowing that the faculty as a whole made the decision, and, as a result, he held much disdain for Theo and his star pupil, Szymanski.

Reuben's personality was dark, to put it mildly. He hardly smiled, complained about the evils of the world all the time, and anytime something happened to him, it was always somebody else's fault. The word paranoid would describe him well. He was an unfriendly-looking man, rather slightly built, with a pale face and thin eyebrows. In addition, his facial features were asymmetrical. He was not at all pleasant to look at. He walked hunched over, as if he had carried a sack on his back for twenty years. He had few friends and kept pretty much to himself.

In 1895, Reuben's parents hired the services of a *shadchan*—a marriage broker—who arranged a wedding with Wickler and a nice girl from the community. Rena Wasser was not well educated, was a little on the chunky side, and had a poor complexion; but Reuben's parents accepted her, and they were pleased that their son finally had someone, even though she came from a poor family and had no dowry.

Now, God willing, maybe I'll have grandchildren, his mother thought to herself optimistically. *And now maybe my son will find some peace from all his troubles,* she added to her thoughts, but not with any great conviction.

After his marriage to Rena, Reuben persevered at Charles University, and he received his doctorate in astrophysics in 1896.

Reuben and Rena Wickler had their only child in 1897, a son they named Stanislaw. He was born shortly after the family arrived in Kraków, where Wickler would be teaching in the same department, at Jagiellonian, as Szymanski and Zilber. In 1900, when he moved his family from the Kazimierz District to a nice middle-class apartment on Krupnicza Street, near the main university campus, Wickler became an assimilated Jew. Stanislaw had just turned three years old when they moved out of the Jewish neighborhood. The move made it easier for Reuben to walk to campus, or so he said, but he didn't want to be identified with the Jewish population of Kazimierz anymore.

He taught his required courses in an uninspired fashion; and for his research, he observed the spectrograms of star clusters, hoping to develop a theory of what star clusters consisted of and what their cosmological origins might be. However, as far as star clusters, he never had any underlying hypothesis that he wanted to test. As a result, his research had no direction. To say he was mediocre would be a compliment.

But he minded his own business, raised little notice, and occasionally published a paper on stellar clusters, mostly pointing out recent new discoveries and getting them cataloged.

* * *

"Nice article in the *Journal of Astrophysical Research*, Reuben," Szymon said to Wickler one morning. "Maybe we should get together sometime and talk about collaborating on something; what do you think?" Szymon was just trying to be collegial since he knew that nobody bothered with the poor guy, and he felt rather sorry for him.

"Yes, yes, uh … maybe we should do that," Wickler responded. "But, uh … let's wait a bit. I'm busy myself right now. I'll let you know," he added.

Szymon intimidated him, for he was afraid that he might not be able to live up to the kind of work that Szymon Szymanski was known for. Besides, he was sure that if he collaborated with Szymon, Szymon would get all the credit, no matter how much work Reuben had done. He remembered reading an early copy of Szymon's dissertation at Charles and finding some parts of his theoretical framework hard to agree with anyway, so delay was best for now.

Wickler joined a reformed temple in the city, but because he felt so distant from Judaism in any form, he hardly ever attended services. He later found a small Catholic church—the Church of St. Jadwiga—whose priest was delighted that he had come to him for lessons in Catholicism, with the intent of conversion. After the requisite waiting time, completion of his lessons, and passing his test on the catechism, Professor Reuben Wickler was admitted into the Catholic religion and allowed to take communion.

His wife and son, who were reluctant to convert, were there for his first communion, and they were pleased with the ceremony because it made Reuben appear important. They watched Reuben approach the altar and kneel down in front of the railing with the few others receiving the Eucharist that Sunday. They watched as the priest placed the wafer in his mouth and then held the cup for him to sip the wine.

With hands clasped in prayer, Reuben returned to his pew.

* * *

In the fall of 1902, Reuben Wickler appeared to be losing his grip on reality. He came to work in messy clothes that had not been properly attended to. His hair was unkempt and long, and there was a look in his eyes that scared many of his colleagues. His students were complaining that he was mumbling a lot in class, and he seemed outraged by some outside influence. They claimed that he was not being responsive to their needs—he was not showing up for office hours, and he failed to give clear homework instructions. Many asked for transfers to other classes or simply dropped his courses. In addition, he stopped going to the observatory, and his scheduled observation times remained unused.

Professor Paul Stoepel was the rector now, and he felt that something had to be done, but he was at a loss. There was no precedent for removing faculty who were deemed mentally unfit, especially if they became senior faculty. Fortunately for the institution, Wickler had only been at Charles five years, and he was not yet eligible to be a member of the senior faculty. In order to avoid a serious scandal yet be totally fair to Wickler, Paul—knowing that Szymon had already approached him with an offer of collaboration—asked Szymon if he could possibly intervene. He asked Szymon if he could find out what was going on with Wickler before they took any rash and irrevocable action against him.

On a rainy fall day late in October, Wickler showed up at the observatory because he'd received a note from Szymon, asking to meet with him.

"Reuben, how are you on this damp, rainy day?" Szymon inquired. "We haven't seen you around much, and we were worried. If you're running out of research, then how about if you and I discuss some joint projects together?" Szymon was solicitous, but he kept his voice low and even so as not to upset Reuben.

"I'm fine, Szymanski," Reuben responded, but not very convincingly. "Actually, I'm having some … eh, problems. My son started in the parochial school at our church, and the children are giving him a terrible time. They know we're converts, and their teasing him about his Jewish ancestry has completely upset him, which in turn upset my wife even more." Reuben was half mumbling, half talking to the ceiling. It was obvious that he was highly distressed. He was shaking his head slowly back and forth when he continued. "My wife wants to return to Luboml and take our son with her. She wants to put him in a heder, but I'm totally opposed to it. We left the synagogue to make it easier for us to live in Poland and Europe. Why would we want to go back now?" he asked vaguely. "As for you, Szymon, why should you be so concerned? You're a large part of my problem as well."

Szymon was caught completely off guard. "I'm sorry you feel that way, Reuben, but why do you think I'm part of your problem? What have I done to you that would cause you to feel that I'm responsible for your family's current situation?"

Wickler then went on a long tirade about all the Jewish scientists at Charles. "Don't you see that they distrust you and the others? Don't you see that they are trying to make my life miserable because of you? Yet you and your friend Zilber continue to attend that shul that practices Kabbalah and sorcery and other *kishufim*. They know about it, and they want it stopped." (The "they" Reuben was talking about were the Christians.)

"And they blame me for your stubbornness … and for you not converting to the true God." Wickler went on and on about how Orthodox, and even reformed, Judaism was an anathema for him and his fellow Christians. "You don't believe that Christ is God's son; would it be so hard for you to accept that simple fact? My life, my family's life, your life, and all our lives would be so much easier if you would simply accept Christ as the *Meshiach*, as it was forecast in the Torah. Then we all could live in relative harmony."

The total naïveté and irrationality in Reuben's tirade completely bewildered Szymon, leading him to believe that Wickler was indeed losing his mind. "Reuben, I'm sorry for your family but also for you. I think you have a more serious problem than just trying to decide if your son should attend a heder. Let's talk again when we both have more time, all right?" Szymon then walked away before he got any angrier.

The next day, Szymon related his conversation to Paul. "I think he's sick—maybe he should be given a leave of absence to take care of his family's problems. I don't know if that would end it, but it might get him out of here, which would not be a bad thing."

"I don't know," Paul said. "A leave of absence would require a request on his part, stating a reason for the leave, where he would go, and how it would enhance his chances of promotion. From what you say, I don't think he'll do it, but I'll try."

He didn't hold out much hope that Reuben would apply for a leave, and even if he did, Paul wasn't sure he could get the administration to go along with it. Reuben was not a stellar candidate, and in all likelihood, he would not be recommended for promotion to the senior faculty next year anyway. Later that week, Paul asked one of his colleagues at the School of Homeopathic Medicine if paranoia was a disease or a personality disorder; and if it was a disease, was it curable? Paul was not encouraged by his colleague's answer—that they really didn't know at that time.

* * *

Reuben's behavior was getting more bizarre, and by the end of October, most of the faculty and all his students had noticed it. He had been relieved of his teaching duties so he could put together a request for a leave of absence. Paul had talked with him and suggested that it was the only way for him to have any hope of getting a promotion, so Reuben grudgingly agreed.

Reuben was furious at Szymon because he felt Szymon had betrayed him by telling Paul about their conversation. Every time he was at the observatory, he made some cruel remark about Szymon, ranting to anyone who would listen. "He thinks he's so good ... so smart; he thinks he's a king. But wait. They'll find out he cheated on his dissertation. They'll find out about his *kishufim*—the evil sorcery that he practiced in Prague. They'll find out ..."

In the meantime, his appearance deteriorated even further—he often came in unshaven with long, unwashed hair and obviously dirty clothes—and he began to drink to the point where at times he was noticeably impaired.

They learned from his priest that his wife and son had left him, returning to Luboml to live with his wife's parents. Rena made sure she kept enough documents and a ledger with many misspelled words in it about Reuben's behavior and his conversion to Catholicism. She did this so it would be easier for her father to ask the rabbi for a *get*—a Jewish divorce—from Reuben. Women had a much harder time obtaining a *get* than did men, but Rena's father was a good person and a respected member of the congregation, so it was granted. But the rabbi and her father knew she would probably never marry again, and she would likely have to live in her parents' house the rest of her life. Her son, Stanislaw, was enrolled in the rabbi's heder and soon became just one of the gang—a much better situation than he had had in Kraków.

* * *

Without his family, Wickler's only ties to sanity were removed, and his mental health diminished rapidly. He drank excessively while he tried to console himself with his hatred for Szymon. On a clear, cold night in November, Reuben was haranguing Szymon in the observatory users' room. Szymon didn't even have his coat off when Reuben started in. "You did it … you and your **Kabbalist** sorcery," he spewed. "You cheater, you liar, you dirty Jew … That's what you are, a dirty Jew, and if it wasn't for you, my wife and son would still be here. I've lost them because of you, and now I'm losing my job because of you!"

Szymon had come to the observatory to make some comparative observations and had scheduled the late period after midnight to get his data. He knew it would be good seeing because it was exceptionally clear and cold that day.

Szymon had no patience today for Reuben's outbursts and his continuing harassment in front of the staff, students, and faculty present at the observatory. Even though everyone knew that Reuben was crazy, they never fully understood why Reuben blamed it all on Szymon. Szymon was just not in any mood to contend with Reuben that night, so after giving him a scornful look, he said loudly for all to hear, "Reuben, if you weren't so insane, I would teach you a lesson for trying to besmirch my name, my work, and my heritage. Now get out of my way before I really get angry."

His anger was making him shake visibly, so Szymon simply turned around and walked out of the observatory. He was glad that he would have to walk the one and a half kilometers to his house, for it would give his temper a chance to cool down. The air was clear, and it felt good to breathe it. Then he heard Reuben behind him. The city was quiet that night, with no noticeable foot traffic or any vehicles in sight.

As was usual on such nights, everyone went to bed early to keep warm. With the exception of the gas street lamps and the occasional harsh glow of the newer electric lamps, there were few lights visible on the streets. The smell of sulfur from the coal-burning stoves hung in the air.

* * *

Szymon saw no one out on Barska Street as he walked briskly toward the Grunwaldzki Bridge over the Wilsa River. Reuben quickly caught up to him, still ranting and raving. "Liar! Cheat! Why don't you confess? Tell everyone the truth about your famous dissertation. Tell them how you cheated, how you lied!"

As they both entered the bridge from the west side and started to cross, Szymon again accused him of insanity and urged him to seek help. Then Szymon said, as if he were talking with someone normal, "Why do you say I'm a cheat and a liar? What are you talking about?"

"I read your dissertation at Charles … and that lemma you used to prove one of your theorems. It's … it's garbage. It's no proof at all. And without a solid proof, you have no dissertation. How did you get it by them?" he asked, his manner suggesting that he had memorized what he was going to say.

"What copy of my dissertation did you read? I redid that section with a full and complete proof. Paul sent copies to the entire committee. You must have seen one of the early versions." Szymon was amazed that Reuben had looked at his dissertation and actually spent time checking all his work.

"Yes, you're acting like you were expecting to have to answer that question some day, and so you prepared just such an excuse. Well, I don't believe you. And your famous noise suppresser—where is it? How come Roethke is given the credit for inventing it and owns the patent?" Reuben pressed. "If you did it, why is there no mention of it anywhere in the literature?"

"I gave my design to Roethke, and he improved on it and patented it. He even fully credits my design in his patent application. I didn't want to patent it; my early papers with Theo created such a buzz that I just decided to let anyone have the design and validate my observations.

You should understand that." Szymon was almost pleading with the man.

"Ha! Another well-thought-out answer that would be hard to disprove. You were worried about people finding you out, weren't you?" Reuben sneered. "Now I know I was right all along—you are a liar and a cheat like all the other Jews. If it wasn't for *kishufim*, you would have nothing. How we Christians put up with your type I'll never understand."

Szymon could not take much more of these maniacal accusations about witchcraft, and he continued to cross the bridge. He was no more than one hundred meters from the end, just past the middle of the bridge, when he had to ask Reuben, "And what *kishuf*—what *spell*—are you talking about? You keep saying *kishufim*. This completely befuddles me; in fact, you befuddle me. I don't know why I'm even bothering with you."

"Yes, and I suppose you forgot that too, or do you have another clever answer for your involvement with the Kabbalists? I know, as do—eh ... does—everyone else at Charles that last night you got your final observations. You claimed that in the old cemetery, the Maharal's dybbuk left his grave and entered you! You had everyone believing that you could bring the golem in the shul's attic back to life again. You had them terrified you were going to have the Maharal's golem kill all the Christians if they threatened you. You are an evil Kabbalist sorcerer! You are ..." And with that last rant, the distraught little man charged at Szymon, fists raised and flailing in the air.

Szymon was so flabbergasted by what he had just heard that he simply put out his long, powerful arm and pushed the crazed Reuben Wickler to one side. Reuben ran headlong into the low railing, clearly about to go over. Szymon saw that he was about to fall and could have reached out with one arm and grabbed him, but he didn't.

Instead, Szymon watched with complete detachment as Reuben went slowly over the railing and into the Wisla. Knowing he probably could have grabbed him before he fell in, Szymon was a little relieved when he saw that Reuben was alive and waving his arms as he came through on the other side of the bridge. He thought how the cold water—cold but not lethally frigid yet—would sober him up and make him come to his senses, if he had any left at all.

Szymon continued home as if hypnotized. He was so taken aback by what Reuben had said that he felt dazed. He was trying to recall that night ... He remembered joking about the lightning and thunder, and he might have said something about being by the cemetery when it struck. Could that story have gotten out and become the myth that Reuben just cited? Or maybe it was about how, afterward, he was able to see his dissertation so clearly that he thought some spirit—some angel—had entered his body and helped him get through all the details.

As he crisscrossed through the tiny streets and alleys on the way home, he thought about getting help for Reuben. He wondered whom he would ask at this time of night. Finally, he realized that maybe it was best just to let Reuben fend for himself. The water would sober him up, and he'd come out of it a little saner, or at least a little cleaner.

The house was dark when he got home at one in the morning. He looked over at the Remuh Synagogue and the old cemetery across from his house. He stared for some time before going inside and getting into bed with Irenka. He never told her about what happened that night.

* * *

Two days later, on Thursday, November 27, Szymon was doing some paperwork at home when he heard a knock on the door.

"Come in," Szymon answered automatically. "The door is open."

Again Szymon heard the knock, so he got up, walked over to the door, and opened it. Just as he was about to chastise the person for not coming in, he saw two uniformed police officers. "Yes, may I help you?" Szymon said somewhat sheepishly. Uniformed police knocking on the door of a Jewish house was not a good sign.

"Herr Doktor Professor Szymanski?" one of them asked.

"Yes, I'm Professor Szymanski," Szymon said, repeating, "Can I help you?" He was a little surer of himself now since they knew who he was, knew his title, and were showing the proper respect for his position.

"We would like to talk to you concerning your colleague Herr Doktor Professor Reuben Wickler," said the first one, who was probably the senior officer. "This morning we found his body about five kilometers downriver from here, in a marsh off of Niepolomska, and we are inquiring about how it came to be there. May we come in?"

A chill came over Szymon. "Oh, yes ... of course. Please do come in," Szymon said. "You completely surprised me. You say Reuben's dead? But how could that be? I just saw him two days ago," Szymon offered without being asked. Szymon led them into the tidy parlor where he had his office. He had a small coal-burning stove in there, and he had started a fire since the cold air that arrived on Tuesday had remained in Kraków. "Yes, yes ... please sit over here ..."

The events of that previous Tuesday night came into his head all at once—going to the observatory, arguing with Reuben, leaving the observatory in anger, the incident on the bridge when Reuben fell in. "How did he die?" Szymon asked.

"We think he drowned, but the coroner will have to confirm that. In the meantime, we have to consider it a suspicious death. We've talked to some of your colleagues at the Kraków Observatory of the Jagiellonian University, and they say you saw Professor Wickler two days ago. From what we have deduced so far, it would seem that you were the last person to have seen him alive." The talkative officer pulled out a small notebook and a pencil and continued talking. "Remember, of course, our investigation is just starting, so there could have been others who saw him after you. We would like you to tell us what you and he discussed Tuesday night. If you would prefer, we can go to the station and discuss it there."

"No, no ... we can talk here—I would prefer to talk here in my house. You'll have to excuse me. It's not every day that one learns that his colleague is dead and may have been murdered," Szymon said carefully, trying to collect his thoughts.

"We never said he was murdered, only that his death was suspicious. Why do you think he was murdered?" the senior officer asked.

Szymon felt that chill again. "I thought when you said his death was suspicious that you were implying someone, or, uh, something killed him." Szymon thought he must keep his mouth shut, answer only what he was asked, and make certain his story was consistent and as truthful as possible. He also realized that the part about Reuben starting to attack him, and then tripping into the river, must not be told, for that would certainly initiate an inquest into murder.

"Yes, of course. Well then, would you please relate to me all the events of that night up until the time you last saw Professor Wickler?" the officer asked.

Szymon told the entire story of Wickler—how he was apparently going crazy, how he came in drunk and ranting, and how he kept verbally attacking Szymon. Szymon also related the abusive nature of his attacks on Tuesday ... and how he, Szymon, left the observatory just to avoid any more abuse.

At this point, the story veered from the truth. "Shortly after I left the observatory ..." Szymon was talking very slowly and deliberately now, for he knew he had to remember exactly what he said and never change it, "... Professor Wickler apparently followed me out, and at the foot of the Grunwaldzki Bridge, he started screaming at me once again. I just ignored him and continued to cross the bridge until I didn't hear him anymore." Szymon stopped there, waiting for the officer to visualize the scene.

"He did not follow you across, or onto, the bridge?"

"No ... at least I don't think so," Szymon replied. "I never looked back, even after I couldn't hear him anymore."

"And what time would you say that was, Professor Szymanski?"

"I'm not sure—I know I was at the observatory until a little before midnight, so I'm guessing it was maybe twelve thirty or so in the morning," Szymon responded, trying to think hard about the actual time but leaving some wiggle room for error, just in case he needed it later. The two officers compared their notebooks and mumbled under their breath to each other; they were probably comparing their notes from their other interviews.

They both stood up abruptly, put their notebooks away, and the senior officer said, "Thank you very much for your time and cooperation with our investigation, Herr Doktor Professor. We will keep your rector notified of our progress, and he, in turn, will notify you of our findings. We can find our way out, thank you, and good afternoon."

When they left, Szymon sat there for a while, trying hard to remember exactly what he had said. He was angry with himself for not telling the whole truth, but he knew that if he had, there would have to be an inquest. And since Reuben was now a Catholic, the event would be considered one of a Jew possibly murdering a Christian. Historically, that kind of incident never worked out well for the Jew.

Irenka came downstairs with Jozef, who, at five, only went to school in the mornings. "Who were those men in uniform I saw through the window, and why were they here?" she asked.

Szymon told her the entire story—that is, the story he told the police—but not the true story of how Reuben Wickler ended up in the Wisla River.

* * *

The death, or murder, of Reuben Wickler was the only topic of conversation the next few weeks before the Christmas holiday at the university. It was on everyone's mind, but it was on Szymon's mind the most. He was getting a little paranoid.

"Why are they looking at me that way?" he asked Shlomo one day. "Do they think I murdered him?" Students and faculty alike were talking about the events of Reuben's last night at the observatory, especially about Szymon's threat: "Reuben, if you weren't so insane, I would teach you a lesson."

From an administrative point of view, the director of the university just wanted it to go away. After all, their world-famous observatory was where Copernicus and many other famous scientists did their most important work.

"The last thing we need is a murder scandal hanging over us," the director told Rector Paul Stoepel. "Just get it settled and over with—it was just a horrible accident befallen on a sick and demented man. He was a Jew, after all, even with his so-called conversion, so why make all the fuss when our racial relations have been getting so much better?" The director knew that the police were concerned that Szymanski, a Jew, might have killed Wickler, a Christian, and they were probably being a little too aggressive in their investigation.

"I'll do my best, Herr Director," Paul said, "but the police seem to have something in their heads about it not being an accident. They say his arm was bruised in a way that looked like he was trying to stop himself after a push or shove. They don't know who pushed him, or why he might have been pushed, but unfortunately, they suspect Szymanski. They know he argued with him, and that they despised each other.

In any case, they want to continue the investigation." Paul's tone was sad, for he really liked Szymanski, and his solid scientific reputation was good for the institution. Paul was also feeling a little guilty, for he had been the one to ask Szymon to intercede when Reuben's behavior became a problem. "I'll have another talk with Szymon to make certain there is no doubt about his story; and if it is true, I'll try to use my influence to not hold an inquest."

A few days later, shortly before the Christmas break, Paul called Szymon into his office to ask him again if he knew anything more about the death of Reuben Wickler. "I know, Szymon," he said with some irritation, "but I promised the director that we would discuss it one last time, and if we are both convinced that nothing more is known, I will use my influence with the police to stop the investigation. So please tell me once again what happened."

"I have gone over it again and again in my mind, and I cannot think of anything else to add," Szymon said with a controlled level of impatience in his voice. "I don't know what else I would have to tell the police to have them stop harassing me about this tragedy. Why are they spending so much time on such a worthless person ... at my expense?"

"They feel that something more than what you told them must have happened," Paul explained, "since there was this bruise—"

Szymon interrupted, almost shouting. "Just because they saw a bruise, they think I murdered him? He could have gotten that bruise anywhere—from a fall, a bump into a door—he was so drunk it could have happened even before he saw me that night!"

"All right, all right ... I will contact Inspector Janiak to stop the whole thing, but remember that I am putting my professional life on the line. If you have not been completely honest with me, or the police, then I'm finished. Do you understand what I am doing?"

"Yes, Paul, I know what you are doing, and I swear to you on everything I hold dear and holy, I did not murder Reuben Wickler." And with that, Szymon, for the first time that he could remember as an adult, broke down and cried.

* * *

After the long Christmas break and early into January of 1903, Paul Stoepel, true to his word, got Chief Inspector Janiak of the Kraków police department to call off the investigation. The death of Professor Reuben Wickler was recorded as a tragic accident, and the cause of death was listed as drowning. There was no mention of alcohol being involved, nor was there any mention of Professor Szymon Szymanski being suspected of murder. With that, the incident was closed—but not for Szymon. He knew that by not saving Reuben when he could have, Szymon had murdered him as surely as if he had stuck a knife in him. Nor was the case completely closed for the police. They planned to keep a close eye on Szymanski, watching for the slightest indication that they were right, and then ... they would arrest Szymanski the Jew.

There was nothing left for Szymon to do but leave Kraków. In fact, he had to leave Poland, maybe even Europe. He had been upset with the political events in Europe, particularly how these events were affecting Jewish families. Everyone knew that persecution of the Jews was happening again, and even though Germany and Poland appeared to be safe refuges, he had to wonder how long that would last.

* * *

At last fall's physics conference, in October of 1902, at the university in Bratislava, Slovakia, Szymon had met John Hall, a young American astronomer who was trying to recruit a senior faculty member for Case Western Reserve University in Cleveland, Ohio. "You know, Szymon, the next meeting of our relatively young American Astronomical Society will be held at Case next year, and it would give me the greatest pleasure to introduce you to the group as our newest senior faculty member. What do you say?" Hall asked.

"I'm extremely flattered that an American university, especially one with an astronomy department as well known as Case Western Reserve's, would want me to come there," Szymon responded. "But my work is at Jagiellonian in Kraków and throughout other European centers, and that's enough for me. Thank you for considering me; I am truly flattered."

Hall then said, "Well, if you ever change your mind, please let me know."

Barely three months later, it was time to let Hall know. After exchanging just two letters and reaching various agreements about salary, title, tenure, and the like, Szymon quickly accepted Case Western's offer by cablegram, and told Hall that the political situation in Europe had convinced him to go to America like so many other eastern Europeans were doing. He sold his half of the house at 3 Jakuba Street to Shlomo for a reasonable sum, which he would pay off over the next five years. He gave the university notice that he was resigning his appointment and would be accepting a senior faculty position— Szymon was only thirty-six years old then—in the United States. He said he would be leaving Jagiellonian by the end of January. The family had booked passage on the *SS Celtic II* out of Liverpool on February 23, 1903.

They had a number of tearful going-away parties at the university, at their home, and with their families and friends in Warsaw and Prague.

"You really don't have to go," Paul said. "All this nonsense with Wickler is a thing of the past now. Could you please change your mind? We honestly believe that both you and the university would be better off if you stayed with us."

"Paul, you have been most kind and supportive these last fifteen years we have been working together. But the Wickler affair is just one reason I'm going. I think my family—because of our Jewish faith—will be in danger in the next couple of years, so it's better to go now while I have the opportunity than go as a refugee like so many of my fellow Jews in Russia, Romania, and other parts of eastern Europe," Szymon explained.

He gave the same explanation to Shlomo, Theo, and his parents, who did understand his position and knew that their own situation was just as tenuous. But only Shlomo thought the timing was right—the others thought he should wait a bit longer. In fact, Shlomo and his family immigrated in 1910 and settled in New York. By 1910, the political situation in Poland and the Austro-Hungarian Empire was unbearable for Jewish scholars.

"Things will quiet down; they always do. And you have such a bright future with Kraków—why would you give it up now?" Szymon's father wanted to know.

But Szymon never told anyone the real reason he was leaving—that it was time for him to seek refuge in a new country. He had read in the *Zohar* that seeking asylum in a city of refuge after an accidental murder was one way of asking the victim's family for forgiveness. That was the real reason he was leaving; he needed absolution.

* * *

Szymon honestly believed that by going to a new country across the ocean, he would be able to put the death of Reuben Wickler behind him and get on with his life and career. However, he would soon learn that such major events never really leave one's mind. They may be forgotten for a day or so, but some little thing—a picture of a bridge, something in the news about a drowning—inevitably re-created the entire gruesome scene.

FIVE: *I am with thee, and will keep thee in all places whither thou goest.*
—Genesis 28:15

The family packed up and left Poland in 1903, and after nearly three days of traveling across Europe and England, they arrived at Liverpool on February 22. The next day, which was bright but cold, the Szymanski family—all six of them—left Europe forever.

When the Szymanskis arrived at Ellis Island in New York, they were quickly processed. All their papers, passports, and letters attesting to their good character were in order, including a certified copy of Szymon's letter regarding his appointment at Case Western Reserve University, signed by the university president himself. They were all in good health and had sufficient funds with them, as well as good European banknotes that could easily be converted to dollars to avoid posing financial burden on the United States. They also had a guaranteed sponsor with a place to stay in Cleveland, so they easily passed through all the hurdles on the island and entered the country.

"Wasn't that a marvelous sight, seeing the Statue of Liberty as we came into the harbor?" Szymon, with tears in his eyes, remarked to his family as they left the island by ferry for a choppy ride over to the Battery Park Pier. They took a cab uptown to the relatively new Waldorf Astoria Hotel, where they would stay for the night. The next day, they took the Illinois Central rail line at eight in the morning, departing Grand Central Station and heading to Cleveland, Ohio. It was a scheduled ten-hour ride, but with first-class accommodations, it would be comfortable, and the food, although not kosher, would be more than acceptable.

At six that evening, Professor John Hall met them at the station with a motor taxi. He had the taxi take them to temporary faculty housing on the campus, where they would settle in for a few days until they found permanent housing. "Oy, dis is so lovely," Irenka said to John. "Having to share house in Kraków wit good friends for such long time … now all dis room just for family will be treat." Her Czech-German accent was quite pronounced when she spoke English because she had little cause to practice the language; Szymon's accent was much less noticeable since he had practiced his English, even lecturing and presenting papers in English at some international conferences.

"I'm delighted you like it, Mrs. Szymanski," John said, "I certainly hope that you and the children will enjoy Cleveland. You'll find lots to do here, and there is a sizable Jewish community that will welcome you with open arms."

Irenka was surprised that he brought up the Jewish community as if it were an issue. *Was he just being polite, or was he worried about something?* Irenka thought. In any case, having a Jewish community nearby was indeed welcome to both Szymon and Irenka. "Please, Professor Hall, I am called Irenka …," she began, only to have Szymon interrupt her.

"No, no, no … you must call us Simon and Irene, and from now on, our last name will be Shemansky." He spelled it out before adding, "In a new country, we start with a new name and a new reputation to build, and having names with Americanized spellings will make it easier for all of us, especially for the children, to be accepted into your community. So … I'm Simon, this is my wife, Irene, and these are our children: Morris, Rebecca, Hannah, and Joseph. Get used to new names, children, for you will be using them the rest of your lives. However, Moishe and Yosie, you'll still have your same names in heder as you had in Kraków." And with that, the Szymanskis of Kraków, Poland, became the Shemanskys of Cleveland, Ohio, USA.

With a little help from the B'nai David congregation, an Ashkenazi synagogue in the Jewish community of Cleveland, the family was quickly indoctrinated into the Cleveland network. The boys were enrolled in the B'nai David Heder located in the basement of the shul, as well as the Cleveland public schools, which all four children went to in the fall of 1903. They were almost all able to speak passable American English after a summer of playing with the other children in the neighborhood. Morris was the one exception—he found English difficult, and his accent and age (he was fourteen then) made it harder for him to fit in.

"Papa, do I still have to do heder now?" Morris begged Simon. Since he had had his bar mitzvah the year before in Kraków, Simon let him drop out of heder. He should have been starting high school, but they had recommended he stay back a year in the eighth grade. Unfortunately, Morris's large size and accent made him a little different; he had made few friends and remained pretty much to himself, with his music and his photography.

The other children fared much better, particularly Joseph—or Yosie, or Joey, or Joe, depending on which circle of friends he was with at the time. Maybe it was because he was the youngest, but at six years old, he quickly adapted to America and the American school system. He excelled in math and science, just as his father would have expected, but his good looks and charm inherited from his mother made him one of the most popular kids in the neighborhood.

* * *

In 1904, the Shemansky family moved into the Glenville area near Forest Hills Park on 117th Street, where the schools were good, the neighborhood Jewish, and it was easy to get public transit to the university on Euclid Street. Simon had no problem getting into the swing of the university, and he was well liked among the students.

"Professor Shemansky, are you any relation to Szymon Szymanski from Kraków?" a student asked him. "You know, the one that came up with that celestial mechanics model of the universe?"

Simon chuckled and said, "Yah, yah ... I know him vell. We are closely related ... so close that I am *him*!" he declared, setting everyone laughing.

Simon's research was not as prolific as it was in Kraków because he missed his longtime friend and collaborator Shlomo Zilber, and he was getting older. Geniuses in math and the sciences seem to do their best work when they are still in their twenties, and Simon turned forty in 1906. But with his doctoral students, he continued to publish and present papers at many professional conferences. In addition, he traveled a lot in the Midwest, giving guest lectures at places like Columbus, Ohio, and Ann Arbor, Michigan. Simon also traveled for meetings with potential graduate students at the many undergraduate colleges in Ohio, such as Oberlin University and Ohio Wesleyan. In fact, it was as guest lecturer at Ohio Wesleyan in 1929 that he ran across a young female astronomy major, a rarity for a woman at that time, by the name of Mabel Coulson, who went on to become his protégé at Michigan.

* * *

Irene was closer to Morris than she was with her other children—they were truly kindred spirits—because of his understanding of her love for music and painting. She knew that Morris was a homosexual, and she was the only family member who had met Morris's partner at his twenty-first birthday party dinner in 1910. It was a small party with a few close friends at one of Cleveland's finer restaurants.

When war broke out in Europe in 1914, Morris was already twenty-five years old, and he might never have been drafted when the United States entered the war in 1918. But he was so outraged by the war that he volunteered for the French Army. After finding out about his photographic expertise, the French gave him the honorary rank of technical sergeant, as a photographer.

In June of 1918, just three months after the United States entered the fight, and when everyone thought the war was winding down, Morris was asked to photograph what was thought to be a decisive battle. He was asked to accompany the Twenty-first Corps of the Sixth French Army, which had joined up with the Fourth U.S. Marine Brigade on a mission at a place called Belleau Wood, near the town of Chateau-Thierry on the River Marne. The battle at Belleau Wood was one of the bloodiest battles of the entire war.

Morris was killed by a mortar blast on June 16, 1918. When she received the news, Irene was totally devastated.

Simon was probably aware that Morris was a homosexual, but he would never have acknowledged it. Simon claimed his disappointment in Morris was because Morris didn't want to study science like his younger brother, Joseph. But Irene knew there was more to it than that. She never got over Morris's death, just as no parent ever gets over the loss of an adult child.

Simon acted as devastated as Irene—and in truth he was—but he also felt a little relieved that now nobody would find out Morris was a homosexual. That feeling of relief at Morris's death also made him feel guilty, so he cried even harder at the funeral. All he could think of at the funeral was Reuben Wickler falling off the bridge, and he, Simon, not trying to save him.

Irene grew distant from Simon after the funeral, and she was never intimate with him again.

* * *

Joey went to Ohio State in the fall of 1916 and majored in electrical engineering, graduating in 1921 with his master's degree. He didn't go on for a PhD as Simon wanted him to, for he was satisfied with the education he had and wanted to work.

"Maybe later, Papa, I'll go back for my doctorate, but right now I'm excited about just going to work for Western Electric." He was talking about the Western Electric Research Laboratory in New York. "They're working on all kinds of modern communication devices like radios and telephones, and I want to get in on the ground floor. It's the future of modern electrical engineering, and that's where I want to go." He was excited about the offer he had received from them for $1,350 per year. "Papa, I'll be making so much money that I'll be able to send some home for you and the family. Maybe Becky will want to go to school too."

His older sister had not married; both of his sisters were sweet and talented, but they were not very good-looking and were extremely shy, even with their mother's help in dressing and makeup. In spite of these disadvantages, Hannah, the younger sister, married a young pharmacy student from Detroit.

"Don't worry about Becky. I can take care of her," Simon said. "And if she wants to go to school, I wouldn't stop her. I'm just concerned about you living alone in New York. And so is your mother. Who would take care of you if you got sick or anything?"

"Joey, if you should need help right away, we have friends on Long Island," Irene told him. "You've heard us talk about the Zilbers many times. He is in the mathematics department at a place called Polytechnic University. I have their address and you should go and meet them anyway."

What Irene didn't tell him was that Shlomo Zilber, now Professor Seymour Silver, was his biological father. Irene knew it from the day he was born, and she was more convinced as he got older. Friends and relatives said that Joey looked more like Irene, but she knew he looked more like her close friend and housemate, the sweet and gentle-looking Shlomo Zilber. In any case, she felt he had to meet him eventually, and this would be the perfect time.

SIX: *Unto the third and fourth generation ...*
—Deuteronomy 5:9

When Professor Reuben Wickler converted to Catholicism, he wanted his wife Rena and son Stanislaw to be Christians too, but it didn't work out for Rena and Stan. Rena left her husband and took Stan back to Luboml with her in 1902, when Stan was just five years old. They stayed with her parents, who helped raise Stan as best they could on limited means. But even with little money, they made sure Stan attended heder at Rena's father's shul, as well as getting an education in a local Polish school.

When the police in Kraków investigated the death of Reuben Wickler, they traveled all the way to Luboml to interview Rena. They told her about her husband drowning and asked if she knew Professor Szymanski. They tried to scare her into saying something incriminating about Szymanski, so they told her, "It seems this Szymanski, who is a big man, argued and fought with your husband because he was Catholic. Are you sure you don't know him?"

It didn't take them long to realize that poor simple Mrs. Rena Wickler knew nothing at all about what her husband did, or whom he had any dealings with. She had left him almost four months earlier, and she was shocked when they came to deliver his few belongings and conduct the interview in January of 1903.

Rena had just received word that her *get* was granted, and when the police gave her Reuben's things, she asked, "Please sir, if I'm now divorced should I still take Reuben's things? Am I now Reuben's widow?" These questions along with her general affect during the interview convinced them to forget about her as a possible source for pinning a murder on Szymanski.

On the train back to Kraków, the two investigators compared their interview notes. The senior officer sat back and said, "What a simple-ass Jew she turned out to be—and she's a professor's wife?"

"If she was my wife, I would have turned to drink and committed suicide. Maybe that's what happened," the other investigator said, and they both laughed.

Rena got work as a housekeeper for some of the wealthier Jewish families in the synagogue, and she had a reputation for being honest, thorough, and reliable—although not very bright. Her father let her keep the money she earned because he knew that someday she would be on her own.

"Renala," her father asked, "what are your plans? You shouldn't stay in Luboml forever. Stanislaw needs a proper home and a father who he can look up to, not a simple tailor like me. If you want to save your money so someday you can move to a better place, that's all right by me. But I cannot support the two of you forever, so tell me, what are your plans?" He was not being cruel, just realistic. Single mothers in Poland, especially divorced Jewish mothers, had little chance of ever getting married again.

"I'm not sure, Papa," Rena said, "but if that man they say killed Reuben did it because he converted, then maybe he wants to kill me and Stan too. I think that when I have enough money to leave Poland, I'll do that. Should I change my name? Do you think that would help?"

Rena's father realized then that because of Rena's fears and naïveté, he, in all likelihood, would be taking care of his daughter and her son for the rest of his life. He was not as concerned about the financial impact it would have on him as he was about the sad fact that Rena would never have much of a life for herself.

* * *

Six years later, Rena had saved enough money to take Stanislaw to the United States. One of the people that Rena cleaned house for knew of a modestly wealthy Jewish family, named Rosenberg, that needed a live-in housekeeper in Cleveland. They hoped to find someone Jewish, preferably from Poland, to fill the post.

In spite of Rena's initial fears (about Reuben's murderer finding them) letters were written, and soon Rena learned that she had the job. Rena and Stan would have to go steerage all the way to America, but she didn't mind since the Rosenbergs were more than willing to help pay their way over.

Stan was twelve years old and had been studying for his bar mitzvah. He didn't want to go, but Rena could not afford to turn down this opportunity to leave Luboml. On the other hand, Rena's parents were ecstatic for her and Stanislaw. A new life in America, with the possibility of their daughter meeting someone to care for her, was more than they could hope for. So they blessed the Rosenbergs, telling Stanislaw, "Staszek, finish your bar mitzvah studies in America and be happy for your mama." And with that, Rena and Stan got on a train with all their papers, money, letters, and other possessions and headed out for Cleveland, Ohio.

Rena and Stanislaw Wickler moved in the Rosenbergs' large house in the Shaker Heights section of Cleveland. Rena told everyone, including the Rosenbergs, that her name was Wicken, not Wickler. Stanislaw was enrolled in the public schools, but he was also enrolled in the local heder because he still needed to be bar mitzvahed. He had a modest bar mitzvah in the summer of 1910, a year after they arrived.

Stanislaw did poorly in the public schools—he had no knowledge of English before his arrival, and he was having difficulty fitting in, even though most of the kids in his school were Jewish.

"Staszek, would you like to maybe stay for longer in heder?" his mother asked.

"Sure, why not," he replied. He felt safer in heder because at least there he could speak Yiddish and learn Hebrew, and the rabbi protected him from the meanness of the other kids.

At thirteen, Stan was an overweight, homely child. He had his father's dour expression and his mother's bad complexion. Being friendless was bad enough, but even worse, Stan was probably the poorest kid in the neighborhood. Living in Shaker Heights with his mother may have been a nice benefit for them, but with the little income that Rena received, there was nothing left over for Stan, not even for simple things like movies, candy, or treats, which all the other kids at school had. He came home right after heder and stayed in his room, doing homework or reading the few books he had gotten for school; reading was his only leisure-time activity.

When Stan was sixteen, he was legally allowed to quit school. He was only in the ninth grade, and he was just getting by. He got a job working in a warehouse, stacking boxes, helping load and unload trucks, sweeping up the place, and doing anything else the owner needed. He was paid thirty cents an hour, which was good money for a *schlepper*—his unofficial title—in those days. But he was strong and did what he was told, so he was worth it to the boss. But more significantly, he loved the job.

Stan felt important because now he had his own money and could give some to his mother to help her out as well. He paid her two dollars a week for room and board, for which she was most appreciative. Sadly, Mrs. Rosenberg wasn't.

"We were pleased to have Stan stay with you, Rena, when he was in school, and he even helped you a little around the house. But now that he has a man's job making a man's salary, well, we just feel we can no longer have him stay here for free. I'm sure you can understand that," she said in perfect Polish.

"Oh, yes, madam, yes … I can see that. Does this mean he has to move out? Can he stay if he gives you two dollars a week for his room and a little food?" Rena implored.

"I'm afraid not, Rena—you see, we plan on hiring a live-in cook soon, and she would take the other room in the apartment, so two dollars would hardly work for us. You understand, of course, don't you? You can tell Stan he can stay until the end of the month, and then he'll have to move out. I'm sure he'll be able to find a place that he can afford. In the meantime, he can continue to have his meals here with you, and he's welcome to visit you whenever he wants; won't that be nice for you? You should be very proud of him—only sixteen and making a man's wage, how marvelous that is," Mrs. Rosenberg said with a self-satisfied grin.

Rena cried that night, not having the courage to tell Stan that he had to move out. When Stan came home from work the next day Rena said, "Staszek, Mrs. Rosenberg says you can't sleep here anymore after the end of the month. That's only three weeks away; you think you can find a place to stay? Maybe they know a place from where you work."

At sixteen, Stan was very understanding. If nothing else, he knew how to accept the pain of rejection, but this time he felt bad for his mother; he was her only friend. "Mama, don't worry so much about me. I'm doing real good at work, and they'll find me a place—someplace closer to work so I can sleep longer. I can still come and visit you, can't I?" Stan asked in a mix of Polish and English.

"Of course you can, and Mrs. Rosenberg says you can even eat here with me sometimes."

Actually, Stan was taking it better than Rena might have expected. He liked the idea of moving out and being on his own at sixteen. He had no trouble getting around Cleveland on the trolley cars, or figuring how much money he needed for things he wanted. His fat was turning into muscle with all the heavy lifting, and he was becoming a real *shtarker*—a strongman.

His boss, Avraham "Abe" Gorski, who was also a Polish Jew, enjoyed talking Polish with the young man. "So you need a place to stay," Abe said. "Yeah, I know a nice boardinghouse, but it will cost you seven bucks a week, and you only get six meals; that's half your salary. Do you think you can handle that?"

Stan thought for a minute, worked out his expenses in his head, and said, "Yes, I can handle that. I'll even have a few cents left over to give my mom."

So, at sixteen years old, Stan Wicken was on his own, living in a quiet boardinghouse in an older neighborhood in the warehouse district of Cleveland. There were eleven boarders in the house, seven men and four women, the others being significantly older than Stan. Even though he had little in common with them, other than the fact that most of them spoke with heavy European accents, he got along quite well. And for the first time in his life, he was socializing with other people and not feeling like an outsider.

* * *

When Stanislaw moved into the Payne Boardinghouse on East Twenty-first Street, just off Payne Avenue, he had a short five-block walk to the warehouse on Lakeside Avenue and East Twentieth Street. He knew that by moving to the boardinghouse, he would save sixty cents a week trolley fare, and that sixty cents was the difference between having a sandwich for lunch and not eating. Stan also began to realize he was not a dull-minded person, even though some kids had called him a moron. He learned the warehouse layout quickly, and he could tell you almost instantly where any item in the huge building was stored. He had no trouble reading—after all, reading was about all he did at home—and his ability with numbers and maps was exceptional. He had memorized almost the entire map of Cleveland, and just given an address, he could easily tell someone where any building was located.

His only problem was speaking English—he understood everything, but he just couldn't say it correctly. He could not translate his thoughts from Polish quickly enough to make himself coherent, even though he knew exactly what he wanted to say. Although Abe's accent wasn't much better than Stan's, he was able to think in English, so he spoke faster and a little more succinctly.

Stan ran all kinds of errands around Cleveland because he knew the trolley lines and locations. He never got lost and never allowed anyone to cheat him, even *accidentally*, as some of them tried to claim. Because of his size and expression when he knew he was being overcharged or shortchanged, the response of the prospective swindler—"Oh, yeah, right. Sorry, kid, my mistake. Here, I'll make it right!"—was not uncommon. He gained Abe's trust in handling money, and he was becoming a very strong young man that nobody would think of trying to push around.

One time, when someone tried to overcharge Stan, he came back and told Abe, "The asshole didn't think I could add up all the charges, and he tried to charge me a whole dollar more than it came to. When I gave him my tough look and said, 'You wrong, sheethead, make it right,' he got so scared he even gave me back ten cents more than the dollar." They both laughed at that one.

* * *

By 1915, Stan was Abe's senior employee, even though all the other warehouse workers were older than he was. He had no problem telling the others what to do, or doing it himself, such as lifting three fifty-pound cartons at one time, if they needed some convincing as to who was the boss. Even at the boardinghouse, the house employees and his fellow boarders respected him. When he told stories in Polish, his compatriot at the table, Mr. Miron Sobieski, would translate for the others. They enjoyed his stories, and they smiled when he spoke English, even though there were times when they didn't fully understand him.

The war had started in Europe, and everyone was concerned about their relatives and friends. They also knew that the United States would eventually be in the fight, and that would just add to their grief. But Stan didn't worry—he knew his grandparents in Luboml would probably be safe, and if the United States wanted him to fight, he would. "Eef I go army," Stan said, "I return to Luboml and see *Bubbie* and *Zaydie*. War not be bad for me."

In 1918, when the United States did get into the war, Stanislaw was twenty-one years old, unmarried, and he had completed almost one year of high school, making him prime draft material. Stan was drafted, as expected, in June of 1918. He went through basic training, and like most draftees, he went overseas right after that. The battle of Belleau Wood had just been fought, and word was going around about how bloody it was for the United States. Stan wanted to get in and do some fighting himself, but his commanding officer found that his Polish and German language skills were far more important.

Stan spent the war, which only lasted until around October of 1918, with the full armistice coming in November, being a translator along the Western Front. His English was good enough by then to be able to do a credible job, even with his heavy accent. Stan was mustered out early in 1919, and he went back to Cleveland, where the first thing he did was visit his mother. Stan then went back to the Payne Boardinghouse to see if they still had a room for him, which they did.

* * *

When Abe Gorski saw Stan, he couldn't believe his eyes. He had been gone less than a full year but the youth of twenty-one was now a full-grown man. He simultaneously looked slimmer yet bigger. His face was narrower, but he still looked tough and menacing. Abe was delighted that Stan had returned, and he immediately asked him if he wanted his old job back at the princely rate of fifty cents an hour, twenty cents more than what he was making before the war.

"Oh, Mr. Gorski, thank you so much for your very kind offer," Stan said in Polish, "but my friend from the boardinghouse—you know him, Mr. Miron Sobieski—has found a good job for me."

"Is that Sobieski the bookkeeper?" asked Mr. Gorski. "If it is him, then you know the job he has for you is with gangsters. What did he say you're supposed to do?"

"He says he needs a big strong man like me to make gonifs pay up—like, you remember, when they tried to charge me too much for something. He'll pay me forty dollar every week. That's a lot of money. I can take care of Mama—she isn't well anymore—with forty dollar a week, can't I?" He knew it was not totally legit like the warehouse job, but he wasn't afraid to use his muscle to make money for him and his mother.

"Look, Staszek, my offer is less than half that, but you don't have to risk your life with me. What would your mama do if you got killed? Tell Mr. Sobieski thank you very much, but you need to work for me—*dobrze?*"

"*Dobrze* … okay," Stan said with a feeling of both relief and regret; he would have liked to have made the big bucks since his mother was getting sicker every day with her weak heart and severe rheumatism, and he knew she would have to stop working soon.

Finally, in 1923, as expected, Rena was too sick to work anymore, even though she was only fifty years old. Stan moved her to the Jewish old folks' home, but he was expected to pay at least four hundred a year for her care. He could afford it, but it did put a strain on his budget.

"Mama, how much money do you have saved up from all those— what is it?—fifteen years you worked for the Rosenbergs?" he asked her in Polish.

"I got almost eighty dollars—I couldn't save too much because they gave me so little. But I still have the money I brought over from Poland."

She started rummaging through one of her drawers, then handed Stan an old envelope. Inside, Stan found some crisp banknotes issued in 1908, from the Österreichisch-Ungarische Bank, which totaled a little more than two thousand kronen. "I took all my *zlotnys* and had your grandfather put them into kronen because I knew it would be easier to exchange them here in America," she said with a big smile.

"Papa told me that they were worth around four hundred American dollars, so with my savings, I have around five hundred dollars. That should take care of me till I get well," she said.

Stan knew that the Austro-Hungarian banknotes were now worth nothing, or damn close to it. When he took them to the bank, they told him that the notes were worthless since the Österreichisch-Ungarische Bank had officially closed down in July … and here it was September.

"Maybe a collector would give you twenty or thirty dollars for them," the teller told Stan, "or you can save them yourself. Who knows, they may be worth more in a few years."

Stan would never tell his mama that she blew it by not converting the money years ago. He just took care of the bills, and as it turned out, she didn't get better. Her health continued to deteriorate rapidly, and she had to be admitted to the hospital section of the old folks' home. They told Stan that her expenditures would go up to six hundred a year, and he would probably have to pay more medical costs as well.

In 1926, Stan told Mr. Gorski that he had to get a higher-paying job in order to take care of his mother. "You treated me like a father," Stan said, "and I will always remember you. But Mama's hospital bills are too big, so I told Mr. Sobieski that if he still needs me, I would take his old job offer."

Avraham Gorski had tears in his eyes when he hugged Stanislaw good-bye. "Look, Staszek, if you ever want your old job here, you're welcome to come back, okay?" After working for Abe for thirteen years, Stan had tears in his eyes as well.

* * *

Speaking in Polish, Miron Sobieski asked Stan, "Did you ever hear of the Purple Gang in Detroit? They used to do some work for us in Cleveland, but now they're mostly involved with their own work in Detroit."

"I never heard of a purple gang; what kind of work do they do?"

"They sell illegal liquor that they get from Canada. It's the same place where we get our liquor, only we have a longer boat ride over Lake Erie, so it can be more dangerous. You understand what I'm talking about, don't you?" Miron asked.

"Yeah, sure. You sell illegal liquor—that's how you get your money. And it's dangerous because it's a federal crime. I read the papers, you know. So what did these *purple* guys from Detroit do?"

"I don't sell the liquor—the people that you and I work for sell the liquor. I just keep the books. What the guys from Detroit did for us was make sure that our customers didn't buy from someone else. Or made sure they paid their bills. Well, that will be your job now. You visit the ones that have threatened to buy elsewhere and convince them they made a wrong decision. Also, if they didn't pay their bill, you have to convince them that it wouldn't be wise for them to continue holding out. You follow me?" Miron asked.

"You say 'convince'—meaning I scare them like I did the clerks, right?" Stan said.

"Well, sometimes you may have to do more than scare them. You may have to break an arm or some furniture. I'm saying you have to be a little rougher than you were with the clerks … but no killing. Are you all right with that?" Miron pressed.

Stan thought about it for a few moments and answered, "I can do that. I learned how to be a fighter in the army, and I've always been strong. Yes, I can do that for the money you're paying me."

The first few places Stan was told to visit were fairly easy. His presence was enough to scare anybody, and in his new clothes that Miron helped him buy, he looked like the guys from Detroit, wearing a three-piece single-breasted suit, fedora hat, and striped tie. His new clothes would also be worn to shul for the high holidays. For his first job, he was told how to get into the speakeasy—given the password—and when the bartender saw him, he knew immediately who—or rather *what*—he was.

"Yes, sir, what'll it be?" he asked nervously.

"You boss here?" Stan asked.

"Uh, no … I just work here. What do you want to see the boss for?"

Stan pulled out a piece of paper and looked at it, and then he said menacingly, "I need two hundred seventy-five dollar for liquor bill and one hundred fifty dollar interest for last month not paid. You got money to give me, or do I have to take it from you?"

"Hold it just a minute. Let's not do anything rash," the bartender said. There were only a couple of customers in the place plus the bouncer.

"Mario," the bartender called out to the bouncer, "go see if Roscoe is in the back, and if he is, get him out here fast. And you stay with him; you know what I'm saying?"

Stan was no dummy—he knew that "Roscoe" was mobster slang for a handgun. As Mario walked past Stan on his way to the back door at the side of the bar, Stan quickly grabbed his upper right arm, and with his enormous strength, he squeezed it hard enough to let Mario know that with a slight twist of his hand, which was the size of a ham, he could break it. Mario wasn't small, but he clearly knew when he was outclassed, for he stopped dead in his tracks and waited for his orders.

"Tell that asshole behind the bar that if he no give me my money now, your arm is gone; you understand that, no?" Stan spoke with enough conviction that Mario told the barman what he was to do.

Most of Stan's encounters were just that simple, but not all of them. One time, one of his boss's competitors was waiting for him to show up at a club that had switched suppliers. When Stan started to explain why he was there, four large men jumped him. Stan was able to break some arms and ribs on two of them, but the other two were able to get Stan down and beat him up badly. They threw him out with the advice not to show up again or he would be dead.

When he explained to Miron what happened, Miron told him, "Don't worry, Staszek, I'll tell our boss, and he'll take care of it. Don't you go back there, okay?"

The club was burned to the ground two days later.

The syndicate let Stan heal for a week before asking him to go back on the street to continue his work. They also gave him a raise because now they had fewer defections and more rapid payments for their products. They attributed these changes to their customers' knowledge that retribution was no longer dependent on the Detroit mob showing up. Stan's reputation as the biggest and meanest guy on the block had gotten around. Stan was now making close to three thousand dollars a year—a lot of money for that era.

* * *

Stan had Rena moved to a private sanatorium, where her care was much better. Her excellent care would cost Stan over a thousand dollars a year, but he never complained. Stan visited her every weekend, and she was quite lucid up until her death. On a number of those visits, Rena would tell Stan about their home in Luboml and how her father, the tailor, was more like a father to Stan than a grandfather. On one occasion, Stan wanted to know more about his real father, Reuben Wickler. He only knew that he was some kind of a teacher in Kraków, but that was it.

Rena started out by telling Stan of her arranged marriage and their move to Kraków, where Reuben was to teach. "He was a very important man at the famous Jagiellonian University. We had a nice apartment in a place called Kazimierz, with lots of Jewish people around. But he wanted better, so we moved out to a Christian part of the city. I had no friends, and you were just getting ready for school. You had many children to play with in Kazimierz, but when we moved … you and me … we had nobody." Rena was telling the story for the first time, and she had trouble remembering everything.

"You once told me he became a Christian," Stan said. "Is that true?"

"Yes, a Catholic, yes … You and I went to the place where they made it true, and we watched them give him something like wine to drink. I think that started him on his drinking habit." She was a little wistful then, but she continued. "In school, the children were nasty to you because you were Jewish; do you remember that?"

"That is one thing I do remember," Stanislaw said. "I wish I was as strong then as I am now. Then maybe it wouldn't have happened."

"No matter," Rena went on. "I was not happy being a Christian, so one day I took you and some clothes on the train back to Luboml, where I knew you would be happy. My father, *alah v'shalom*, was able to make the rabbis give me a *get*, and he gave us a place to stay. I worked, and in a little while …"

"So what about Reuben Wickler? What happened to him? Did he come looking for us? Didn't he care that we left?"

"Yes, Reuben … He was drinking a lot and thought the world was against him now that he was Catholic. He once told me that a dybbuk inside one of the other teachers was trying to destroy him with a golem. Can you believe that? That's how bad he was. Well, the police came—"

"The police? In Kraków?"

"No, no ... it was the Kraków police, but they came all the way to Luboml to tell me he was dead! They said he was murdered by a professor by the name of Shaszemski, or something like that. That's why I changed our name to Wicken ... so he wouldn't find us."

That conversation was the only one that Stan ever had with his mother about his father. He never pressed her about whether Reuben was a good father to him. Stan just got used to the idea that in 1902, when he was five years old, he became fatherless.

Rena died from many physical ailments in 1930, when she was fifty-seven years old, but heart failure was listed as her cause of death. She looked much older than her age when she died, but that was to be expected, considering the hard life she'd endured. When Rena died, Stan was thirty-three years old. He'd devoted so much time and money to his mother that he'd never thought about marriage or at least about getting a real girlfriend—other than prostitutes. Now that Rena was gone, Stan decided it was time to get a life for himself—to get married and, if possible, to raise a family of his own.

SEVEN: *One generation passeth away, and another generation cometh ...*
—Ecclesiastes 1:4

When Joey Shemansky first arrived in New York in the fall of 1921, he made contact with Professor and Mrs. Seymour and Rebecca Silver of Great Neck, Long Island, and they invited him for dinner.

"Call me Sy. Actually, you know, that was your dad's nickname back in Prague, but it's mine now," Seymour laughed. "Come, get reacquainted with the family—you probably don't even remember us anymore. This is my wife, Becky, and here's Adele, our youngest, and that's Estelle. Our son Mordechai—well, Melvin now—is the same age as your brother, Morris. He's married and lives in the city with his family." Then Seymour paused. "Oy vey ... I'm so sorry. I forgot for a moment about Morris. What a tragedy." Of course, he had heard about Morris being killed, because the family received notes and cards regularly from Irene. Szymon only wrote to Seymour occasionally, about technical issues and work-related problems.

When they sat down to dinner, Sy said, "So, let's see, you were born in 1897, right?"

"December of 1897. I'm an old man of twenty-three ... Well, almost twenty-four now," Joey said. "Mom wants me to get married so she can have grandchildren while she can still enjoy them—or at least that's what she told me. She said the same thing to Channa—everyone still calls her Channa—when she got married! Mom also insisted I should meet you and your family. She said you'd take care of me if I got sick." They all laughed as the family continued with the small talk.

"December 1897—I remember that very well … your birth, that is," Sy commented. He was now staring intently at Joey, and the hair on the back of his neck started to rise. *My God*, he thought, *Irenka wants me to see that he is my son!* "You interested in math, Joey?" he asked in a strange way.

"Sure, that's why I'm an electrical engineer—it's mostly math now," Joey answered. "But you're a math professor; I'm sure you know all that."

Sy nodded in agreement and was quiet for much of the rest of the dinner.

Becky asked, "Joey, honey, how's Irenka? Is she doing well in Cleveland? And the girls are they all right too? You remember that we all lived in the same house in Kraków, don't you?" She spoke in fairly good but heavily accented English.

"Mama is doing well. She has her music, and there are some marvelous museums and art galleries for her to go to. In fact, my sisters opened their own gallery with many of Morris's photos. I remember little of Kraków, but Moishe—Morris—promised me that one day he would take me there. Maybe I'll go there someday," Joey said a little sadly. "You knew that Channa married a boy from Detroit—Saul Portnoy— last year. She met him at a Zionist youth camp in Fremont, Ohio. So now Rivka runs the gallery with some help from my mother."

Joey was more subdued now as well because he sensed something strange was happening between him and Sy. He sensed that Sy was acting more like a close uncle rather than just a family friend, and it made him somewhat uncomfortable. But after learning more about how they all lived together in Kraków, he could understand Sy's attitude. He left their house a bit early, with good wishes and a standing invitation to come and visit. Sy also invited him to visit the Polytechnic campus to talk more about what he was doing at Western Electric. It seemed Sy was more interested in Joey's math skills than anything else.

* * *

Around nine months later Joey called Sy. "Professor Silver? This is Joey Shemansky calling from New York—the city. I want to accept your offer, if it's still available, to visit with you on campus. I'm considering going on for a doctorate and would like your advice. Can we meet someday soon?"

"Joey … Yosie, my boy—yes, sure, please come visit with me. I would love to talk with you about getting your doctorate here. Let's see …" Seymour paused briefly to check his calendar. "Can you come here Wednesday morning around ten?" Seymour gave Joey directions as to what train he should take, and where on campus to meet him.

When they met on Wednesday, Sy was more than cordial, once again acting like a long-lost relative. He kept looking at Joey, trying to see himself in his face, his voice, his mannerisms; but try as he might, it just didn't seem to be there. If anything, Joey was more like Simon in his demeanor than anyone else. But he didn't think that was unusual, and he was still convinced that Joey was his son. He recalled that at times he'd looked at his son Melvin and wondered if he was really his father.

They talked for over two hours, and then Sy invited Joey to stay for lunch. They went off campus to a small delicatessen in Brooklyn, where Sy said the corned beef was supposed to be "out of this world."

"That was a great sandwich, Sy," Joey said when they finished eating and talking more about Joey going on for a PhD. "Thanks for bringing me here. Also, thanks for your advice about going back to grad school, but I think I'll wait another year and see how things work out at the lab before making any commitment right now."

"You're more than welcome, Yosie. Remember, we're almost family, you know," Sy said with a feeling of some sadness, or was it a feeling of emptiness? "If you change your mind about the doctorate, you can always come back and talk with me, and I'll help you get settled into a program that fits your needs, okay?" Seymour Silver realized that he could never be a real father to Joey, even if he was his biological father, but he could always be like an uncle. That is, if Joey wanted him to be like an uncle.

* * *

Joey never did go back for his doctorate, and he visited the family only a couple of times over the intervening years. The Silvers were invited to Joey's wedding in New Jersey nine years later, in 1931, when Joey was almost thirty-four years old. Seymour attended the wedding, but Becky, who was having back problems, didn't feel well enough to go. Simon had turned sixty-five, and Irene was sixty, and she still looked youthful and as beautiful as ever. Seymour and Simon were delighted to see each other, and they couldn't stop talking about the old days at Jagiellonian. They were talking in Polish and thrilled to be doing it.

"We did all that fantastic research that's still being cited in the literature. I was at a meeting a couple of years ago under my American name—Professor Seymour Silver—and somebody asked, 'Does anybody know what ever happened to old Zilber?' and I said, 'Oh, he's fine,'" and they both laughed as if they were students again.

"I got this offer from Polytechnic because they recently started to be an all-science and engineering school," he explained to Simon. "They needed good applied mathematicians, so we left Kraków. You know, it's over twenty years ago now. That seems so hard to believe."

They brought each other up-to-date on relatives and friends back in Poland. "You know, Theo and my mother-in-law left for Palestine before 1920," Simon said. "They went to help in the creation of a Zionist state. It has been hard for them—they were both in their sixties then, you know—but they love every minute of it. Can you believe they're living on a kibbutz? Here they are … in their seventies … and they're farming." He smiled broadly.

"When I left Kraków, life was getting uncomfortable for Jews living in Kazimierz, but even more so for the Jews that had moved out and tried to assimilate," Seymour told Simon. "I think we left at just the right time. From what I understand, that crazy anti-Semite Hitler is gaining more power every day in Germany. They say he might even run against President Hindenburg next year. If he gets the presidency, it will not go well for our Jewish brethren."

Irene came over to the two men. "You both look as if it's the end of the world. Stop your serious talk and come join the party. Remember, it's Joey's wedding we're celebrating, not a funeral."

Seymour couldn't take his eyes off Irene, and when the opportunity came, he quietly said to her, "I know why you wanted me to meet him. He is a marvelous boy; we should be very proud."

"Yes, Joey is a great person. He looks like me, don't you think? But he has inherited his dad's interest in science and math—and isn't that just wonderful for Szymon?" Irene had responded with a tight smile on her face, so Seymour dropped the subject.

* * *

With the birth of their son, Edward, in October of 1935, the New Jersey Shemanskys were totally thrilled. Joey and his wife, Sarah, were both in their mid-thirties, and they had been trying to have a child since they were married. The pregnancy was difficult for Sarah, and she was told that she would be better off not trying to have any more children. She almost miscarried three or four times in her first trimester, so the anxiety-wrought pregnancy ended in great relief with the birth of Edward. He was a healthy baby weighing in at over eight pounds.

When Edward started kindergarten in the fall of 1940, Joey complained that he was not thrilled with the educational facilities in the Murray Hill School District, even though they were all new and modern. "Talking with that Miss Middleton, I wasn't impressed with her attitude. That school is just not as good as the schools that I attended in Cleveland," he stated.

"So what do you want to do? How about if we enroll him in a private school?" Sarah offered.

"Actually, I have a better idea. A new government laboratory is opening in Cleveland. It's going to be headed by George Lewis, an engineer that I met some time ago. Like it or not, the United States is going to be in a war soon, and this place is supposed to be involved in cutting-edge research on new modes of flying. They need communications experts, and he offered me a great job there. You want to try living in Cleveland for a while? The schools are better," he said with a gleam in his eye that belied the phony bad school issue he'd raised.

"Joey, if it's a good move for you, then by all means let's do it," Sarah said. "I think I'd rather raise Eddy in Cleveland anyway. This New York area is just getting too harsh for me." She was mostly offering this to assuage any guilt that Joey might have about leaving Bell Labs and Sarah's home state of New York.

* * *

Joey, Sarah, and Edward moved to Cleveland in the summer of 1941, barely six months after the new National Advisory Committee for Aeronautics laboratory was dedicated. Young Edward was in his first semester of grade school in 1941 when the attack on Pearl Harbor brought the United States into the war. Joey, at forty-four, with a heart murmur and one child, was ineligible for the draft. In addition, he was considered to be in a vital occupation for the war effort, and that alone would have disqualified him. But he couldn't help feeling a little guilty about not being able to fight for his country as his brother Morris had done in the First World War.

Simon was proud of his youngest son, and even though he, Simon, had retired at age seventy-two in 1938, he enjoyed talking with Joey about all the modern technical devices Joey was working on. But most of all, he enjoyed his grandson, Edward, who was growing up rapidly and loved sports. Edward was a large, strong young man like Simon, but he had the strength and good looks of both Simon's and Sarah's fathers. Sarah, who also came from a family of big men, and who was a good-looking woman in her own right, never disagreed when Papa Simon pointed out how much Edward had taken after him and Irene. She would simply smile and say, "Yes, Papa Simon, Edward certainly does take after you two." Joey would smile at her with a knowing look, appreciating how she made Simon feel about his only grandchild. Sarah's father, whose name was also Edward, had died when she was an infant, so Simon would be his only grandfather. Making Simon feel solidly identified with Edward was the least she could do.

* * *

Joey and his family moved into Shaker Heights, a Cleveland neighborhood just south of his old Glenville community, where Simon and Irene were still living. Shaker Heights had a large Jewish population and a reputation for outstanding schools, just like Glenville. Edward grew up playing sports and being a good student—not a great student, and certainly not blessed with his father's science and math capabilities, but good enough to get into almost any college he applied to. Joey thought that Edward was smart enough to get a scholarship, and he encouraged him to apply to Ohio State, where Joey went to college. But Edward was a little stubborn and had a mind of his own. As an only child, he had some difficulty in getting his parents to stop treating him "like a baby"—his words. So, to show his independence, and probably to piss off his dad, he applied to and was accepted at the University of Michigan in Ann Arbor, Ohio State's perennial football rival.

He wasn't recruited with a football scholarship—Michigan had already committed all its football scholarships by the time Edward applied. But one of Michigan's recruiters, who had seen him play football in high school, told him that he could get on the team as a walk-on. He told Edward that as soon as he started school in the fall, to come down to Ferry Field, where they practiced, and he would take him under his wing.

"What position do you think I'll be playing?" he asked the recruiter. "I've been a halfback through all my high school playing. Do you think I could make halfback at Michigan?"

The recruiter laughed. "Why don't we wait until you meet with Coach Oosterbaan; he may have some other ideas as to how he might use you, okay?"

Edward told his parents about being accepted at Michigan, and that he would probably play varsity football as well. Of course, his parents were not aware of his college varsity football aspirations, as they just assumed he would be attending college to get an education, preferably in science or engineering.

When his father acted a little startled at his decision and began to question the wisdom of his plan, Edward shouted, "I'm not a baby! I can take care of myself. I knew you'd be pissed about Michigan, but I thought you would understand my feelings for a change!"

"Eddy, Eddy," Joey said evenly, "we're so proud of you. Getting into Michigan was no small thing, and you did it all on your own. We're delighted that they think highly enough about your football skills to let you play on their team. But ..."

"Yeah, here comes the 'but,'" Edward said.

"Let me finish," Joey pleaded. "*But* ... we know it will be hard to do both—playing varsity football, and getting a solid education in the sciences, or any other academic program you want to pursue. Look, we'll support whatever you want; we're just telling you how we feel based on our experiences, that's all."

Sarah added, "Honey, mazel tov on being accepted to Michigan. I know you'll do great in whatever you try, and if you want to play football, that's okay with me. Just go and have a great college experience. Be careful and try to live your dreams. You know we love you very much. Maybe, though, you should wait before you tell Papa Simon about the football thing. Is that all right?" Sarah was simply cooling down the situation.

Edward was still unsettled and a little disappointed that they didn't jump for joy about his decision, but he could live with his mom's request about holding off on telling his grandfather.

In the fall of 1953, Edward went to Ann Arbor to study whatever he wanted and hopefully become a star football player. Maybe, he hoped, even one of the few Jewish players that go on to the pro teams.

Wow, would that be something great, he thought, *playing football for the Cleveland Browns, my favorite team.* They were the champions in 1950, but they lost the championship to Detroit in 1952. Edward began to daydream. *With me on the team, they'll make a comeback.*

He made the Michigan team as a walk-on, but the position he was told he would play was backup tight end. As a freshman, he saw no action in 1953 because of eligibility requirements. However, he practiced hard, and the regular tight end all-star, Ray Barber, liked his attitude. But it was clear that unless Barber got hurt, which was highly unlikely at that time, Ed wouldn't get to play in any regular season game.

In the fall of 1954, he stayed with the team, practicing and doing what he was told. He also started to date a freshman he had looked up on the advice of his parents. Her name was Clarice Adams, and she was related to one of his grandfather's friends. He was told that she was the granddaughter of some professor by the name of Silver, who lived in New York.

Part II

EIGHT: *Therefore shall ye keep all the commandments which I command you this day …*
—Deuteronomy 11:8

Benjamin Jacob Bernstein enrolled in the College of Literature, Science, and Arts at the University of Michigan in the fall of 1954, after finishing his four-year tour of duty with the U.S. Navy. His parents, along with his brother, who was the rabbi of a small congregation in a younger Jewish neighborhood on the west side of Detroit, drove Ben up to Ann Arbor on a bright fall Sunday and helped him move into his dorm. It was not quite the same as Theo helping Szymon get settled in Frau Kohn's boardinghouse, but it was nice to have his family with him when moving into a new place to live.

"You'll be living in relative luxury compared to where you've been living for the last four years," his older brother, Marvin, told him as they entered Strauss House in East Quad. Marvin Bernstein had a big smile on his face, pleased that his little brother was home and going off to college.

The university called them residence halls then, which made it sound more like officers' quarters to Ben. He agreed with Marvin that living in East Quad would be nice for a change after living the life of an enlisted man, mostly in the cramped quarters of a relatively small destroyer.

Ben's parents were happy, he was happy, and now his career as a scientist was about to begin. Life looked to be going in the right direction for Ben. Little did he realize then that science and religion would turn out to be his most valuable resources for dealing with the coming events in his life.

Szymon and Ben had both started out in major universities; Szymon began at the graduate level, while Ben was starting out as an undergraduate. As a navy veteran, Ben was four years older than most of the other freshmen. Conversely, Szymon started at the doctoral level at only eighteen years old, considerably younger than most other graduate students.

Once Ben was moved in and had said his good-byes to his family, he settled into his room. He got excited reading about the college orientation process. But he told himself not to appear too enthusiastic for this new adventure or he might look foolish to the younger students.

* * *

Ben finished the three-day orientation period, along with a few thousand other freshmen, and he was ready to register for classes. The freshman advisor said, "Let's see what's on your list. You want to start your natural science sequence because you indicate here"—he pointed to Ben's worksheet—"that you want to be a math or science teacher, right? What area of science are you interested in?" He then began a litany of natural science courses that might be available to Ben.

Ben wasn't sure what area he wanted. He'd liked chemistry and biology in high school, but his work as a sonar man in the navy, and the things Lieutenant Malloy had taught him, made him think that physics would be best.

He recalled his last conversation with Mr. Malloy. "Ben, I'm expecting you to keep up your studies in science. I understand that you're thinking about going to Michigan when you get out. It's a good school for either a science or an engineering program. Keep me posted on your schoolwork—I'm really interested." With that, Mr. Malloy extended his hand to Ben, and both of them were smiling as Malloy left the ship.

"Well," the advisor said, "lots of freshmen are taking astronomy this year. It's a great nat sci course for beginners because you don't need a lot of math or other scientific background. Do you want to try that?"

"Sounds okay to me," Ben answered, remembering how much he enjoyed looking at the night skies aboard ship.

* * *

Ben finished registering for classes and going through the lines at the various stations along the corridors and stairwells inside the big gym where registration was held. Several other less important stations, like religious activities, clubs, football tickets, and other nonacademic events and organizations, were represented along the way. Ben stopped at the Hillel table and inquired about it, for he planned to attend religious services occasionally.

Religion to Ben was a major part of his life while he was growing up, just as it was to Szymon Szymanski. Ben was born in Detroit in 1932 and, like Szymon, was raised in a middle-class Jewish family. They were an Orthodox Jewish family, but not ultraorthodox. Ben didn't wear the long sideburns or have a yarmulke on his head all the time. His family had joined the B'nai Moshe Synagogue, a relatively liberal Ashkenazi shul located on the corner of Dexter and Lawrence streets, near the edge of the Jewish section of Detroit.

Ben had attended Hebrew School since he was six years old, but in 1942, his grandfather, Volvo Bernstein, enrolled Ben in the Yeshiva Beth Yehudah Hebrew school near his grandfather's grocery store on Dexter. "You'll like it here, and if you study hard, maybe you too can become a rabbi like your brother, Mordecai," his *zaydie* told him after Ben's bar mitzvah in 1945, when he was informed that he would be in a parochial school. The family frequently interchanged their Hebrew names with their American names like his *zaydie* did when referring to Marvin as Mordecai.

The parochial school at the yeshiva wasn't a completely accredited school like some of the Catholic parochial schools. Ben would go to the yeshiva all morning, and in the afternoon, he would have to go to Durfee Junior High, a public school, for certain academic classes. Later in the afternoon, he'd go back to the yeshiva. When he was enrolled in the parochial school, Ben frequently went to the Saturday services in the yeshiva, where the younger members stayed all day long in shul, studying the Talmud and various other commentaries on the Mishnah.

"So, tell us, Rabbi," Ben once asked at one of these Shabbos afternoon Torah sessions, "do we believe in a heaven or some other place where we go when we die?" Ben didn't say *hell* because in those days, doing so constituted swearing, which they weren't allowed to do.

"Places such as heaven and Hades are described in the Torah," the rabbi told them, "but these are not places where your soul necessarily goes when you die. If you were to read the Midrash and the book of Zohar, you might interpret such places for the soul to exist after one dies, but on the other hand, sections of the Talmud tell us otherwise."

This type of monologue went on for some time, and in the final analysis, Ben never did get a straight answer. All he got were quotes like "Rabbi Eleazar of Sfad, seven hundred years ago, in 5047, tells us, 'The soul is not transient, but exists elsewhere for all eternity,' without necessarily telling us where elsewhere is."

Some of the kids snickered at the term "Hades," and Ben told them, "Boy, was I ever tempted to ask him if Hades was the same as hell." Ben didn't tell the boys that he would never disrespect his rabbi by asking that silly question.

Ben attended the parochial school for almost three years, but when he entered the tenth grade, his father allowed him to quit the yeshiva after starting Central High School on Linwood and Elmhurst. His *zaydie* was initially disappointed because he wanted Ben to go on and become a rabbi like his brother, who had attended the yeshiva in New York.

"I'm really interested in being a scientist, even if some of the mysticism associated with the Mishnah does interest me," Ben told his *zaydie*, "but I think I would rather just be in one school right now. Maybe later I'll go on for my rabbinical studies," he explained, and his *zaydie* understood.

Ben's brother was eight years older, and like Ben's yeshiva rabbi, he could never give Ben a straight answer about religious doctrine either. He would end up saying, "You damn junior scientist, always wanting straight, rational, simple answers. Well, there aren't always straight answers; can you ever understand that?"

"Well, no, I can't understand that. If you can't explain things to me rationally, then you might as well just make it all up," Ben responded dismissively, "and maybe that's why I would rather be a scientist than a rabbi."

"So you think I'm making it all up?" Marvin said. "If you believe that, then you're even dumber than I thought. It's a good thing *Zaydie* didn't hear you say that. He would have busted your ass."

* * *

Back at the Hillel table during registration, Ben asked, "Do you guys hold services every Shabbos?"

"Yes, we do. They're conservative services, but we have a deal with the Orthodox shul next door if you want to attend there. They welcome all UM students as well. Would you like us to send you more information about our programs?" The student was very friendly, and Ben told him, "Yes, I would like that." Ben handed the student one of his registration forms with his contact information on it, and then he took some of the handouts they had on the table.

It was still drizzling when Ben left the gym and walked over to Ulrich's Bookstore on the corner of East University and South University. Ben felt genuinely relieved to be registered, and he was looking forward to starting his classes later in the week. After buying all his textbooks—mostly used—he took them back to his dorm and put on the yellow, blue, and white book covers that Ulrich's had given him for free. As Ben filled in his name, room number, and book title on the inside of the book covers, he finally felt like a college student. He was smiling with a mild sense of self-satisfaction when he filled in the course information on the front covers of his new spiral notebooks. *Well, I guess my parents are happy now that I'm safely in college, and not aboard that tin can anymore,* he thought.

Ben's father, Samuel Bernstein, owned a jewelry store on Twelfth Street, near Hazelwood, next to Boesky's Delicatessen in the older Jewish section of Detroit. The area still supported an active Jewish community, and it was the commercial center for Jewish entrepreneurs. The jewelry store was a retail shop, but it was surrounded by a number of wholesale shops, so Ben's dad occasionally sold wholesale to friends and relatives; however, walk-ins always paid retail.

"Sam, Sam the jewelry man," Ben recalled one customer calling his dad. "Got any fancy-looking crap I could sell to the *schvartzes*?"

"You know I don't sell wholesale lots—you also know I sell to *anyone* that comes in my store, except maybe gonifs like you," Sam Bernstein answered somewhat jokingly, but letting the street peddler know he didn't appreciate his characterization of black people.

"Just kidding, my religious friend. Just kidding. Seriously, I need something for my wife's sister. It's her birthday. Got something nice for under twenty bucks?"

Sam Bernstein was not very religious, but the family did keep a relatively kosher house for Ben's *zaydie*. Outside the house, the occasional hamburger or Chinese food in a non-kosher place was something they enjoyed without feeling a lot of guilt.

When Ben finished high school in June of 1950, the Korean War had just started (the government called it a "police action"). Ben decided that if he was drafted, he would prefer not to go in the army. So he enlisted in the navy in the fall, just two months after the start of the war and three months after he turned eighteen.

"What's your hurry?" Ben's dad asked. "They probably wouldn't draft you for two more years, so what's your rush?"

"I just feel that my chances of getting in the navy by enlisting now are better than they will be in two years," Ben replied. Not very convincing, but Ben's dad recognized that he was not ready for college at that time, so neither of his parents argued, although he could tell that they were concerned with Ben joining the military during wartime.

"If that's what you want to do, then okay, do it," Sam Bernstein said. "Four years is a long time. I just hope that you'll still be interested in college when you get out. And maybe by then you'll have a better idea of what you want to be."

On an unusually hot and dusty September day in Detroit, Ben's parents, along with his brother, drove him downtown and dropped him off at the Federal Building. They kissed Ben good-bye; his mother Rose was crying, and his brother shook his hand firmly and then hugged him. With tears in his eyes, Marvin said, "Take care of yourself, you little schmuck, and come home safe or I'll beat the piss out of you."

"Nice talk for a practicing rabbi, even if you are in a reformed shul," Ben said, holding back his own tears.

* * *

After Ben's parents dropped him off at the Federal Building, a bus took him and the other new recruits to the train station for their trip to Great Lakes, Illinois, for basic training. Ben went on to Sonarman School in New London, Connecticut. After school and a brief tour of duty on a training ship, Ben ended up on a destroyer in the Sixth Fleet.

Aboard the destroyer, Ben developed a close friendship with hospital corpsman Mike Rabin. The two of them talked for hours about science, poetry, and whatever came into their heads. Mike's background was similar to Ben's, as both were Jewish and from Detroit.

One night, Mike and Ben were sitting up on the foc'sle deck, looking at the stars. They were also enjoying the bioluminescent plankton light up the water breaking over the bow as the ship knifed through the ocean. "I wonder what that shit is," Mike said, looking at the greenish-white light of the plankton. "Do you think that stuff can be used for anything?"

"Everything has some use," Ben said. "I'd bet that right now some scientist somewhere is studying that stuff and will probably come up with some use for it." Ben paused for a few moments and then said, "Maybe as a source for energy 'cause there's so much of it ..." They continued gazing at the stars, which were always magnificent on cloudless, moonless nights like it was that night.

"Hey, look!" Ben shouted. "There's a shooting star—see it?" He pointed up in the sky, but it was too late for Mike to see it. As Ben was pointing up, he suddenly became aware that they were sitting under the shadow of the forward five-inch gun turret, and the huge barrel of the gun conspicuously blotted out a portion of the night sky. And the reality hit Ben quite suddenly: the ship he was on was designed for one thing—war. Here he was, with his buddy Mike, enjoying the heaven's and the ocean's secrets, thinking about the good that mankind could do, yet the vehicle they were riding, which offered them these wondrous pleasures, was designed specifically for killing people.

How ridiculous was that? Ben thought.

It was then that Ben realized that he could never be a military person, for he believed with all his heart that "You shall not murder" was God's commandment ... and it could not be broken. Ben wasn't going to become a conscientious objector—that would be too radical—

but he knew that he was never going to be in any profession that might require him to kill someone.

"Maybe I'll become a vet, or a doctor, or someone who works to keep people and their pets alive," Ben told Mike, nostalgically remembering Stormy.

The two spent the next couple of hours talking before turning in, and both agreed that it seemed in some way sick to be on a killing machine and talking about science and the good it can do for civilization. Ben thought about this the whole night … and what he might do once he was out of the navy and in college. He knew that no matter what he studied, his dad would be pleased that he still believed strongly in living by God's commandments.

* * *

At dinner that night in East Quad, Ben met a number of other students, both upperclassmen and freshmen, who had all arrived during that week and were filling up the house. The staff gave a number of talks in the lounge about the rules and the code of behavior students were expected to follow while living at Strauss. They met the housemother, the resident advisor, and the rest of the housing staff—affectionately called "staff asses," which was shorthand for staff assistants. Seeing the diversity of the other students and staff, Ben couldn't help making the connection between them—a number of whom were veterans like Ben—and the guys he had met while in the navy. The new students he was meeting made him think about some of the young sailors he met as he recalled his trip to downtown Detroit, and then off on his navy adventure.

Ben felt alone that night in his room in East Quad, even though all the students seemed to be nice kids and easy to get along with. He had been sitting around the lounge with some of the other vets, which made him feel like he truly belonged, but Ben couldn't help but wonder, right before falling asleep that night, if they believed in God's commandments as he did.

NINE: *There is no new thing under the sun.*
—Ecclesiastes 1:9

Once classes started, Ben found his favorite teacher, an astronomy professor named Mabel Coulson. On that first day of classes, Ben came early and took a seat in the fourth row of the large lecture hall, watching as the room filled with students. At promptly 10:10, Professor Coulson walked in. She was a short, somewhat round woman who looked to be in her fifties, with a jovial girlish face. She was dressed in a somewhat unexpected outfit: an unremarkable dark skirt, a simple white blouse, an unbuttoned sweater, and oddly, saddle oxfords with white bobby socks. Around her neck, she wore some kind of pendant hanging from a piece of thick string. Hanging from her waistband, her Phi Beta Kappa key was attached to a silver chain that was somehow—perhaps with a safety pin?—hooked to her skirt. Even from the fourth row, where Ben was sitting, he noticed the safety pin and key; Ben fell in love with her instantly.

"Okay, quiet down, quiet down," she said. "I'm Professor Coulson, and this is Astronomy 11—freshman, or beginning, astronomy—the solar system. For those planning to take Astronomy 12 next semester, we'll cover the stars, nebulae, and galaxies then. Is there anyone here who thought this was something else?" she asked. Seeing no hands go up, she continued in her well-practiced way to tell the students how the course would be conducted, what they needed to do in order to pass, and to always take the same seat when they came to her lecture.

She passed out a seating chart with a box for every seat in the room (including those along the back wall) and instructed the students to print their names in the corresponding box. She also warned them that attendance would be taken, and attendance was mandatory unless they had an excusable absence. The room had around one hundred seats, and Ben wondered how, with that many people, she would take attendance every time.

Ben soon found out that Professor Coulson had a remarkable memory. She would take attendance by simply looking around the room; and without the aid of the seating chart, which she had memorized by the second day of classes, she would announce who was absent and ask if anybody knew why.

"I see Miss Adams is missing today, and so is Mr. Shemansky. Are they skipping class together?" she asked in an impish way one day.

One student said, "I saw them having coffee at the Union."

Another added, "He's at practice, and she's watching him."

"Well, you tell them that they better start practicing their attendance here because the football plays Miss Adams is watching Mr. Shemansky learn on the practice field won't help either of them in the fields of science." And then she started her lecture for the day with a smile on her face and a romantic gleam in her eye.

Doc Coulson (everyone called her Doc Coulson, even her students) had a host of talents that she revealed to the class little by little. Many of the students had heard about her from friends and relatives, and they knew about her fantastic teaching ability. They were aware that she was ambidextrous—she could draw two different charts on the blackboard simultaneously. They were all aware of her wide-ranging memory; and they knew that she was the national secretary for Phi Beta Kappa, the academic honor society, and proudly wore her ΦBK key every day. They also knew that she wore a green eyeshade visor when she graded exams or term projects, looking like some kind of Mafioso accountant. But most importantly, they knew she was a brilliant woman who loved teaching and loved her students, no matter how eccentric she might be.

* * *

Ben learned that she'd never married. She lived on campus with her mother, in a house on East University, just down the street from East Quad. People knew it was Doc Coulson's house because in the second-story window, they could see her brass sextant, which she used to check out the declination of planets and other celestial bodies. But when she was in class and it came to discussing anything the least bit sexual, she would blush and giggle like a fourteen-year-old schoolgirl. There were always a number of jocks in her class, and they would be the first to initiate a giggling event.

"Doc Coulson, is it true that the constellation Virgo was named after a beautiful Roman goddess? And didn't she have a lot of godlike lovers?" one of the jocks asked.

"No, no," Doc Coulson answered, a hint of red showing up on her cheeks. "She was a Greek goddess, but you're talking about astrology, and this class is about astronomy." She was clearly anxious to get on with her lecture.

"Do you mean that in astronomy we can't talk about love and the relationships the gods had with each other?" the jock persisted. "Is there a course on astrology that I can take that covers those things?"

"If you're so interested in 'those things,' you can take my history course after you successfully finish the freshman astronomy sequence," she said with a straight face. "And if you're truly interested, then see me later for some readings you could start with." At this point, she started to giggle, and the class started to laugh. It was contagious, and the laughter and her giggling would continue for a while, until Doc Coulson got the class back on track.

Ben and the other vets in the class had to have their monthly course attendance and progress forms signed by their instructors, or their GI allowance for the month might be withheld. So at the end of each month, there were always vets and jocks hanging around her desk.

On one brisk Monday morning, following a Saturday football game, with the usual crowd hanging around her desk after class, Doc Coulson started to kid one of the football players. "You missed that pass, Mr. Mants. That would have given us the win—why did you do that? Next time hang on to the ball," she teased. But Mants's dropped pass hadn't lost the game for Michigan, and everybody knew that.

Mants smiled sheepishly, but he knew her joshing was not meant to be cruel; Doc Coulson would never be cruel to a student.

The small crowd of mostly male students gave the appearance that she might be playing favorites with the men. The banter was great, and the few women brave enough to be up there joined in on the fun.

One time, Ben noticed Doc Coulson was wearing a necklace that looked like a piece of lead hanging from a leather strap. She always wore some kind of doodad around her neck, but this time he had to make a comment while waiting to get his attendance form signed. "Gee, Doc Coulson, that's an interesting piece of jewelry you have on—what is it?"

"Oh, you mean this piece of lead," she said, holding it up for all the gang around her desk to see. "One of my graduate students was doing a project, and he noticed that this piece of lead had a pockmarked surface that looked like the surface of the moon. So he gave it to me. I just drilled a hole in it and hung it from my neck with this old lanyard string," she explained, smiling. "Do you think it looks like the moon surface, Mr. Bernstein?"

"It certainly does, Doc Coulson. Is that the crater Tycho I see there?" Ben said in jest. Doc Coulson just smiled at him, catching his humor, and looked admiringly at her piece of Selene jewelry.

Clarice Adams—one of the jock's girlfriends—whom Ben had been tutoring, was also at her desk that day to simply comment on how nice Doc Coulson looked in her new sweater. Doc Coulson got that girlish look going. Blushing and giggling, she said, "Oh, this is just some old sweater I haven't worn in a while. Do you really like it?"

Ben was impressed that Clarice, whom Ben liked, would go out of her way to make Doc Coulson feel good about her looks. Ben didn't think any other student would have done that.

* * *

Living in a university residence hall, Ben and his fellow housemates had the opportunity to invite faculty members for an occasional dinner. The person who came up with the recommendation would join the invited faculty with a small number of other students and some staff assistants for a discussion after dinner, over coffee and dessert.

Ben suggested Doc Coulson as a possible dinner guest. Ben was on the house student council by then and had heard other students also admiring Doc Coulson. Students were interested in some of the more modern questions concerning astronomy since rocket science seemed to be the current topic of interest, and going to the moon was approaching a reality. When Ben suggested Doc Coulson, he was surprised to hear a negative comment.

"She's really not a scholar, you know," said one upperclassman. "You know, she's somewhat of a joke to the science community here on campus. She did her dissertation on stellar spectral analysis—you know, spectroscopy—but she hasn't published a scientific article in years. You know she's only an associate professor," he added with some disdain.

Ben was taken aback, but he didn't respond to the other student's remarks, including the fact that he said "you know" too many times. Neither did anyone else for that matter, and some even nodded in agreement. Ben was new to university life and had no idea what was meant by "only an associate professor." He thought a professor was a professor, so what was the big deal?

Ben also had no idea what stellar spectroscopy was, but it certainly sounded quite sophisticated and scientific to him. "Maybe she hasn't published because she hates to write," Ben speculated. In any event, Ben pressed his case for inviting her and got the student council's approval. The housemother—they called her Mrs. Mac, which was short for McHenry—who had to do the inviting was surprised when she heard that the council had approved Ben's recommendation. When she saw Ben, she congratulated him on such a fine choice—a female faculty member. But she too had heard the nonsense about Doc Coulson's reputation as a football-loving, easy-grading teacher, and she asked Ben why he picked her.

"You know, Benjamin,"—she never called him Ben—"there are a lot of famous faculty members here at Michigan, and I'm curious as to why you want me to invite her. You're not doing this in order to get a better grade, are you?" Mrs. Mac chided Ben with a motherly smile on her face.

"Oh, no, of course not," Ben said defensively, "I'm doing very well in her class, and I'm even tutoring one of the students. I just thought that some of us would like to spend more time with her on a social level and talk about modern astronomy—rockets to the moon, what the other planets are made of, and the kind of stuff that we don't always talk about in class." Ben made that up on the spot because of what that upperclassman said about her not being scientific anymore. Ben just thought she would be fun to have over for dinner, and he wanted to chat with her about her life here in Ann Arbor.

"Well, then that should be of interest to the other boys," Mrs. Mac said. "I'll invite her for our regular Wednesday night faculty dinner."

On Wednesday evening at six sharp, Doc Coulson knocked on the housemother's apartment door, where Ben, some other student council members, most of the staff assistants, and a couple of other students were waiting for her to arrive. There were twelve of them in all, counting Doc Coulson, which was the largest number of people they were allowed to have at these dinners. All the men were wearing their required evening dinner dress—jackets and ties—but some of the guys looked as if they had slept in their jackets and eaten dinner off their ties.

Doc Coulson was wearing exactly what she wore in class, looking just as disheveled and uncaring about her clothes as she always did. Mrs. Mac, on the other hand, wore a stylish dress, high heels, and tasteful jewelry. Her silver hair was elegantly done up. She looked like the widow of a renowned faculty member—which is exactly what she was. Since Ben was the one who'd suggested inviting Doc Coulson, he had to do the introductions.

When Ben took her coat, he could see Mrs. Mac smiling admiringly at this gentle soul of a woman. There were brief introductions all around, and then Doc Coulson said, "I had your brother Albert for a student, Mr. Chalmers, in 1949, and if I'm not mistaken, your sister Rebecca was in my class in fifty-one—she did very well. Why didn't you take my class?" she asked with a mock hurt look on her face.

Dicky Chalmers sputtered some lame excuse about why he was taking another natural science sequence. Doc Coulson smiled at Dicky, and he seemed to relax, clearly looking forward to talking with this Michigan legend.

"Astronomy is certainly becoming an important field today, what with all the interest in rockets and atomic science," Mrs. Mac said to

Doc Coulson. "Why, just the other day, Benjamin was saying how interested he is in those things, weren't you, Benjamin?"

"So you're interested in rocket science, Mr. Bernstein?" Doc Coulson asked.

"Well, yes, and other sciences too," Ben said. He couldn't believe he said "other sciences too." How awkward was that? So Ben went on trying to talk less like a dumb kid, saying, "I think I would like to be a science teacher," believing that sounded more mature.

Doc Coulson beamed at Ben when she heard that, and for the first time, he noticed a twinkle in her eye, which he hadn't seen before. "I imagine you might enjoy what I have to say to you and your friends later today."

When dinner was over, it was the custom for the guest to make a brief opening remark to set the tone and then answer any questions the students might have. Mrs. Mac got things going by saying, "So what would you like to talk to us about today, Professor Coulson?"

Ben wasn't sure what the gang expected to hear, but they were all a little surprised when Doc Coulson took out a piece of paper, put her eyeglasses on, and read:

> *If the stars should appear one night in a thousand years, how would men believe and adore; and preserve for many generations the remembrance of the city of God which had been shown! But every night come out these envoys of beauty, and light the universe with their admonishing smile.*

"Ralph Waldo Emerson wrote that many years ago. When I first heard that, I knew I wanted to be an astronomer. I wanted to describe what the heavens looked like on that once-in-a-thousand-years event that everyone would want to see. And that's what I think teaching science is all about—making things seem like they only happened once in a thousand years."

Doc Coulson was looking right at Ben and smiling when she said that. She went on for another five minutes or so, talking about the beauty of the stars, the planets, and her favorite heavenly bodies— the comets. How she marveled in them, and how they inspired her to learn more and to tell others about them. She said absolutely nothing about the scientific elements of astronomy, just the aesthetics, but the students were fascinated. It was then that Ben realized why he liked her so much: he knew that she was an incorrigible romantic.

* * *

Doc Coulson's reputation did not need any more boosting to convince people she was a unique person at Michigan, but her popularity among coeds who wanted to be scientists was legendary. In some sense, it was due, in part, to a negative image. Some of them felt that if *she* could be a scientist, then they certainly could. But it wouldn't take long for students to realize what an outstanding scientific mind she had, and how interesting her courses were.

One thing most people didn't know about Doc Coulson was that she had a vast knowledge of mythology and ancient religious practices. That knowledge and her understanding of history often gave her insight into why some people appeared to act irrationally. From Ben's perspective, her astronomical background played an important role in this particular analytical ability, giving her another method of inquiry into problem solving. Problem solving—or, more appropriately, problem identification—was one of her strongest talents.

* * *

On Monday, November 22, after the Ohio State game, one of Michigan's football players, backup tight end Edward Shemansky, never returned from Columbus. He was not on the train coming back from Columbus, but that in itself was not unusual. Many Michigan players—including Shemansky—were from Ohio, and many of them stayed in Columbus after the game. The Thanksgiving vacation started on the following Wednesday, so it was a short week, and a number of students took off early for the long weekend.

But the events surrounding Shemansky's failure to return to Michigan were far more devastating than simply skipping three days of school. In addition, the need for Doc Coulson's unique capabilities would soon become apparent.

TEN: *Arise and thresh, O daughter of Zion.*
—Micah 4:13

Clarice Adams was a good-looking eighteen-year-old girl with an outgoing nature. Her personality complemented her boyfriend's character. Edward Shemansky was not as outgoing, and he was always a little too serious for the guys in his fraternity house. But Clarice charmed them all, and Ed was given a lot more credit for being her steady. The two of them hit it off immediately, and they were definitely attracted to each other, but they seemed to think of each other more as a friend than as a boyfriend or girlfriend. They had absolutely no idea that they were blood cousins.

Miss Adams, as Doc Coulson called her, was from Great Neck, New York, and she had a common learning disorder—an inability to visualize a three-dimensional object on a two-dimensional surface, like on a blackboard or a page in a book.

In a beginning astronomy class, a lot of time was spent on spatially locating celestial bodies on an imaginary globe in space, called the celestial sphere. Ben was in the same class and lab that Clarice Adams was in, and at their first lab session, the lab instructor (a graduate teaching assistant) said, "Ben, you and Clarice should pair up." He could see that Ed was Clarice's boyfriend, but he thought it best to have her work with someone else, so he arbitrarily picked Ben.

Ben thought Clarice was one of the most beautiful girls he'd ever seen, and he got that tingling sensation in his stomach when the instructor assigned the two of them to be lab partners. It was early in the semester, but Ben knew Clarice was going with Ed, and that made him feel a little uncomfortable, but he was thrilled to be working in the lab with her anyway.

It didn't take a genius to see that no matter how much skill Clarice had in algebraically calculating celestial positions, try as she might, she could not visualize a sphere—or a globe—when it was represented as a circle with an ellipse drawn in the center.

Ben saw Clarice's problem immediately when she tried to explain what she saw. It was apparent to him that she would never be able to do the problems using the methodology taught in class and the lab. So Ben worked with her on how to numerically calculate the coordinates and then draw them on the 3-D diagram, and it worked beautifully for Clarice.

"Ben, would you be able to tutor me in astronomy?" Clarice asked one day. "I'll pay you of course—we'll work something out. Is that okay with you?"

"I don't mind helping you out in astronomy … hey, but don't forget I'm just learning this stuff myself," Ben replied. "Uh … let's not worry about any money. We'll play it by ear and see if it works out."

From the time Ben became Clarice's astronomy tutor, they also became good friends. Ben could never be her boyfriend, or so he thought, because he felt that at twenty-two, he was probably too old for her—but he could be more like the big brother she never had. He was also keenly aware that she already had a boyfriend in Ed Shemansky.

Ben also became her sounding board for an entire list of social and academic problems and, in particular, her relationship with Ed. "One of Ed's fraternity brothers was asking him how to find girls," Clarice said, "so Ed asked me to help out … fix him up with someone I know."

"So did you?" Ben asked.

"No, I said I'd try, but I haven't. This friend of Ed's is on the team, and he's a real loud-mouthed bully. I wouldn't fix him up with any of my friends."

"Just tell Ed that you wouldn't fix up any of your friends with anyone you wouldn't date yourself. Ed should understand that."

"You're right! That takes a load off my mind. Thanks, my friend."

In any case, Ben thought that if tutoring Clarice gave him a chance to know her better, and maybe even a chance to date her in the future, then that would be marvelous.

* * *

During one of their many study sessions Ben learned that Clarice was Jewish, even though Adams didn't sound Jewish. She said her grandparents changed their name from Adamski when they emigrated from Poland around the turn of the century. "So I'm Jewish like you," she told Ben, "though you'd never know it by looking at me."

Clarice's blond hair, fair complexion, slender frame, and small nose made her look more like what Clarice's mother thought was the look of a typical shiksa. Clarice's mother, whose maiden name was Silver, picked the name Clarice simply because she liked the sound ... and the fact that it had absolutely no Jewish or Hebrew equivalency. Clarice's parents were raised in a time when assimilation was not only considered acceptable, but socially preferable.

Clarice grew up on Long Island, and although most of her friends were Jewish, she had little in the way of any formal Jewish upbringing, other than attending the weddings and bar mitzvahs of her friends and relatives. The only exception was speaking Yiddish with her mother's parents, Professor and Mrs. Seymour Silver. Of course, Clarice would never think of denying her Jewish roots, nor would her mother, under any circumstances, expect her to.

"My dad will be pleased that my astronomy tutor is Jewish. He was upset when I told him my boyfriend was a football player, even though he's Jewish too! My mom knows Ed's family and couldn't care less—in fact, she doesn't like to talk about who's Jewish and who isn't. She says my chances for having a career in the movies would be better if people didn't know. She keeps telling me all about these famous actresses who are Jewish but changed their names so they could make it in the movies." Clarice looked uneasy while telling Ben about her mother's foibles. "She told me that Lauren Bacall's name was Betty Perske, and she knew about her 'cause she was from New York." After a brief pause, Clarice said emphatically, "Well, I don't give a damn about being an actress. I would rather be an artist ... or even a scientist, if I thought I was smart enough. But Mom says actors and actresses have it made, so I should either marry a doctor or become an actress."

They both laughed at that because it was a well-known Jewish stereotype that Jewish girls were supposed to marry Jewish doctors.

It was late October and it was getting chilly in Ann Arbor. They had been studying at the library and were sitting outside on the huge concrete staircase that ran up to the front doors of the main library.

"Oh," Clarice said, "I almost forgot this," and she handed Ben a skinny gift-wrapped box she had been carrying with her books. "You'll be needing it now that it's getting colder. I understand that Ann Arbor can really get bitchin' cold in the winter."

Ben opened the box, and inside was a beautiful blue plaid cashmere scarf. "What's this all about?" he asked, feeling a little embarrassed about getting a gift and not knowing why.

"It's for tutoring me—you never would accept any money, so it's the least I can do. Why, don't you like it?" She had the cutest grin on her face and seemed pleased with herself for surprising Ben like that.

"No, no ... I, uh, I really love it. It's the nicest scarf I've ever had. I don't have one, you know. We never wore scarves in the navy, at least not the enlisted men." Ben carefully folded it back up and put it back in the box. He was touched by her thoughtfulness.

Clarice then gave him a peck on the cheek and said, "I'll see ya tomorrow." She walked off to her dorm on the hill.

It was then that Ben realized that he was more than simply attracted to her.

* * *

Ben went home that weekend to visit with his folks. He also planned on going to a Halloween party on Saturday night, even though Halloween fell on Sunday that year. It was Saturday morning, and his father was at the store—Sam Bernstein rarely went to the store on Shabbos—so just Ben and his mother were sitting around talking that morning.

"Ma, haven't I heard you mention the name Shemansky? Isn't it someone related to us?"

"Of course, darling," she said. "Your Uncle Saul the druggist—you know his drugstore on Linwood, where we would go for ice cream— married a Shemansky girl. That was your Aunt Channa's maiden name.

You know, my brother Saul was your father's friend from high school. In fact, Saul introduced your father to me, but you knew that."

"How did they meet? I mean Uncle Saul and Aunt Channa. Was she from around here?"

"No, no … she's from Ohio. She met Saul at a Hashomer Hatzair camp that was held on a farm near Fremont, Ohio, when they were teenagers. She's older than Uncle Saul, you know, but they seemed to hit it off anyway."

So she was from Ohio … *She has to be related to Ed,* Ben thought. "Wasn't the Hashomer movement a Zionist youth group? Did they want to go to Israel?"

"Yes, Saul was active in Zionist organizations, and Channa's *bubbie* moved from the old country to Palestine, so the two of them—"

"Did you meet Aunt Channa's family? Did any of them have a son named Edward?" Ben asked excitedly.

"Yes and no … I met them at the wedding. The family went down to Cleveland for the wedding at Channa's house. Her father was a professor at Case University, and her mother—I think her name was Irene—was a very nice, cultured woman from the Old Country. I was just seventeen then, I think … Hmm. But Hannah—that's what her family called her—didn't have any married brothers or sisters then."

Rose thought a bit more, and then said, "I heard later from Uncle Saul that Channa's younger brother Joey got married in New York. I think he moved back to Cleveland, and I heard that he had a son. Channa told me that Joey's son was her parents' only grandchild. Uncle Saul and Channa never did have any children and …"

Rose was beginning to ramble, and Ben interrupted. "Do you remember if Joey's son's name is Edward … or Ed?"

"I don't remember. Why, is he one of your friends at school?"

Ben mentioned Ed and Clarice, and the possibility of Ed being part of Ben's *meshpucha* (extended family). If Ed's father was Joey, then Ed and Ben had a common aunt and uncle; and even though they wouldn't be blood related, they would be, in some sense, cousins. Maybe then Ed wouldn't be too concerned about Ben tutoring Clarice, and it might even mean that Ed would get Ben better seats at the football games. Ben looked forward to going back to Ann Arbor and talking with Ed. *Who knows,* Ben thought, *we might even become close friends.*

* * *

The one thing Ben noticed about Clarice that made her seem different from the other girls was that she swore more than they did. She never swore like the guys Ben knew in the navy—as in "Pass the fuckin' butter." She simply said hell, damn, and shit—and she loved the term bitchin'. Ben thought that maybe the term bitchin' (he'd never heard the expression before) was a New York thing, and that other girls from New York used it too. In any case, Ben liked the fact that she didn't care what other people might think about her swearing. It showed that she had a mind of her own, and Ben admired that.

Another thing about Clarice that Ben admired, but wasn't sure why, was that she posed naked for an art class.

Clarice had signed up for an art class, and on her first day, the professor asked her if she would be willing to pose in his life drawing class a little later in the semester. He told her that the students were mostly upperclassmen and grad students, and they would not act silly or embarrass her. Clarice told Ben she wasn't concerned about being embarrassed, and when she found out how much she would be paid for six hours a week—twenty-five dollars an hour—she quickly accepted it.

"That's more money in one week than I could make in a month working full-time at home," Clarice told Ben. "It's all very nonsexual, you know, but don't you ever tell Eddy—he'd have a real shit fit. I walk into class from a private dressing room in the back, wearing this big old terry cloth robe. Then the professor sits me down on some cushions, poses me, makes sure I'm comfortable, and when I'm ready and feel I can sit like that for a while, I just open my robe and drop it down." She gestured as she spoke, showing him the process, and Ben, watching her motions, started to become turned on. She said, "In some of the poses, I felt a little uncomfortable, like maybe they were trying to do a crotch shot, so I just didn't do it."

That last declaration made Ben sweat as he visualized the process. "Maybe I'll try to come over and watch you work sometime," he said with a grin.

"Don't you dare do that!" Clarice said. "If I saw you sitting out there, I would be totally embarrassed and upset. Don't even kid about it."

"Okay, okay," Ben said. "I was just teasing." Ben then realized how childish his remark was. Here she was, talking to him about this job that she obviously felt a little uneasy about, and here he was, making it sound dirty. "Look, all kidding aside now, I think that posing nude for an art class is okay—even though you didn't ask me—and there's no doubt modeling pays well. The course is supervised, so there's nothing wrong with it. I also realize that if I was dumb enough to walk in on the class just to hassle you, the art students would probably kill me, as well they should. And knowing you the way I do, even in the short time we've been working together, I know you take your job seriously, and that it's hard work. But even more importantly, you have the looks and talent to be a model, so you should definitely take advantage of the opportunity."

Clarice let the subject drop, but by the slight smile and look of relief on her face, one could tell that she felt better about her job after Ben's clarification.

* * *

Clarice and Ben were studying in the library for their astronomy midterm exam when Ben asked her about Ed and the other jocks, and if she ever studied together with them.

"Not really. They have their own way of studying for exams. They look at old exams and just redo them—and I don't think that would help me."

"Maybe Ed would like it more if you did study with him. What do you think?"

"You're right," Clarice agreed. "I sometimes feel guilty that Ed and I don't study as much together as maybe we should. I mean, if we're going steady, then you'd think I would want to spend more time with him." However, her eyes told Ben that she really didn't feel that she wanted to be with Ed all the time.

"You know, when I went home at Halloween, I was talking with my mom, and she told me that Ed and I have the same aunt and uncle," Ben casually told Clarice.

"You mean you're Ed's cousin, and you're just telling me now?" she asked, somewhat shocked.

"Well, not by blood. My mother's brother is married to Ed's father's sister; we're just *meshpucha*, I think. And I just found out recently myself."

"Sounds complicated to me; either you're related or you're not—which is it?" she asked. "Oh, forget it. I just was feeling funny talking to you this way about Ed if he's your cousin. Makes it a little harder being so open with you about how I feel about him, but ..."

"Well, it really hasn't changed my feelings about you ... or him ... or us," Ben said. "After all, I just met him this year. Whether or not he's my cousin, or some unrelated family member, doesn't change a thing for me. I can still be your friend and confidant without any false sense of family loyalty, so don't worry about telling me how you feel, okay?"

They then got back to studying in their fixed routine—Ben would give her new problems, and she would work out the answers. Ben would then check her answers with his. Ben would use the drawings and Clarice would do the calculations. By the end of their study time, she was getting her answers to the problems almost as fast as Ben was.

They both aced the midterm: Ben got 95 percent, and Clarice got 97 percent. She had a better grasp of the nontechnical elements, like the names of stars and constellations, than Ben did. Ed got an A too, but Ben never did know how many points he got, though it had to be at least 90.

Ben had talked with Ed before the midterm exam in early November about his Uncle Saul, and Ed was surprised to find out that he and Ben had a common aunt and uncle.

"Yeah, yeah ... Uncle Saul the druggist; I haven't seen them in years. They used to come and visit us for Pesach, but it's been a few years since they've done that," Ed said. "Small world ... small world, isn't it? So we're almost cousins, right?"

Ben just smiled and nodded his head, and that's about as close as they got. However, there was a sense of kinship there, and Ben did feel that Ed was more relaxed with him being Clarice's tutor. Maybe their friendship would flourish, but Ben wasn't counting on it.

* * *

It became apparent later that fall, just before the Thanksgiving break, that Clarice and Ed's commitment as a couple was cooling down. Clarice made it clear to Ed that he should be dating others because she didn't want to go steady anymore. She wanted to stay friends because she did feel something for him and, let's face it, having a nice-looking football player for a boyfriend was not something that most girls would just throw away. Also, her grandparents, the Silvers, and Ed's grandparents, the Shemanskys, were good friends, and so, in some respects, Ed was more like family.

But what she did begin to notice was that her feelings toward Ben were getting more intense. She told him that she missed him when they didn't have to study some nights, and she was looking forward to next semester, when the two of them would be taking the next astronomy class from Doc Coulson.

"Supposing I have trouble in that class too—with those shitty 3-D diagrams—would you still tutor me?" she asked Ben.

"Hey, I would tutor you in any subject you took if it meant I got to see your delightful face even more than I do now," Ben said in his typical half-serious, half-joking fashion.

"I mean it," Clarice protested with a smile. "Can I depend on you to help me get through other science classes?"

"Clarice, you should know by now that I enjoy working and studying with you, and not just because you're the nicest person I know," Ben answered, still half joking. After a short pause, he got more serious. "One thing I found out is that I learn more tutoring you than I would if I had to study alone. So, yes, yes, and yes … you can definitely count on me."

ELEVEN: *And thou shalt teach them diligently unto thy children.*
—Deuteronomy 6:7

In the meantime, Ed Shemansky, who didn't return from Ohio after the UM-OSU game on November 20, had more than astronomy, football, and Clarice to worry about because other generations of Reuben Wickler's would soon come into his life.

This new Wickler menace went by the name of Robin Wicken because his grandmother, Rena Wickler, had changed their family name for fear that the person she thought murdered her husband, Professor Reuben Wickler, back in Poland would come looking for her and her son.

Rena never knew her grandson Robin, who was born in Cleveland on March 3, 1935, and although his father, Stanislaw, made a good living, Robin didn't stand much of a chance of becoming a success. Robin's paternal grandfather was either murdered or had accidentally drowned many years earlier. One of the reasons that Robin—they said his name was sort of an anglicized form of Reuben—didn't have a chance at success was because his father didn't do a very good job of raising him.

Stanislaw Wicken's income working for the mob allowed him to have more financial freedom than he was used to, and when his mother was gone, his income was boosted by 25 percent. He once asked Miron why he continued to stay in the boardinghouse when he could afford a much better place to live. "I'm still sending money to my parents and family in Poland—I would rather they had it than I should spend it on luxuries," he explained. "Besides I like it here; I know everyone, the room is clean, and the food wholesome ... so it's good enough. Why do you ask?"

"I don't know. I think I would like to live in a fancier place with a chance to meet younger girls. This place is fine for old people—please forgive me—I mean people older than me," Stan clarified, "so I'm looking at a place nearer downtown. What do you think?"

"I think you're right; you should move into a place where a young man, who is not so young anymore, might find a wife. Yes, you should move closer to downtown and have more fun," Miron advised. Both were speaking Polish, and when Stan realized that he would be moving away from Miron, he did get a little frightened. He wouldn't have the comfort of someone like Miron, whom he could speak with easily without worrying about his accent.

But Stan did move into a fancier place that was more like a residential hotel. He could eat in the downstairs restaurant or in his two-room suite, which had a small kitchen. He liked eating out now that he could afford it, so he dined at a number of nice restaurants and clubs. He started dating some of the women he met at the residence, and in 1933, he met and married Nadia—a young Russian immigrant who was anxious to marry an American.

In 1933, the Volstead Act was repealed, and liquor sales were now legal again—which meant that the people he and Miron worked for would be changing their business model. They kept two major enterprises: a legal liquor distributorship and an illegal off-track gambling operation. They were also in the neighborhood protection business, extorting money from the small businesses in the older Jewish neighborhoods. It was in the extortion business that they had Stan doing what he did best—putting the muscle on store owners to pay up.

Much to her dismay, Nadia got pregnant in 1934. In 1935, their baby boy, Robin, was born. Nadia got citizenship through Stan and almost immediately started looking for a more exciting life. She had no idea what Stan did for a living, but whatever it was, she knew she could do better. She started staying out late, going to dance halls and clubs, and sometimes staying out all night. Stan could only take so much of this. When Robin was just two years old, Stan let Nadia know what he did do for a living.

He first beat her to within an inch of her life, explaining in a mix of Polish, English, and Russian, "See, this is what I do for a living," and then he put her on notice. "I'm moving out, so you can fuck whoever, but I'm paying you to take care of Robin, you understand? I will keep the money coming as long as Robin is okay, but if I see he is not okay, or you're not taking care of him, you will not only lose the money, but I'll kill you and get some other *nafka* to take care of the boy, you get the picture."

Stan had made it very clear that it was in Nadia's best interest to raise her son as best she could, with obviously enough money for a relatively comfortable life. She was free to keep looking, but odds were she would never get a better deal.

Nadia did try to give Robin (she called him Robbie) a good home, mostly out of fear of what would happen to her if she didn't. Once she stayed out all night with a guy she thought would take her away from Cleveland, to a glamorous life in New York, or at least that's what he promised as soon as he got enough dough together. When Nadia tried to contact him the following week, after he never called her back as he had promised, she found out that he had "left the area." She wasn't sure exactly what that meant, but if it meant what she thought it did—that he was dead—that was enough to scare her out of ever leaving young Robbie by himself again.

"Robbala, my baby, I never leave you alone again, you hear?" Nadia told Robbie and hugged him tight. "I only left you alone one time—for work, if somebody ask. You believe me now, okay?"

Robbie went to school in Shaker Heights because the schools were better there, and his father made sure his mother lived in the Shaker Heights School District. He wasn't a bad student, but he wasn't a good one either. In 1940, when he started school, he was rather slim and had a fair complexion. He looked a lot like his mother, except one could tell that he would be much taller than she was. Nadia was not interested in his schoolwork, and she did little to encourage him, other than to tell him that if he didn't behave, his father would come back and beat him.

Maybe it was because he didn't have a father in his life, or that his mother didn't seem to care much about what he did, or that somehow the greasers he ran around with were some kind of substitute family, but that was the company he preferred. By the time Robbie finished high school and went out on his own, his future was well determined.

* * *

When Robin Wicken turned nineteen in 1954, he had been out of school for over one year. He told his mother he was leaving home and going out on his own.

"Look," he said, "I'm just in your way here, and I think I would rather be living by myself. I don't need your money so don't worry about that, and don't start with the 'you know, I love you' shit because we both know it ain't true."

"Okay honey, okay … If that's what you want, I'm okay. But if someone should ask you, I never treat you bad. You tell them I never treat you bad … I no kick you out, okay?" Nadia said in her Russian accent.

Robbie didn't know what she was talking about, but she always seemed to be worried about someone thinking she was not a good mother. Every time he cried when he was little, she would worry and say pretty much the same thing about not telling anyone she treated him badly. Whatever. He wouldn't have to put up with her two-faced bullshit anymore.

Robbie had discovered marijuana in high school and started smoking it or eating it laced in brownies. He would buy it from some guy who wasn't in school but who hung out near the school, selling it to the other kids. Robbie had also noticed that some of the high school jocks, like Ed Shemansky, would buy from the same guy, so they would occasionally exchange a "hi."

The guy who sold them the dope was beginning to look his age, which was around twenty-two, so he had to stop selling at the school before it looked conspicuous. He asked Robbie, who was one of his regular customers and still looked young enough to be in school, if he wanted a job. "You'll get to keep 20 percent on all the joints you sell. That means you get ten cents for each joint. If you buy a nickel bag, that's your cost; you can make around twenty skinny joints, so that's a bargain for you if you want to roll your own."

After figuring out how much money he could make in a week during the school year, Robbie had grabbed it. There was no legitimate way that he could make that kind of dough while out on his own.

Robbie found a small apartment in one of the four-story apartment houses in a nice neighborhood on Essex Road, between Glenville and Shaker Heights. He told the people there that he was studying to be an electronics technician, and his family thought it would be better if he had his own place.

He didn't hang out in Shaker Heights because people knew him around there, so he went to the large newer schools in Cleveland Heights and other wealthy suburbs around Cleveland. Business was good, and he was recognized by most of the students as the campus swingman, but he was careful enough not to raise any questions. His contact, the old Shaker Heights swingman, had moved up in the organization to a supplier. He made contact with Robbie by leaving notes in envelopes slipped under his apartment door. All the supplier wrote down was a date and time—for example, Oct 6 210 meant that Robbie was to be at the warehouse on Wednesday, October 6, at 2:10 in the afternoon. It was always on weekdays and at times when people would be in the area, so that two men casually walking around would not create any suspicion. After a few weeks, his contact would frequently not show up at the warehouse, but they had a special place where goods and money could be stashed on a shelf in the warehouse for short periods without fear of discovery.

Robbie was living well for a kid just out of school. He had a brand-new 1953 Chevrolet convertible, he had nice clothes, and he threw some wild parties for a select few of his dope-using greaser friends.

Then one day in mid-November 1954, he had an unexpected visitor. He heard a knock on his door, but before he could even ask who was there, three men walked in the door. One was a big man, well dressed in a pin-striped suit, an old-fashioned fedora hat, and shiny black wing tip dress shoes. While the other two men were also big, they were younger. Immediately, Robbie thought they must be his bosses … and they wanted to give him a big promotion. He never even questioned the fact that they entered through a door he always kept locked, and that the two younger men were wearing long raincoats when it wasn't even raining.

"You da kid that sells joints at da school?" the big man asked in an Eastern European accent.

"Who's asking?" Robbie countered, a bit scared.

"Your mama asked me to look in on you to see if you all right. Are you all right?"

"Oh, shit … yeah, yeah I'm fine … and no, she never beat me or treated me badly. Is that what you wanted to know?" Robbie thought that finally the people his mother had told him about were there to check him out.

"Don't be such a wiseass. I know she not beat you. But why you sell shit to kids? What you do is for *schvartzes*, not for smart kid like you. Look, if you want, I get you better job doing hard work, but no trouble with police. I pay for apartment too until you can afford better; what you say, yes?" the big man asked, and Robbie could tell he would not accept a no.

"Who are you?" Robbie asked.

"Just friend of your father, okay? You do what I say, and you and mama will not get hurt. Your mama not get hurt, better for everyone. I be back next week to tell you where to go and who to see for job. Here." The big man counted out five twenty-dollar bills and handed them to Robbie. "This enough to last till I come back, so stop selling shit. You no need to tell your supply man; I already tell him no more supplies and to forget you ever worked for him. He understand."

The three men left the apartment, leaving the door open … and Robbie wondering what the hell had just happened. From what his mother said, he'd always suspected his father was tied to the mob. From the way the big guy talked with that foreign accent, he was sure that was his father. Maybe next week when they met again, he'd ask him.

For a long time before going to bed that night, Robbie sat there and thought about what had happened. He began to fantasize all kinds of future scenarios for his life: being a mob boss, being a big businessman, going into show business, becoming a famous person, or just about anything else he could imagine—except what actually happened to him.

* * *

Later in the week, Robin found the usual envelope slipped under his door with the following note: Nov 18 445. Either his father (or whoever that was) hadn't made himself clear to the swingman, or the note was written before his seller was told not to sell anymore. In either case, he was just going to forget about it and do whatever he thought his father wanted.

Robbie had more important things on his mind that week anyway—the University of Michigan-Ohio State University football game was on Saturday, November 20. Robbie went to all the OSU games, and even though he'd never played anything in high school, he'd loved the Friday night high school football games. He loved the OSU games even more, and ever since he was a junior in high school, he would drive the 140 miles to Columbus and get the high school student tickets for the game. When he started his pot-selling job, he made sure that he had OSU season tickets so he could see all the games. He knew a couple of the players from high school, and he would go down to the tunnel leading to the locker area before the game and wave at them when they came in.

On Saturday, he was pleasantly surprised to see the Michigan team coming down the tunnel. It was cold and snowy that day, so not many people were hanging around. When he spotted Ed Shemansky, he yelled at him, "Hey, Shemansky, over here! Good luck to you!"

Ed was a little surprised that someone recognized him at the OSU stadium. "Hey, Robbie, what's shakin'?"

"Meet me after the game and I'll tell you. Do you want a lift back to Cleveland?"

"Come down here after the game. Maybe I'll go with you," Ed called back as he trotted down the tunnel. Ed was feeling a little dizzy and feverish, as if coming down with the flu or something, and the thought of going home made him feel a little better.

It snowed during the game, just as it had during a number of other UM-OSU games. But the snow this time had little to do with number-twelve-ranked Michigan getting beat again by number-one-ranked OSU, twenty-one to seven. It wasn't a very exciting game, even though the score was close through most of the game. An exciting game to Ed Shemansky meant he would be able to fill in for Ray Barber. But he felt feverish and was just not up to playing anyway.

When halftime came, the teams went to their respective locker rooms for the usual pep talk, equipment corrections, and a little rest.

After Coach Oosterbaan's half-time talk, Ed told one of the assistant coaches, "I'm feeling a little sick—dizzy and nauseated—so maybe I'll just stay here for a while, okay, coach?"

The coach thought it would be a good idea, and he asked Ed what his plans were for after the game.

"I think I'm going home to Cleveland. There's an old high school friend of mine here, and he said he'd drive me home. I'll just stay with my folks till after the Thanksgiving break."

"Sounds good, Shemansky," the assistant said. "You take care of yourself and we'll see you after the break."

Ed got dressed in his street clothes and was lying on the bench listening to the second half of the game; it was being broadcast into the locker room. During the fourth quarter, Ed heard a knock on the locker room door. Ed got up and opened the door.

"I didn't see you on the field all through the second half," Robbie said. "You okay?" He was afraid to go in because he knew he wasn't allowed there.

"Hey, yeah, man, thanks for coming to get me. I'm not feeling 100 percent, so if you still want to drive me home, that would be great."

Ed put his coat on and followed Robbie out of the stadium to his car. It was around three thirty in the afternoon, and with the heavy clouds, it was already getting dark out. They got into Robbie's car and drove toward Cleveland. Since they left about a half hour early, there was little traffic. "How long you think it will take us?" Ed asked.

"Less than three hours, unless we hit a snowstorm," Robbie said. "Should have you home around six, in time for dinner."

With that, Ed leaned back and closed his eyes right after he heard the final score on the car radio. The car was warm, even though it was a convertible, but it was noisy on the highway, so Robbie turned off the radio after the game wrap-up and let his companion sleep.

* * *

About an hour into the drive, Ed woke up and said quietly, "I feel much better. Maybe all I needed was that little bit of sleep." He felt like talking, so he went on. "So, Rob, whatcha been doin? You still getting high?"

"I got my own little business, and yeah, getting high now and then is good," Robbie grinned.

"I haven't been able to score since I came to Michigan," Ed said, "but I've been so fuckin' busy with school and practice and all that other shit that I just haven't found a seller. Does that guy who used to come to school still hang around? I bet he's fifty years old now."

"No, man—that dude is long gone," Robbie said. "In fact, the dude who replaced him is gone now too." Robbie felt he had to tell someone, so he told Ed the whole story about taking over the dope business, and how his father was getting him a good job. He said his father had ties with the mob, so he should be doing a lot better real soon.

"No shit, man!" Ed said. "Hey, too bad you gave up the business. I would be one of your best customers."

It began to snow a little, so Robbie slowed down because he hadn't switched to his studded winter tires yet. They drove in silence until the snow stopped, then Robbie speeded up again as they approached the outskirts of the greater Cleveland area.

"You know, maybe I can help you out one last time," Robbie offered. "I can still get my hands on some stuff if you want to go with me to pick it up. You interested?"

"Hell, yes, man—let's do it."

It was around six in the evening when they drove up to the old warehouse. It was pitch-black out, and the area was totally deserted. The two got out of the car and walked up to a side door. When Robbie opened it, he was surprised that it was still unlocked. He was supposed to make his pickup two days and about three hours earlier. For a split second, something made him hesitate, like someone else was influencing his movements.

"What's the problem?" Ed asked.

"Oh … nothing. I just realized I didn't bring my money. That's okay. I can pay later," Robbie said, trying to act casual.

The two of them walked in, closed the door, and Robbie turned on the flashlight he'd brought from the car.

There were boxes and crates everywhere. Some held small appliances, and some had fancy cans of meats and wines. There were also a number of steel racks in different spots, their shelves filled in some places, and empty in others, with small items: watches, jewelry, and expensive perfume. But for the most part, it was a lot of empty space.

Robbie walked over to one of the racks and tried to act surprised— even though he expected it might be empty—when he saw nothing on his shelves. "What the fuck? Shit, I guess they decided not to fill my order."

Just as they reached the empty rack, Ed started feeling sick again. He was dizzy and nauseated, and it pissed him off. "What kind of shit are you trying to pull here, man?" he said to Robbie. "Why are you jerking my chain, you stupid-ass greaseball—" All of a sudden, he felt a pain like a red-hot poker sticking him in his left shoulder; he started to scream, but all that came out of him was a bone-chilling moan.

Ed tumbled and fell forward. Robbie tried to stop him from falling, but Ed was so much bigger than Robbie that he just couldn't stop him. All he was able to do was redirect his fall into the end of the rack. Sticking out of the end of the rack was an angle iron bent upward at a sixty-degree angle, and Ed's forehead went right into it with the full weight of his body.

Robbie thought for sure his skull would split open and his brains would pour out all over the floor. He stood there looking at Ed in the light of his flashlight, and he knew that Ed was dead. He turned off the light and just remained there in silence for about a minute, or an hour—he couldn't tell.

"What the fuck just happened?" he was wondering aloud. "Did Ed get killed falling on that metal thing? Maybe he's not dead? What should I do?"

All he could think of was getting out of there as fast as he could, and getting Ed's body out as well. He grabbed a flat cart, and with some difficulty, he was able to haul Ed onto the cart in total darkness.

Robbie took his flashlight and looked to see if anything would give his visit away. He couldn't see any blood on the angle iron, which surprised him. Other than some scuff marks on the concrete floor, there was no real evidence of anyone having been there. Robbie also noted that Ed's forehead wasn't bleeding either—there was only a strange purple indentation from the angle iron.

Robbie wheeled the cart out of the side door and over to the trunk of his car. Again, with difficulty, he got Ed into the trunk, the only light coming from a distant streetlamp. Robbie looked around and was sure there was not a soul in sight. He then put the cart back where he got it, took one quick last look with his flashlight, and left the place with the door closed but still unlocked.

* * *

After going on an aimless drive of about thirty miles outside of Cleveland, he spotted an unmarked dirt road going south. Robbie turned left down the dirt road and drove for about a mile. He pulled off to the side of the road, stopped the car, and waited there for about a half hour. He saw no one on the road in all that time, and the only lights he saw were off in the distance, coming from a farmhouse.

It was getting cold, and Robbie was freezing. He quietly opened his car door, opened the trunk, and dragged Ed's body out of the car. In the moonlight, he again noticed the strange mark in the middle of Ed's forehead. It looked a little like a backward Greek gamma. He had learned the Greek alphabet once, just for laughs, and now it seemed that it had some use. Silly and useless thoughts like that kept filling his mind as he tried to get Ed's body off the shoulder and into the drainage ditch a little farther down. There was a good dusting of snow in the area, and with any luck at all, more snow would come and cover up Ed's body, and no one would find him until next spring.

Confused, tired, scared, and in shock, Robbie got back in his car and started to drive. He slowly drove home, composing himself, trying to decide what he was going to do. *If Ed is dead, they're going to think I killed him,* Robbie thought, *and on the outside chance he's still alive, they're going to wonder why I didn't take him to the hospital. Either way, I'm fucked! If the cops don't get me, the mob will. Just when life seemed to be working out for me, this had to happen.*

TWELVE: *Honor thy father and thy mother: that thy days may be long upon the land which the Lord thy God giveth thee.*
—Exodus 20:12

The Michigan team, a little dejected, left Columbus by train late in the afternoon and arrived back in Ann Arbor around ten that night. Nobody was concerned that Ed Shemansky was not on the train; he was from Ohio and would probably stay there after the game. A few other guys from Ohio stayed behind as well, going home early for the Thanksgiving holiday weekend.

A week later, on Monday, November 29, Doc Coulson was taking attendance. "Where is Mr. Shemansky?" she noted. "He wasn't here last week either, so where is he now?"

"He stayed in Columbus after the game—maybe he's still celebrating Thanksgiving," one of the jocks said.

It was later the next day that everyone read in the *Ann Arbor News*, or heard on the local radio, about Shemansky's body being found in Ohio after his parents reported him missing just before the Thanksgiving holiday. He hadn't planned on staying in Ohio after the OSU game, as was first thought, so his parents weren't expecting him then, but they were expecting him to come home Wednesday night. When he never showed up, they notified the police. Since he hadn't been missing long, no investigation would begin until after the holiday ended on Monday, November 29. A farmer had discovered Edward's body on Sunday,

129

November 28, on the edge of his land just outside of Cleveland. It had been over a week since Michigan played the OSU game.

* * *

Earlier in the week, on Wednesday, November 24, the day before Thanksgiving, Robbie had a visitor. The big man Robbie had met the previous week, the one who said he was a friend of Robbie's father, sent over one of the other men to get Robbie.

Robbie was just beginning to relax on that Wednesday, after seeing nothing in the news about Ed and not hearing anything from his former dope supplier.

There was a knock on his door, but this time whoever was knocking didn't just walk in as he did last week. Instead, he waited for Robbie to answer. Robbie was glad that the time had come, and when he opened the door, he recognized the man immediately.

"Get your coat on and come with me," the man said.

They went down the elevator to the foyer, where the man had his car parked out front. It was a black 1955 Cadillac sedan with whitewall tires. They both got in the front seat, and then drove off.

"Tell me, was the big guy who did all the talking last week … was he my father?" Robbie asked. Robbie wanted to believe with all his heart that the powerful-looking man was his father—someone who would protect him no matter what.

"Who did he say he was?"

"He said he was my father's friend," Robbie replied.

"Then that's who he is. Look, you want some advice? Keep your mouth shut, your eyes open, and learn. Don't ask questions; do what you're told, and you'll live a long and happy life, okay?"

Robbie now felt certain that the big guy must be his dad.

They soon ended up at the place where Robbie's father had worked for over thirteen years: Abe Gorski's warehouse. The place was all but shut down for the long weekend, but when Robbie and the driver walked in, a small number of people were working. The two walked over to the offices on one side of the warehouse. The hood knocked on the first one, then told Robbie, "Go on in. I'll be waiting here for you to take you back."

Robbie did as he was told.

Abe Gorski looked at him and shook his head when he saw he wasn't built anything like his father. "So you're Robbie," he said. "Well, Robbala, you're gonna work for me now, you understand that?"

Robbie just nodded his head.

"We're mostly shut down for the holiday season and open up again early next year. So you'll come here again … when is that … Monday the third? Yeah," Abe said in his Polish accent, looking at a 1955 calendar. He then took out a roll of bills and counted out five fifty-dollar notes. "Here, this should take care of you till next year. It's not a gift—it's an advance. You know what an advance is? It's an advance of five weeks' pay so you'll have money for the holidays. You got someplace to go for Hanukah?"

"Uh, yeah," Robbie lied. "My mom always does something for the holiday."

Abe didn't challenge him this time, but he could see by Robbie's size and demeanor that his agreeing to take Robbie on was going to be more of a chore than he had hoped for.

"So, all right, I see you next year. You come in seven in morning on Monday the third from January. You know how to get here," he said, more as a declaration than a question. He then shook Robbie's hand. Robbie gave a weak handshake since no one ever taught him how to shake hands like an adult.

The man who brought him there took him back and let him out in front of his apartment. "You know how to get to the warehouse yourself?"

Robbie nodded, got out of the Caddy, and went upstairs to his place. He had mixed emotions—on the one hand, he was glad that his father would be back in his life, but on the other hand, he wasn't thrilled with where he was supposed to work. In any case, with Ed's death still heavy on his mind, he was glad to have the diversion of a new job and possibly new friends.

* * *

Robbie had planned to relax over the next five weeks, keeping a low profile and staying out of trouble. But on Monday, November 29, there it was, in the *Cleveland Plain Dealer*, right on the first page:

LOCAL UNIVERSITY OF MICHIGAN FOOTBALL PLAYER FOUND MURDERED

Edward Shemansky, son of Mr. Joseph and Mrs. Sarah Shemansky of Shaker Heights, was found dead yesterday in a ditch on a farm road off Edgerton, at the edge of Cuyahoga County …

There was even more on the six o'clock news, with pictures of the scene where the body was found. The reporter, all bundled up with a scarf and hat, was pointing to the ditch and saying, "Cuyahoga Sheriff Deputy Elmer Stilwell told us he answered a call yesterday afternoon from Mr. Joachim Schwarz, whose farm abuts the road where the body was found." The camera panned over the grounds and then focused in on the distant farmhouse. "According to Mr. Schwarz, he had let his dogs out while he was working on his woodpile, and when he heard them howling in the distance, he went over to investigate. Mr. Schwarz discovered the body near the road, about two hundred yards from his farmhouse." The camera panned back to the reporter standing by the ditch. "The Cuyahoga Sheriff's Department has no suspects at this time. It seems the Shemansky family was just notified of their loss."

Robbie went out and bought the other Cleveland newspapers, and he found that they had all published something similar to the *Plain Dealer*. He watched the major news channels at eleven o'clock, which basically repeated the six o'clock news. Nowhere did he hear what the cause of death was, or why they thought Ed was murdered. One station showed Ed's parents' home in Shaker Heights, but no one was visible on camera.

For the next five weeks, Robbie watched the news constantly and scoured the papers for any more information about the investigation. The only other piece of information given over that period was that an autopsy was being done to determine the exact cause of death. Aside from that, it would seem that Ed's passing was, for all practical purposes, forgotten.

Robbie got his stuff together—his clothes and TV were about it—on Monday, December 6, went to the manager of his apartment, told him he was leaving, and paid him for the six days he'd lived there in

December. He moved to a new place on East Thirty-seventh Street, a furnished apartment in a working-class neighborhood, under the name of Robin Wickler—a name he once heard his mother use, but then she quickly corrected herself. Before leaving, he took the clothes he'd worn to the UM-OSU game, including the shoes, and threw them into the apartment's incinerator chute, where he knew they would be burned on Wednesday.

On Tuesday, he went shopping for a new car. He first sold his convertible—making sure to turn in the license plates—to a used car dealer for a reasonable price. He went to the bank, paid off his car loan, and still had a little money left over. He had saved up some cash, and along with the $100 from his father and the $250 from Abe, he was able to buy a used car from another dealer. He bought an older 1950 Chevrolet coupe, using his new alias, Robin Wickler. He figured that if he was asked later about the wrong name on his title, he would just claim it was a typo.

After completing those chores, Robbie bought some groceries, settled into his new apartment, and kept a low profile for the next month.

* * *

Winters in Cleveland could be brutal at times, especially when the cold Canadian air came down from the north over Lake Erie, as it was on Robbie's first full week of work in January of 1955. He was both anxious and relieved as he drove to work for the first time on Monday. Even though he lived less than ten minutes from the warehouse, he left home at six forty in the morning to be sure to be there before seven. It was still dark out, and the lake-effect snow squalls hindered his vision every time they swirled up in front of his car's headlights. He had dressed casually in jeans and a laundered blue denim work shirt, prepared for anything Mr. Gorski would ask him to do.

There was plenty of parking in front of the warehouse when he drove up at six fifty in the morning. The streetlamp down at the end of the block cast an eerie pink hue on the light snow that was falling. It was easy for him to remember where the warehouse was because it was less than four blocks from where Ed's murder took place.

When Robbie walked in, the only light in the entire place was coming from Mr. Gorski's office.

"You're early," Abe said with a smile. "I like that. Shows you're serious about job. Here, get some coffee, and I start to show you job, okay?"

And so Robbie's new career began. He wasn't thrilled with all the hard work—schlepping crates, sweeping floors, and just being a gofer—but he found that time passed quickly. The last five weeks had seemed like an eternity for Robbie so starting work was a blessing. The more time that passed with no additional news about Ed, the better for him—or so he thought.

THIRTEEN: *A time to kill, and a time to heal ...*
—Ecclesiastes 3:3

Ed Shemansky's murder was being investigated under the experienced supervision of Detective Sergeant Martin "Marty" Kowalski. Marty was originally from Hamtramck, Michigan. He was a big guy—over six feet tall and around two hundred pounds—who stood out among the many other big guys from his high school graduating class of 1938. Marty always wanted to be a cop, so right after graduation he applied for and was admitted to the Detroit Police Academy for training.

"Hey, Marty, how do you like working in Detroit?" one of his hometown buddies asked. "Why don't you come back here where we need you? They're letting jigs work up at Dodge Main now, so we need you to bust heads when they get outta line."

"Hey, I'm doin' just fine in Detroit, and you can take care of things yourself here," he said. "Colored people have worked in Hamtramck since forever so don't give me no shit about trouble unless you're causin' it." He chuckled.

Hamtramck was an independent city completely surrounded by Detroit, and it had one of the largest Polish populations in the United States. Almost all the people in the small city spoke Polish, including the children.

Marty was assigned to the Twelfth Precinct, which was located on the edge of Sherwood Forest, one of the wealthiest neighborhoods in Detroit. Marty spent much of his time patrolling along Woodward Avenue, and he saw little in the way of any interesting crime scenes until a person was murdered in a posh home on Canterbury Road in the spring of 1940.

Marty was assigned to the murder investigation with the criminal investigation detectives from the Twelfth, and he loved it. Criminal investigation was what Marty wanted to do for the rest of his career.

Marty had been with the Detroit Police Department for two years when the war broke out in 1941, and early in 1942, Marty was drafted into the army. Private First Class Martin Kowalski was sent to military police training immediately after boot camp. He spent the rest of his army career as a military police officer, honing his skills as a professional criminal investigator.

* * *

Marty was mustered out as a first sergeant in 1946, and he arrived back in Detroit in August, an entire year after VJ day. Marty went downtown and applied for his old job back at the Twelfth and was, by federal law, allowed to claim that job since he was drafted. He got his job back, but there was no pay raise, and he was sent back on mobile patrol, exactly where he had been four years earlier. He submitted numerous requests for transfer to either crime analysis, major crimes section, or a detective squad. He even submitted copies of his wartime military record, noting all his citations and experiences in order to bolster his chances of being assigned to the detective squad, but was routinely turned down.

Marty was told by his precinct commander, "Look, Marty, I know you want to move out of patrol, but all this postwar racial tension has got us all on edge. The job situation here in Detroit hasn't helped much either. I'm sorry, but I need you more on the streets, helping us keep the peace—if that's what you want to call it—than investigating crimes. Don't worry, your chance will come because you're a good cop and you deserve a break, okay?" Marty's commander was referring to the postwar race riots that permeated Detroit. His commander was serious and sympathetic, but it didn't make Marty any happier with his situation.

"Hey, it's open season on niggers," one of his fellow officers said during one of the many small violent outbreaks between blacks and whites, which were still occurring three years after the major riots.

"Hey, man, don't be such an asshole. We got enough problems keeping the peace without you yelling out racially charged shit, so can it, okay?"

"Cool it yourself, Kowalski. I learned the word nigger from your Polack friends in Hamtramck, so don't yell at me—yell at them," the officer countered.

Marty had heard these arguments all his life, and it seemed that the race-baiting and ethnic threats would never stop. In a city like Detroit, with so many different ethnic neighborhoods, one would think they would celebrate their diversity instead of belittling everyone else.

In 1949, a recruiter from Cleveland was in Detroit, looking for experienced police officers to join the Cleveland Police Department. Cleveland was experiencing a slowdown in population growth—its population of around a half million was about half that of Detroit. The city was attempting to recruit greater industrial and manufacturing diversity, resulting in some major social changes. Crime was on the rise, so more police at all skill levels, especially investigators and other specialized police personnel, were needed. Marty immediately applied for a job as a detective, and he was offered the position. He happily accepted.

In the summer of 1949, Marty headed to Ohio and moved into an older Polish neighborhood on Kenyon Avenue, in what was called the Warszawa Neighborhood. He joined the St. Stanislaus Church, where he met and married his wife, Clara. By 1954, Martin Kowalski had become the senior homicide detective in the Cleveland Police Department, and he had been promoted to detective sergeant. He was known across the country for his thorough investigative skills in solving complex murders. In the late fall of 1954, he was about to undertake one of the most complex murder investigations of his entire career.

* * *

On Tuesday, November 30, the Cleveland Police Department officially took charge of the murder investigation from the Cuyahoga County Sheriff Department. Detective Sergeant Kowalski's team secured the crime scene and relieved the county of the responsibility for maintaining the area.

After thoroughly interviewing Sheriff Deputy Stilwell and Schwarz, the farmer, along with his family, they released the crime scene. They had gathered as much physical evidence as they could from the scene, including plaster casts of tire tracks, shoe prints, and dirt samples from various locations in the area. Shemansky's body was already at the Cleveland morgue, and Marty showed up the next day at the autopsy.

"What's that mark on his forehead, Doc?" Marty asked Fred Mandel, the medical examiner. "Do you think he was whacked with something?"

"It's hard to tell. The mark was made postmortem ... but barely. It's apparent from the other marks on his body that he was dragged, pushed, dropped, and carted around from one place to another, but what actually killed him was a rare heart defect," the doctor reported. "It's called cardiomyopathy; I'm not going to bore you with all the various technicalities here, Marty, but suffice it to say that the disease, if left untreated, would probably have killed him sooner or later."

"He was a jock; you'd have thought they'd have discovered it by now. What are the symptoms?"

"Actually, they wouldn't necessarily have discovered it," the doctor answered. "Sometimes there are no symptoms until the patient has an attack. The type of disease he had is usually congenital in origin, and there may have been no symptoms until just recently, or he may never have had any symptoms at all. But something triggered it the day he died—high stress, extreme emotional, or physical, arousal ... Oh, and the early symptoms could be fatigue, weakness, dizziness, shortness of breath—symptoms not atypical of what a young college jock might feel when final exams and a big game are in the works."

"I'm still puzzled by the mark on his forehead," Marty said. "You say it was done postmortem ... Do you think it was some kind of a ritual thing, maybe a cold branding or something like that? All kinds of cults and weirdoes out there."

"No, no ..." The doctor shook his head. "I doubt if it was some kind of a satanic or other ritual. But, you know," he said, pausing, "it looks much like the Hebrew letter *vav*, if my ancient Hebrew school memory serves me correctly." Dr. Mandel took out his pen, and on a piece of scrap paper, he drew the Hebrew letter *vav*: ו.

"*Vav*?" Marty asked. "Does that have any significance to you?"

Again, Dr. Mandel shook his head. "No, no … just a childhood memory, that's all."

* * *

Marty gathered his homicide team in the small conference-interrogation room in the homicide section's space at police headquarters. The team currently consisted of Marty, two other detectives, and a uniformed patrol officer from the second precinct. The team could grow if necessary, but this was all the help Marty needed for now.

On the blackboard, he had drawn a matrix with a timeline down the far left column, listing dates and times of key events, including Nov. 20, after 2:30 PM, probable murder time; Nov. 24, 8:00 PM, missing person's report filed. Next to each event, he added any pertinent details. For instance, after the date and time of the autopsy, he wrote the words *vav, forehead*. He also listed all previous interviews by the sheriff's department, the Cleveland police, his own personnel, and an Ann Arbor police detective who was asked to help out while memories were still fresh.

Marty started his meeting promptly at one o'clock. "Okay, listen up … Here's what we have so far," he said, pointing to the matrix. "I have copies of the detailed interviews for all of you to read, but right now I want to focus on this one here." He pointed to the Ann Arbor detective line on his matrix. "I want to follow up on his interview with the assistant coach who claimed Shemansky got sick and stayed in the locker room after halftime. He said Shemansky told him a friend was taking him home. We have to find out who that friend was, and how sick Shemansky was. We need all the who, what, why, when, where, and hows—so let's get crackin." Marty looked over at the two detectives and said to the younger one, "Frank, I want you to work on this." He then looked at the older detective, Dave Gordon, one of his most experienced investigators. "Dave, I want you to do the parents again—his parents are in real grief, so be as gentle as possible. They're very distraught since Jews want the burial to be within three days after death, and they don't believe in autopsies … but you know all this, Dave."

Marty looked over at the uniformed officer and said, "Patrolman— your name's Patrick, right? You come with me. I have a tedious but extremely important job for you." Marty gave him the assignment of driving down to Columbus and getting as many names as possible of those who were at the game on Saturday, November 20.

And so the investigation into the murder of Edward Shemansky was under way. Ed had been dead at least eleven days by then, and they needed to be well under way on the investigation if they hoped to get this one solved.

* * *

Thursday morning at eight sharp, the team met again. Marty started the meeting by asking, "What have we got? Frank, did you talk with that Ann Arbor detective?"

"Yep, and I'm headed up there today to meet with him and the coach. The detective didn't add anything to what we already have from the interview notes, but I still want to talk with Coach. You know, in-depth kind of stuff—who were Shemansky's friends, where did he hang out, that kind of stuff. Then I might try to see a couple of his friends or classmates and do the same thing."

"Good," Marty said. "You know what to do ... so just do it."

Marty got a quick report from Dave, who explained that Ed's folks and his grandparents were in total shock. Dave had told them that he would do whatever he could to get the body released for burial. The ME said he had all he needed so there was no reason not to release the body.

Patrick, the patrolman, displayed a huge box filled with sheet after sheet of names and contact information. It was the list of all the season-ticket holders, broken down into students, staff, alumni, and fans. He also had the list of mail-order requests filled for the UM-OSU game, as well as a list of any other people who might have gotten a ticket or pass—press corps, professional athletes, Boy Scouts, and the like. Patrick explained that well over ninety thousand people had attended the game, and that many of the people listed didn't even go to the game but either sold their tickets or gave them away.

Marty explained to the others that they would compile a list of Shemansky's friends and associates who might have been at that game, and Patrick would check them against the lists he had.

"Patrick's got a fine start, and if he needs help, I can get it for him. We'll have him concentrate his efforts on trying to find the friend that supposedly drove him home." Marty paused for any comments, and then said, "Well, that's it. Continue with what you're doing, and as leads and names come up, we'll make a list and interview them. Good work, guys."

By the end of the week, Patrick, with the help of two other patrolmen working overtime, had put together a list of twenty-seven names. Twelve of them were students from Ed's high school graduating class. They were enrolled in OSU and had season tickets. Ten of them were former students at Shaker Heights, but were in different graduating classes, and they also had season tickets. The other five were family members of former students who had tickets. Patrick was sure that they might have missed others, but he felt they had a good start to set up interviews. After contacting all twenty-seven, they found out that twenty-two of them were at the game. The other five had sold their tickets and had no idea who the buyers were. Robin Wicken was not on the list of season-ticket holders, so his name wasn't on the interview list.

All three detectives had shown up at the funeral on Sunday, December 5, to see if anyone of interest might be there. But the family was so well-known in the community that over one hundred people came to the service, and most of them went to the cemetery afterward. It was a cold, overcast day with intermittent snow showers. The graveside services at Jewish funerals usually proceeded quickly, but so many people wanted to shovel in the token shovelful of dirt that it took almost an hour and a half. If any stood out as outsiders or as people who shouldn't be there, it was the three detectives.

* * *

By New Year's Day, Marty was getting discouraged. None of the interviews had turned up anything. They conducted hundreds of them using the so-called "snowball" sampling process: they interviewed someone, and that person gave them two or three other names of people they also interviewed, and they provided more names, and so on. But none of the interviewees said they saw whom Ed had left the game with.

By the first of the year, the list stopped growing, and the other detectives put on the case—Marty had received four more detectives to help through the month of December—were sent back to their posts, leaving just Marty and his original team members left to work on the case. On Monday, January 3, Marty was holding his weekly meeting. OSU had won the Rose Bowl on Saturday, and they were crowned national champions. There was some excitement about that, even at police headquarters. Marty made some small talk about Saturday's game before starting in on the Shemansky murder case.

"I want to pursue that mark on his head—the one that looks like a Hebrew *vav*. I'm going up to Ann Arbor tomorrow to talk with some of his professors before their winter break starts. They may know something more about Ed's course of study that could possibly explain the *vav*. Don't ask me what right now—it's just a hunch. Frank and Dave, you guys sit with Patrick and start all over again, trying to find who, if anybody, drove him home from the game. Check with OSU again, and see if we had all the names to start with," Marty directed. "Also try to follow up on that one lead of the guy who said he thought he heard someone call out to Ed when Michigan entered the tunnel before the start of the game. I know you already did it twice, but with all the other things we now know, try it again."

They did know, from their interviews, that Ed was pretty much a guy who kept his social life narrowly confined to his fraternity brothers and teammates. They also knew he had a nice-looking girlfriend at Michigan, one Clarice Adams, whom they also interviewed. Most of the team knew him as a hardworking player. They also knew he played backup to the star tight end, and even though he never got a chance to play in any of the Saturday games, he never complained to Coach Oosterbaan. He was one of those guys who never missed practice and gave up his body for the good of the starting team. They also learned that in high school he was a star halfback and a popular kid, but he was also known to have smoked a joint or two, and he was stopped for speeding and underage drinking on occasion. They also knew he had no known enemies, never got into any fights with other students, and was never belligerent or aggressive to any of the adults he encountered.

It would appear that there was absolutely no known reason anyone would purposely kill Ed Shemansky. But there had to be a motive and an opportunity for someone, who thought he had the ability, to commit the murder. Whoever killed Ed, or tried to kill him, was just lucky enough that Ed's heart gave out first, especially if that someone didn't have the physical ability to kill Ed.

FOURTEEN: *They shall not labour in vain, nor bring forth for trouble ...*
—Isaiah 65:23

Marty's appointment with Professor Coulson was at three thirty on January 4. Marty always tried to be on time and expected everyone else to be on time as well, so he was pleased when at exactly three thirty by his watch, he knocked on Doc Coulson's door and heard her say, "Come in, Mr. Kowalski. I've been expecting you."

"Professor Coulson?" Marty said. She was sitting there wearing the most unusual outfit he would ever expect a University of Michigan professor to be wearing. She had on a simple skirt, white blouse, and pink cardigan sweater. That was not so bad, even though she looked a little too preppy for her age. But the bobby socks and blue saddle oxford shoes looked a little out of place on her. In addition, she wore something around her neck on a piece of string that was not jewelry. No, it couldn't be ... Was it a roller skate key? To top it all off, she wore a green eyeshade visor to make it easier, he guessed, for her to read all the papers, documents, and books she had in front of her. There were also two other tables pushed up to her desk, just as cluttered with stuff as her desk was.

She didn't look like what he expected, but he had heard she was one of the most brilliant members of the faculty, and she was Ed Shemansky's astronomy instructor, so she was a good place to start. "I hope this is a convenient time for you ...," he began.

"Fine time, fine time," she said, motioning him to sit down at the table closest to her desk, where the tabletop was the clearest. "I'm reviewing the students' proposals for their class projects for my history class. That's the reason for all the mess—hope you don't mind. So, how may I help you with your investigation? I hope you're making some headway. Edward was a delightful young man, and he had a good chance for a real future in science. You know his grandfather is an emeritus professor of astronomy from Case Western Reserve?" Marty nodded, and she continued. "A brilliant astronomer—he even has a law of cosmology named after him—Szymanski's law of cosmological motion. That's S-Z-Y-M-A-N-S-K-I, which is how he spelled his name when he taught at Jagiellonian University in Kraków, Poland. I first met him in 1929, when he came to my undergraduate school, Ohio Wesleyan, to give a guest lecture. We actually stayed in contact until his retirement in—I think it was—1938. Yes, it was 1938. In many ways, he considered me his protégé, and I'm indebted to him for that. Now, what can I do for you, Mr. Kowalski?"

"I knew he was a retired professor, but I didn't know it was in astronomy," Marty said, making a note in his little spiral notepad. "Unfortunately, we seem to be at a roadblock in young Mr. Shemansky's case. I was hoping that maybe with your knowledge of the students … that you could help shed some light on the case and maybe offer us another path to go down in our search for a solution."

Good God! Marty thought. *That was the worst collection of trite metaphors I ever put together in my entire life.* He was trying to talk as if he were a college graduate, but he wasn't, and he should have known that he had nothing to be ashamed of. But coming from Hamtramck he was a little intimidated by the University of Michigan. Looking at Professor Coulson and seeing the understanding in her eyes, he calmed down and continued.

"I guess I'm looking for anything and anyone who might help us," he said, sounding more relaxed. "We know his girlfriend, Clarice Adams, was also in your class. Did he seem to have other friends in your class besides other jocks? We've already interviewed Miss Adams and the entire football team, but was there anyone else he might have talked with more than once?"

145

"Yes, Edward and Miss Adams and Benjamin Bernstein—who is Miss Adams's tutor—would get together after class on occasion. Mr. Bernstein was the only other student, besides the football players, that he seemed to talk to. Mr. Bernstein was a navy veteran and a good tutor for Miss Adams," she threw in. Marty's instincts told him to check out this Bernstein guy because of a possible lover's triangle motive.

They continued talking along the line of other students who might have known Ed, but they soon ran out of any new contacts.

"You told me that Mr. Shemansky's grandfather was also an astronomy professor, and you apparently continued contact with him until ... seventeen years ago? I'm just curious as to why you kept in contact with Professor Shemansky." Marty had asked because he realized through the old spelling of Shemansky that they were Polish and that he taught in Poland. Marty's own Polish roots made him curious about the astronomer, but he knew it probably had no bearing on the case.

"Oh, it was Professor Shemansky who got me interested in astrology, mysticism, and the history of astronomy. He also helped me in my work on stellar spectroscopy—that branch of astronomy in which he was world famous, and in which I did my doctoral work. Yes, we carried on a long correspondence. I just recently sent him a note telling him how sorry I was at the loss of his grandson," she said with a noticeable crack in her voice.

"Astrology and mysticism. Are you interested in that stuff?" Marty asked, getting a little excited, as he knew he needed just such an expert to help him out with the *vav* on Ed's forehead.

"Oh, sure," Doc Coulson replied. "My real love of astronomy came out of its history and grandeur over all the centuries that we've been viewing the heavens. There is a wealth of ancient information— some fact but mostly myth—about how the various heavenly bodies portend our future. Professor Shemansky was studying to be a rabbi at one time, and he knew a considerable amount of ancient Hebrew mysticism, mostly coming out of the Kabbalistic tradition. I spent a lot of time learning Hebrew, and how the Kabbalists used Hebrew letters and symbols for the planets for all kinds of mystic conjectures."

She was about to continue when Marty asked, "Do you know if there is any special significance to the Hebrew letter *vav*?"

"Well, I'm sure you know that *vav* is the sixth letter of the Hebrew alphabet, and since in Hebrew letters are also used for numbers, *vav* is also another way of writing the numeral six. It's numerology that the Kabbalists used to divine future events, or understand current events. And *vav*, like all the other numbers, has so many different ways of being interpreted either alone or in combination." She paused and then said, "Why do you ask?"

Marty then told her about the mark on Ed's forehead.

Doc Coulson said, "I learned long ago that when looking for something mystical, or rational, with very limited information, to use Occam's razor; that means I take the simplest explanation I can find. If it were me, I would assume the *vav* was a six, probably referring to the sixth commandment. In any modern shul today, all the commandments are usually represented by a drawing—or weaving or whatever—of a stone tablet usually placed above the arc, with the first ten letters of the alphabet to symbolize the Ten Commandments. So, let's see ... the sixth commandment is 'You shall not murder.' Does that make any sense to you, Detective?" she asked.

"Yes, to some extent—only 'Thou shalt not kill' is the fifth commandment, not the sixth. The sixth commandment—"

"By your name, I'm assuming you're Catholic, and for Catholics, 'Thou shalt not kill' is indeed the fifth," Doc Coulson gently but firmly informed Marty. "But for Jewish people, it's the sixth commandment: 'You shall not murder.' They're the same, but with some subtle differences."

"Are you Jewish, Professor Coulson?"

"No, no, I'm a Methodist. Remember, I attended Ohio Wesleyan University. In case you're wondering, I learned all that stuff from Professor Shemansky, and it has helped me greatly in my historical research."

With that, Doc Coulson had to finish the first meeting she had with Detective Martin Kowalski, but it certainly would not be her last.

* * *

Because Doc Coulson mentioned Ben Bernstein as someone who knew both Ed and Clarice, Marty hung around Ann Arbor to meet Ben, and he actually invited him out to dinner. Marty felt he needed a reliable student contact at the university, and he took a chance on Ben when he found out that he was also a vet.

Ben suggested going to the Women's League on North University. They always had a good dinner buffet for a reasonable price, and many regulars dined there almost every night. They met in the lobby around six fifteen. Marty came in a little late, but he spotted Ben from his gray sweater and other clothes that he said he'd be wearing.

Marty walked up to the young student and asked if he was Benjamin Bernstein before saying, "Sorry I'm a little late. I was with Professor Coulson till just a little while before I called you." They shook hands, and Marty said, "I had a real problem finding a parking space around here," as a way of explaining why he was a couple of minutes late.

The cafeteria line was quite long by now, but they were fortunate enough to find a small table in a relatively isolated corner. The furniture was Early American—a lot of maple and quite simple in design.

"Maybe we should eat before I start asking any questions since these things tend to upset people, and I don't want to spoil your supper, okay?" Marty suggested.

"That's fine with me," Ben said. "Now, are you with the Cleveland Police Department, or are you local? I didn't quite understand that when we talked on the phone."

"I'm sorry, yes ... I'm with the Cleveland Police—that's where the crime is being investigated," Marty explained. "I should have made that clearer during our phone conversation. The pay phone in that gas station from where I called you was not the most private place to talk. I guess I was just a little too fast in telling you the details."

After dinner and over coffee, Marty took out his pad and pencil and started the interview.

"Professor Coulson tells me that you and Ed Shemansky were friends, or rather, that she's seen you two talking together. Just how well did you know Shemansky?" Marty asked.

"I didn't know him well at all. I help his girlfriend, Clarice Adams, in astronomy class—I guess you might call it tutoring—and we would talk briefly when the three of us were together. Actually, all I knew about Ed on a personal level was what I learned from Clarice. I got the feeling, when the three of us were together, that he was a little jealous of me. I don't know ... maybe that's wishful thinking on my part. I mean, he knew we spent a lot of time together, and, uh … maybe he worried that we weren't always studying."

"Were you? That is, always studying."

"Oh, yeah. We had to study a lot because Clarice has a problem visualizing things in three dimensions from a two-dimensional diagram. I taught her how to do it arithmetically," Ben clarified, "but as I said, I didn't know Ed that well. Why would you think I did? Did Doc Coulson tell you we were friends?"

"Professor Coulson simply said she saw you talk with Ed on occasion, so I just wanted to follow up. You don't mind, do you?"

"No, not really. Um … I just sometimes get a little paranoid when people ask me if I know someone, when all we have in common is that we're both Jewish," Ben responded honestly, but a little hesitantly.

"Now that you mention it, the fact that you're Jewish never crossed my mind till just now. Say, would you mind if I do ask you some questions concerning your faith? Of course, if you mind …"

"No, go ahead. At least that will make me believe that my Jewish paranoia isn't all in my head." Ben smiled.

"Okay, okay … you got me there. Seriously, though, some things have occurred in this case that I think only someone who is knowledgeable about the Jewish religion—Judaism? … Well, anyway, you get the idea. Hey, I'm just a dumb Polack from Hamtramck so help me out here." Marty smiled.

After Marty's declaration, Ben felt obligated to say, "By the way, I should tell you that I recently found out that Ed and I have an aunt and uncle in common. I mentioned this to Ed around the end of October, but it didn't do much in the way of us becoming closer. I'm just telling you in case you found out and wondered why I didn't mention it."

"Thanks for that info—I appreciate your telling me that," Marty said.

"Maybe my years spent as a yeshiva *bucher*—uh … I guess you would say a seminary scholar—will finally pay off. How can I help?" Ben offered.

Marty filled him in on the *vav* on Ed's forehead, and what Doc Coulson had told him about its meaning. They talked for a long time, getting to know each other better. Both men were vets—although Marty was much older—and that had a lot to do with their being able to talk easily with each other. For Ben, it was sort of like having his big brother there with him, only now Ben would be teaching Marty instead of the other way around.

Marty also felt fairly certain that there was no lover's triangle here to worry about.

* * *

Ben told Clarice all about his interview with Marty Kowalski the next day. "You know when they interviewed me in December with Ed's fraternity brothers ..." Clarice started to tear up, saying, "You know I told them that Ed and I were just good friends now, and that we were going to be dating other people." She looked down and said, "Maybe if I hadn't told Ed to start dating other girls ..."

"Don't think like that," Ben said. "Your deciding to break off the going steady thing had nothing to do with Ed's death."

"How do you know that?" she cried.

"Because I just do, that's all ... I just do. I feel bad about Ed being murdered, but it happening in Ohio could in no way be connected with you any more than it's connected to me, and I'm a relative! You gotta trust me on this one, okay?" Ben waited until it sank in and then said, "Hey, look, the detective I met with asked me to check out some Jewish folklore that might be connected to Ed's death. You want to help me with that?"

Ben filled Clarice in on his conversation with Marty. "You know, my brother Marvin is a rabbi in the Detroit area, and I was thinking of going in on Sunday and asking his help on the *vav* thing. You want to go with me?"

Clarice was delighted to go. She'd always had a desire to learn more about Judaism, but she'd never had the opportunity. Maybe now she'd have that chance.

* * *

They got to the temple (Ben still called it a shul) around nine Sunday morning, and the place was buzzing with Sunday school students who were mostly preteens. Ben and Clarice went right to the rabbi's office. "Hey, Mordecai, how's it going?" Ben asked. "Hey there, junior scientist, still looking for a rational world to live in? Who's your friend?" Marvin said, beaming at him and Clarice.

Ben introduced Clarice and then filled Marvin in on everything—who Ed Shemansky was, his murder, and how Detective Kowalski had asked him to research the possible meaning of the *vav* on his forehead.

"Hold on, hold on … Are you telling me that a police detective has asked you, a college freshman, to assist him in a murder investigation? Is he out of his mind? And now you're dragging Clarice into it as well? I've got a good mind to call this guy and find out what Cracker Jack box he got his badge from!" Marvin was steaming. "Does he know that Edward Shemansky was related to us? Did he take that into account when he asked you to do this so-called research?"

"Oh, so you knew about Ed Shemansky and Uncle Saul?" Ben said. "Who told you?"

"I always knew that Uncle Saul married a Shemansky girl from Ohio, and when I read about the murder, I checked it out. I was going to call you, but I didn't know if you knew him or not, or if you knew we were related, and I didn't want to upset you. Now I wish I'd have called. How are you taking all of this?" he asked gently, as both Ben's brother and a rabbi.

"I'm all right with it since I didn't know Ed that well. Clarice and I talked about it—getting involved with the investigation—and let me tell you why we think Detective Kowalski asked for our help. I know it sounds strange, Mordecai, and at first, I thought it was odd too that he would ask me. I wondered why he doesn't ask an expert on Judaic studies in Cleveland to help him, and then I realized that if he did ask someone locally, it would probably get into the newspapers. That could stir up all kinds of anti-Semitic demons in the community. He admitted to me, from one vet to another, that he knew nothing about our religion, saying our astronomy professor was the one who turned him on to a possible explanation involving the *vav*. He simply asked me to do more research on the meaning, or I should say *meanings*, of *vav*, to see if it has any relation to the imprint on Ed's forehead."

"Still the scientist," Rabbi Bernstein said. "Well, okay, but don't you go getting involved any deeper than doing some scholarly research. And if anything you two run across appears to put you in danger in any way, you let Kowalski know instantly, and let me know too. Will you do that?"

Ben assured his brother that he and Clarice would be careful and keep out of harm's way, and that he would keep Marvin informed of their findings as well.

With that assurance, Marvin offered Ben some scholarly texts, some of which were quite old.

"You know," Marvin said, "we grew up orthodox, yet I didn't decide to become a reformed rabbi until rather late in my education. In a way, I now feel that maybe it was *bashert*—meant to be—so that my resources would be open to you two. Maybe your research will help Clarice learn more about her religion … and help our cousin Edward rest in peace."

Marvin corroborated Professor Coulson's theory about the *vav* representing the sixth commandment, but he felt that that might be too simple of an explanation, and that Ben and Clarice should look carefully at all the other options, no matter how complex. Ben speculated that rabbis weren't taught Occam's razor.

Marvin gave them both hugs as they left. "Take care of yourself, you little pu—" He cleared his throat and said, "Pumpkin. Keep your promise to call me often on this one. Clarice, nice meeting you; I hope to see more of you as well."

"Pumpkin?" Ben said with a big grin on his face. Ben knew his brother was going to say *putz*, but then he remembered that Clarice was there, so it came out *pumpkin*. "Nice talk for a rabbi," Ben teased.

On the way back to Ann Arbor, Clarice was quiet for a long time, and then she said, "I like your brother. He really cares for you. I could see that in his face." She was smiling a little now, and Ben was glad that she liked his brother.

* * *

Earlier in the week, on Wednesday, January 5, Marty's team, working together on who was at the stadium on November 20, came up with a new list of names. There were seven more than before—five were missed in the first cut, and the other two were new names that OSU added because they had accidently been left off of the original list of season-ticket holders. Marty told Patrick and Frank to interview the five that were missed earlier, and he asked Dave to do the other two that OSU added.

Marty was the closer on all the serious interviews. That meant that he had someone else do a preliminary interview with a "person of interest," and then he would do an intense follow-up in the hopes of breaking the case. He felt a break in the case was due, and that one of these two ticket holders might be that break.

Dave set up an interview with the first person on his list. That person, who was interviewed the next day, had had no contact with Ed Shemansky and didn't know him. The other person on Dave's list was a little harder to find. His name was R. Wicken, and the phone number Dave called was disconnected. Also, the mailing address was either wrong, or the person had recently moved with no forwarding address, so it would take him a little longer to locate R. Wicken.

It wasn't until Friday that Dave located Wicken's mother, who claimed she had no idea where he moved—and she had no known address or other contact information for his father. That was not completely implausible since she said his father deserted her and Robin—Dave learned that that was Wicken's first name—when he was just two years old. Wicken's mother gave Dave little information, other than saying that Robin had graduated in 1953 from the same high school, Shaker Heights High, that Ed had. "Why you looking for my son?" she asked Dave in her heavy Russian accent. "He good boy ... he never give trouble. Why you want to see him?"

"Your son's not in any trouble, Mrs. Wicken," Dave said. "We're just looking to talk to anyone who might have known Mr. Shemansky. I assure you that it's all very routine in this type of situation."

Dave knew that Wicken had moved out of his apartment in December, leaving no known forwarding address, and had discontinued his phone service. He also knew that Wicken drove a 1953 Chevrolet convertible, but the license plate was turned in when Wicken sold the car in December to a used car dealer. Fortunately for Dave, the car hadn't been resold, and he had the police impound it as possible evidence.

At first, Dave assumed that Mr. Wicken had left Cleveland, and maybe even the state, because no new or used car registrations under the name Wicken turned up. Also, checking the utility companies, he saw that no gas, electric, or phone hookups showed up under the name of Wicken.

It wasn't until the following week that Dave's dogged determination paid off. He switched theories and assumed that Wicken never left town, but somehow, he either purposely, or otherwise, changed identities. Dave knew that a person who changed his or her identity usually stuck closely to the original name, either keeping the same initials or simply inverting a couple of letters in the last name. With that assumption, Dave changed the parameters of the search with the state department of motor vehicles, requesting all new registrations, since November 20, with last names beginning with *W* and first names beginning with *R* from the Cleveland area. His list was only about two hundred names, among which he found Rob Wickler. Checking further, he found that a Robin Wickler had ordered a new phone and other utilities for an apartment on East Thirty-seventh Street.

A little after six o'clock on Monday night, Dave called the new number. "Hello, is this Mr. Robin Wickler?" he asked.

"Who wants to know?"

"I'm Detective David Gordon with the Cleveland Police Department, and I would like to talk to Mr. Wickler about an investigation that we're currently carrying out in the greater Cleveland area. Is this Mr. Wickler?"

"Uh ... yeah, I'm him. How can I help you?" Robbie asked in as cool a voice as he could muster.

"Can I come over to your place now, or would you prefer we meet some other time?" Dave asked. "I would like to do this interview as soon as possible, if that's okay with you."

"Uh ... sure, come on over. I'm at 2342 East Thirty-seventh Street, apartment 304. Do you want directions?" Robbie asked politely.

"I'll find it. I should be there in about ten minutes."

He arrived at six twenty, and after knocking on Robbie's door and being let in, he casually looked around. "You recently move in, Mr. Wickler?" Dave asked.

"About a month ago. I needed something a little cheaper, so I moved here. What's this investigation all about?" Robbie asked.

"We're investigating the death of Edward Shemansky, and we have ..." Dave took out his notebook, pretended to thumb through it, looking for Robin's name. "Yes, we have your name down as someone who might have known him, is that true?"

"Everyone in school knew Ed. He was a great guy ... a great football player. Sure, I knew him. Well, that is, I knew him, but he probably didn't know me other than to say hi."

"So you would say that you were more of an acquaintance of his rather than a friend. You know, of course, that we suspect Ed was murdered, and we're trying to find out if he had any enemies or if someone had it in for him. Are you aware of anybody like that?"

"I can't think of a person who would ever want to harm Ed. He had a smile and a wave for everybody, and he knew everyone's name, even a greaser like me. No, there's no one I know who would want to hurt Ed Shemansky," Robin concluded, looking a bit tense but trying to act nonchalant.

"Well, you seem to confirm what everyone else is saying about him. You say he even had a kind word for a ... what did you call yourself? A greaser? What's that?" Dave asked, as if he didn't know.

"Oh, that's just the term some kids use for guys like me and my friends. We had no money; we weren't jocks ... You know, we hung around cars and stuff. It's just a term," Robbie explained, again trying to act blasé.

"Well, thank you for being so candid with me, Mr. Wickler." Dave looked in his notebook again and then said, "Or is it Wicken? I have both names down here. Wasn't your name Wicken while you were in school?"

"Yeah ... it's a long story. I sort of took my dad's name, even though I haven't seen him since I was a baby. I don't know ... Maybe it was wrong, but I would like for him to know I'm honest and workin' hard, in case he wants to find me." Robbie had that well-prepared response ready for just that moment.

"By any chance, were you at the UM-OSU game in November?" Dave threw this out without warning.

"Uh ... yeah, sure ... I wouldn't have missed it." Robbie started to sweat after this question, almost losing his composure. But he quickly regained his aura of indifference. "Yeah, that was the last game Ed played in, wasn't it? But I was more interested in what my guys from

OSU were doing than watching Ed. Wished he woulda stayed here rather than goin' to Michigan."

"You said you're now working hard somewhere; would you mind telling me where, just in case I have to contact you again? Oh … what time did you get home from the football game on that Saturday?" Dave asked.

Robbie told him where he worked and what time he got home from the game. He spoke untruthfully about the time he got home, but it didn't raise any flags, so Dave finished the interview.

Dave left young Mr. Wicken's apartment feeling that something was just not right with his attitude toward Ed's death. He couldn't explain what it was that bothered him. It was his detective's sense of the way an interview usually goes, and it had nothing to do with what Robbie had actually said; it was more how he said it.

The police crime lab went over Robbie's car and found no evidence linking Ed to the vehicle; however, they did keep samples of the trunk carpet and the floor carpet to compare with any fibers found on the body. The car was returned to the dealer, who was thanked for his cooperation. What Dave didn't know was that Robbie had replaced the tires and carpets before he sold the vehicle, just in case the car was found.

* * *

On Monday afternoon, January 17, a little after two o'clock, Marty was at the University of Michigan Union, looking for Ben and Clarice. He had set up an appointment to meet with them and talk more about Jewish mysticism and the meaning of the *vav* on Ed's forehead. Also, he had gotten to know them a little better through a few phone conversations, and he trusted Ben and Clarice to be his Ann Arbor contacts for any background research on the Jewish aspect of the case. Ben and Clarice had promised Marty a couple of weeks earlier that they would do some research on the *vav*. Marty also told Ben that his reasoning about not wanting to have people in Cleveland do the research was close to the mark. He spotted them at a table with coffee and sweet rolls, and he went over to greet them like long-lost friends.

"Hey, guys, how ya doin'?" he asked. "I hope you haven't been waiting long for me. Clarice, so nice to finally meet with you in person."

After Marty got a mug of black coffee, he asked, "Have you made any headway on the *vav* or, for that matter, anything else in Jewish lore that might be of help here?"

Ben told Marty that they found that most of what they wanted to know was with Doc Coulson. He said, "There's so much shit about *vav* in all the different references that it would take us years to do a thorough research job, but Doc Coulson helped us narrow it down. Did you know she can read Hebrew better than I can? You should see her zip through those old books and find the right page for what we wanted."

"So you say you found something? What is it?" Marty asked impatiently.

"As I said, there's tons of stuff about *vav*, and you already know it's the Hebrew letter denoting the number six … and the sixth commandment is 'You shall not murder,'" Ben said, repeating what he knew Marty had already heard, just to let him know they were on the same page. "But here's the thing. The letter *vav*, in some grammatical as well as mystical way, can change the meaning of something from past to present, or present to future, depending how you read it. She thinks that the *vav* might be a way of saying that what happened in the past is now happening again. Or, more importantly, what you did in the past is now being done to you."

"A revenge killing?" Marty asked. "You think the killing was payback for some murder in the past?"

"I'm not sure," Clarice said. "I don't think revenge killings are allowed. Yet killing is allowed under some circumstances. There are a couple of places in the Torah where killing is specifically mentioned, like these two quotes: 'And if any mischief follow, then thou shalt give life for life …' and 'A time to kill, and a time to heal.'" Clarice had been reading from her research notes. "By the way, did you know that parents could have their children killed if they swore at them? I guess that would help out in the discipline thing for parents."

"Wait," Marty said, "this is all getting very deep and confusing. I need something clearer to go on, not just some quotes that have nothing to do with *vav*."

"Yeah, we agree," Ben said. "We've been going too deep into this, and it's gotten hairy. I think we should stick with the commandment and let it go at that. That's what Doc Coulson thinks too."

Marty thought for a minute. "But your discovery about it meaning something that could change the past to the future, or whatever it is you said, does seem believable. I like the payback motive. Maybe it's because right now we can't come up with any other motive for someone to take Ed's life."

"Maybe it's both—payback and for committing a murder," Clarice offered. "I would think murder constitutes mischief, even though in the context I mentioned before, mischief meant performing, or causing, an abortion."

"So you think maybe that if someone in Ed's past—a family member—performed an abortion on the murderer's past relatives, then killing Ed was simply ... what did you say—giving life for life?" Marty asked.

"Heavy," Clarice said. "That would be real heavy. Maybe not performing an abortion, but doing something that would cause it."

The three of them sat around talking for a little longer, until Marty had to go back to Cleveland. "You both did great, and I really appreciate your effort on this. Thanks."

Clarice and Ben were feeling good about their research and how it might help solve the case. Sitting there and congratulating each other on their efforts became a little anticlimactic, for their feelings of satisfaction soon turned to sadness. It seemed strange when Clarice said, "Poor Ed, *alah v' shalom*," which was Hebrew for rest in peace. "We'll miss you." Clarice had heard the term many times. It was something a parent or grandparent, certainly someone from an older generation, would say. When Clarice said it in Hebrew, she realized that this time she was saying it for someone her own age.

Maybe Marvin was right; maybe it was *bashert* that Ben and Clarice had gotten involved in the heartbreaking affair. And maybe it was *bashert* that Clarice and Ben would also become husband and wife someday.

Ben realized now that more than ever, he wanted to marry Clarice and spend the rest of his life, God willing, with her.

FIFTEEN: *To me belongeth vengeance.*
—Deuteronomy 32:35

After listening to Dave talk about his interview with Robin Wicken, Marty, too, felt certain he was involved. He just couldn't get a handle on what Robin's involvement might be. Marty had been informed by the crime lab technician that the carpets and tires in Robin's convertible were new, which in itself was suspicious.

Marty talked to the salesman who bought it back for resale. "Did you notice that the carpets on the floors and in the trunk and the tires were all new?" Marty asked

"Sure did," the salesman said. "The kid said the old carpets were all stained and the original tires were for shit, so he replaced them—even the spare—with the hope of getting more money for the car. Smart kid. A clean-looking car sells for more money and faster than one that looks like the owner didn't take care of it. I gave him top *Blue Book* dollar for that car. I'm not sure what I would have offered him if he was right about the flooring and tires."

"What reason did he give for selling the car in the first place?" Marty asked.

"He said that he had a new job and couldn't afford the payments, or something like that. I've had it sorta hidden here on the lot because I know I'll get more for it later. I'll take it out this spring and wash it and Simoniz it, and I'll have no problem selling it."

Marty also checked out Robin's old apartment and noticed it had an incinerator chute. When Marty interviewed the super, he asked him, "How often do you burn the garbage?"

"Every Wednesday, we light it off in the basement. It's a gas-fed burner and does a good job. Why do you ask?"

"You don't happen to remember a funny smell coming out of the incinerator on the Wednesday after Wicken left, do you?" Marty asked, not expecting much of an answer since it happened so long ago.

"Funny you should ask, 'cause, yeah, I do. I noticed the stink in the basement almost immediately after it was lit off—burning rubber. Rubber is not allowed, so I was pissed when I opened it up and found a pair of rubber-soled shoes burning in there. Anyway, we pulled them out and just threw them in the dry garbage after I dowsed them. Don't know who they belonged to … or I would've said some stuff to them. I sure would have …"

* * *

On Valentine's Day, Marty got what he was sure was the break he was looking for. Dave had been running the names Wicken and Wickler through the various police department records when he got a hit in the organized crime section. It seemed that a Stanislaw Wickler—aka Stanley, aka Staszek, aka Stan Wicken—was listed as some kind of petty mobster. He was never actually arrested and convicted, but he had been picked up on numerous occasions for assault (strong-arming), extortion, and other similar crimes. Some thought he was associated with the local Fleischer crime family, but it was never proved.

Could that be the father that Robin wanted to impress with the fact that he was "honest and working hard"? Dave thought to himself.

At the team meeting Monday afternoon, Marty brought doughnuts for everyone in honor of Valentine's Day, announcing that he and his wife were going to Poland in April to visit his family's hometown. He also wanted to do some research into something that the two students in Ann Arbor had uncovered for him.

"I'll be looking into a revenge killing," Marty said. "One that may involve someone from Ed's past—possibly a family member—who might have performed an abortion. I know it's strange, but the kids pretty much convinced me we're looking at a revenge killing here."

Dave reported his Stan Wicken lead, and Patrick and Frank were still working on who might have taken Ed Shemansky back to Cleveland after the game in November. Every new lead or new contact had proven useless, but they did have the person who claimed he'd heard someone yell out to Shemansky before the game started.

"Marty, can we get a picture of the Wicken kid? If we can, I'll show it to our contact who claims he heard the voice and see if that doesn't ring a bell with him," Frank suggested.

"Good idea," Marty said. "Dave, can you get a copy of his high school graduation picture from their '53 yearbook? It's just a year old, and I doubt he's changed that much since."

Marty filled the team in on his interviews with the car salesman and the super of Wicken's old apartment. "I'm with Dave on this one. I just have a feeling that the kid's involved somehow."

There was nothing else for anybody to report on the Shemansky case. Until there was any new evidence or other reason for continuing on the investigation, the case was put on the back burner while the detectives concentrated on more recent crimes. However, as busy as Marty was with other cases, there was no way he was going to let this one slip into the cold case files.

* * *

The following week, Marty set up a telephone conference between him, Ben, and Clarice to keep them updated.

"The name is Wicken, or Wickler, and his first name is Robin. He went to the same high school as Ed, and they seemed to know each other casually. See if you can find out for me if Ed's friends knew the kid. Please don't interview them yourself, but if you find someone that knows Wicken, just let them know that I would love to hear from them, okay? You guys got anything for me?"

"We haven't found out anything else, but all kinds of rumors and gossip are floating around."

"What kind of rumors?" Marty asked.

"Some are saying that he was killed because he was Jewish, some say he was killed by the other players because he was better than them, some say players from OSU did it because he went to Michigan, and some are saying that he committed suicide because Michigan was too tough a school for a kid from Ohio," Clarice offered. "All of it a bunch of silly nonsense."

"Right, silly nonsense," Marty repeated. "Well, look, kids, keep your ears open, and if you have anything to tell me, no matter how silly you might think it is, you know how to reach me. I'll be back in contact with you after my trip to Poland."

* * *

All the team members, including Marty, were assigned to other cases, and the team was formally disbanded at the end of February. They still kept working on the case whenever they had a chance, though.

Dave got Robin's graduation picture to Frank, who then showed it to the person who claimed he heard someone shout Ed's name outside the tunnel. Unfortunately, too much time had passed since the game. The potential witness claimed all he heard was someone shouting hey or something, and then he saw Shemansky turn. There was the usual crowd at the tunnel that day, and this guy in the picture might have been there, but the witness just didn't know.

Dave tracked down Stan Wicken, and with Marty's permission, he tried to set up an interview with him. Because of other ongoing investigations Dave was working on, and delays on the part of Stan Wicken, it wasn't until mid-March that the meeting could be arranged. It turned out it was far more complicated than Dave thought.

Dave arrived in the late afternoon on a warm Wednesday, in the middle of March. When he was led into Wickler's house, he was surprised to see that Wickler had a lawyer with him. It was around four in the afternoon, and Mr. Wickler had the doors and some of the windows open to let in the warm afternoon air.

"Thank you for agreeing to meet with me today," Dave said. "Shall I call you Mr. Wickler or Mr. Wicken?"

Stan was about to answer when his lawyer interrupted. "For what reason have you come here today, Detective Gordon?"

"I'm here regarding the investigation into the death of one Edward Shemansky, and we believe that Mr. Wickler's, or Mr. Wicken's, son may have some information regarding the investigation," Dave replied.

"First of all, you claim that the person you want to talk about is someone who supposedly claims to be my client's son, and second of all, you have not told me why you want to interview my client," the lawyer said. "Could you be more specific? Why do you want to interview my client?"

"We believe that a Mr. Robin Wicken may know more about what happened to Edward Shemansky on the day of his murder than he has already told us. We also believe that Stanley Wicken is Robin's father since Robin claims that he took a new job to show his father that he's honest and hardworking." Dave threw that out just to get Stan's attention. Recalling his interview with Robin's mother, Dave continued. "We are also aware that Stanley Wicken moved out of his home when Robin was an infant, and we can respect the fact that he may not want to be identified at this time." Dave wanted Stan to be aware that desertion was not an issue since Stan paid child support and was legally divorced. "All I can say is that I can assure Mr. Wicken that all we want to know is if he has had any contact with his son in recent months, and if he knows anything at all about his son's involvement with Ed Shemansky. That's what this is all about, okay?"

Dave knew he wouldn't get any answers from Stan, but maybe he could grease the skids here to get some father-son action that would help Marty break the kid when he did his interview.

The lawyer and Stan Wicken counseled in whispers for a few minutes, and then the lawyer spoke. "My client regrets to inform you that you have made a mistaken identification, and my client, to the best of his knowledge, is not the father of a certain Mr. Robin Wicken. We regret that you had to waste your time coming over here today, and we wish you success in your investigation. If you should ever have any reason to question my client again, for anything, please contact me first." The lawyer handed Dave his card and bid him good day.

Dave smiled, took the card, and left. Now he would wait it out to see just how long Daddy would take to contact his son. He didn't have to wait long.

* * *

For over two months, Robbie neither heard nor read anything about the Shemansky murder. The police hadn't bothered him since Detective Gordon had interviewed him in January, so he was feeling somewhat confident that things had cooled down and that he was out of the picture.

Robbie had learned his job well. He pretty much kept to himself and took the advice of the gunsel who told him to keep his mouth shut and his eyes open. Abe Gorski was pleased with his effort. He was not as strong as his father, nor was he as smart as Stan, but Abe had other guys who were strong and smart. Besides, he felt he owed it to Stan to look after his son for a while, knowing that the kid would be leaving as soon as something else came along.

Robbie believed everything was going well with work and his relationship with Abe, so he was taken by surprise on Thursday—the day after Dave interviewed Stan Wicken—an unseasonably warm St. Paddy's Day, when he came home and found his father's two gunsels waiting for him in his apartment.

"What's up, guys?" Robin asked nervously. "My dad send you to give me another hundred bucks?" He was trying to lighten up the situation a little. Robbie also wanted to impress upon them that he knew their boss was his father.

With that last remark, one of the hoods grabbed Robbie by his shirt collar, almost lifting him off the ground. "Look here, you little shit. Your old man's through with you—you understand that? Through with you, finished, kaput. You fucked up royally, and now you're trying to get us into your shit." The hood held Robbie's collar tight at the throat with his left hand while he slapped him and then backhanded him hard with his right hand. Then he let him drop to the floor. Robbie wanted to cry, but he was too afraid to do so. And before he could say anything, he felt a swift kick to his stomach, which totally knocked the wind out of him. He thought for sure that he was about to die as he fought to catch his breath, but before he could say or do anything, he got another kick in his ribs from the other hood.

He blacked out for a second as things got quiet, and then the gunsel said, "We don't want to come back here again, because if we do, you won't get off so nice. So listen carefully—forget you ever saw us, you hear? Never mention your father in any way to anybody again. If you're asked, he left when you were two, and you never heard from him or saw him again. Your name is Wicken, like your mother's. You made up the name Wickler for whatever fuckin' reason you want to use. Do you understand what I just said to you?"

Robbie heard clearly, and as quickly as he physically could, he grunted, "Yeah, yeah … I get it, I get it," and then he dropped his head on the floor, still trying to breathe without pain.

The gunsels left, leaving Robbie's door open behind them. Robbie crawled to the door and, while still on the floor, slammed it closed. He knew that he had been lying there for a long time when he saw that it was getting dark, and he finally got up and started to walk around a little. The pain in his ribs and chest was finally easing off. His right cheek where he was backhanded was still red, but that too was showing signs of abating.

Yes, he was alive, but he knew that the Shemansky affair was not over, and that's probably what this beating was all about. The only good news for Robbie was that he was now certain the third guy in the group was his father.

Are the cops trying to set me up? Robbie wondered. *If my old man is mob connected, are they trying to get to him by using me? Maybe it would be better for me to just go to the cops and tell them exactly what happened. I might get busted for some petty marijuana shit, but they'll see that there was no murder. That would get my old man off my case. But I don't want to do time if I don't have to. What the fuck am I supposed to do?*

Robbie tossed and turned all night. He couldn't wait to go to work the next morning, just to take his mind off his problems. His pain was almost gone, and his face was no longer noticeably red. The weather was turning cold—back again to winter—on Friday, March 18, when he got to work. Robbie immediately started moving crates, stacking boxes, shifting piles, and doing whatever he was told by his supervisor—with no complaints or questions. Then Abe Gorski came back into the warehouse looking for him. Someone wanted to talk with him.

* * *

Shortly after Dave finished his interview with Robin's father, Marty made sure that Robin's apartment and workplace were being watched. Marty's surveillance team told him that two unidentified men had arrived around five o'clock Thursday afternoon, and they were there when Robbie arrived home at around five thirty. Before six, they left in a vehicle that they later learned, when the license was checked at the state DMV, had no outstanding tickets or warrants. The owner listed was some company name that was not on any crime watch list either. Marty was still not ready to close on Robbie, and he asked Dave to soften him up even further.

Friday morning, Dave showed up at the warehouse where Robbie worked, showed Abe his shield, and said, "I'm looking for Mr. Robin Wicken. I understand he works here."

"So why you wanna see Robbie?" Abe asked. "He in no trouble, no?"

"We've been talking to him about an ongoing murder investigation, and I just have a few more questions to ask him, that's all," Dave said in a slightly menacing tone.

"I get him for you," Abe said. "You wait here in office. I get him."

In a couple of minutes, Abe came back with Robbie, who was a little pale and walked in with some difficulty because he was still sore. "You want I should stay?" Abe asked no one in particular.

"You may stay if you like, Mr. Gorski," Dave said. "It's up to Robbie."

"Sure, I don't mind," Robbie said, noticeably agitated. "Hang around, Abe. I have nothing to hide from you. What's up?" he asked Dave.

"You remember me, don't you, Mr. Wicken?" Dave asked, using Robbie's legal name. "I just have a few important questions to ask you about the Shemansky murder investigation. Do you mind answering them here, or would you prefer to come down to the station when it's more convenient for you?"

"This is cool," Robbie answered. "Is it all right with you, Abe?"

Abe just nodded and stood there listening.

"Two men visited you yesterday afternoon. We have reason to believe that they work for your father, and even more reason to suspect that your father might have had something to do with Ed Shemansky's abduction and death. Did these men in any way try to get you involved in that affair?" Dave was trying to set a trap that, if it backfired, could put Dave's career, as well as his life, on the line. He knew that the mob played rough with cops that tried to put the squeeze on them, and that they had influence within the justice system. But he took the chance that the pressure on Wicken would pay off.

"Huh? No, uh ... what the fuck you talkin' about, man? My old man ain't got shit to do with Ed's murder. Why are you doin' this? What's happenin' here?" Robbie was looking rapidly back and forth between Dave and Abe. There was little doubt that he was scared.

"Don't get over hot," Abe advised. " Don't say what you don't know. Best keep mouth shut."

"Look, Mr. Wicken, all I'm saying is that if you have any information about your father's activities in any relation to Ed Shemansky's death, you should tell me now. Otherwise ... well, if later we find out you haven't been absolutely truthful with us, it may not go well for you. That's all I'm saying. So, once again, do you know anything about Stanley Wicken's involvement in the abduction and murder of Edward Shemansky?" He asked the question slowly.

"Like my boss said, I got nothin' more to say," Robbie said. "I gotta get back to work ... so good-bye." He just stood there, waiting for Dave to leave.

Dave looked at Robbie, and then he looked at Abe as if to say, *Straighten this kid out or he's in deep shit*. Dave nodded and said, "Sorry to have troubled you," and then he left.

* * *

At an ad hoc team meeting on Monday, March 21, the first day of spring, Marty filled everyone in on Dave's latest push of the Wicken family ... and his certainty that Robbie was somehow involved. Marty hypothesized that it was probably Robbie who drove Ed back to Cleveland; and either when they got back or before they hit the city, something went wrong, or something was planned that caused Ed's death. Even if Ed died of natural causes before the actual murder attempt, as the autopsy showed, it might still be murder one if intent was proven. In addition, if another felony was being attempted, and Ed—as only a bystander—died while the felony was in progress, then it still could be murder under the felony murder rule. Finally, transporting a dead body and concealing it for nefarious reasons could also be a very serious felony.

"I leave for Poland on the fourth, and I'll be back on Sunday the seventeenth," Marty was saying. "Let's give the Wicken kid a month to stew a little, and when I get back, I'll interview him on … what day is that?" Marty looked at the calendar. "Yeah, I'll talk with him on either Tuesday or Wednesday of that week, unless something else breaks. Dave, don't you do any more now. You stuck your neck out far enough."

SIXTEEN: *To every thing there is a season ...*
—Ecclesiastes 3:1

Because Poland had become a People's Republic—a client state of the Soviet Union—after World War II, Marty had some difficulty getting visas. But with the help of his priest and Polish relatives still living in the Warsaw region, he was finally able to secure the visas and travel through East Germany to Poland. What amazed Marty the most was that when he arrived in Poland, it appeared that they didn't speak the same Polish he spoke. He thought he spoke perfect Polish from his days in Hamtramck ... and even now in his Polish neighborhood in Cleveland. Worst of all, they didn't seem to understand his Polish dialect; all they did was smile a lot and nod in agreement at their American cousin. After spending almost a week visiting in Warsaw and talking daily with new friends and family, his confidence and language skills improved enough so that he could now carry on a decent, relatively modern conversation in Polish.

Marty's relatives still lived in the Warsaw area where his grandparents had emigrated from over a half century earlier. It was a farming village when his family left Poland, but the land was placed in a government collective by the Soviet regime. Shortly after Stalin died in 1953, the land became privately owned once again—but not by Marty's relatives. Marty's extended family members that he met for the first time were all merchants, mechanics, or in the service professions. None were farmers; all of them despised the Soviet regime. It was exciting for Marty and Clara to meet these relatives. He had known many of them by name from his parents' conversations. It was also important for both Marty and Clara to reestablish their Polish roots.

The following week, they traveled to Kraków, where they planned to visit Auschwitz and some other World War II sites. However, Marty's primary purpose in going to Kraków was to investigate what had happened to Ed Shemansky's grandfather.

Doc Coulson said that there was some rumor about his being involved in a turn-of-the-century murder investigation there, but she knew nothing of it, and she never pressed Professor Shemansky whenever they visited.

On Tuesday, Marty walked into the Kraków police headquarters without an appointment and introduced himself to the duty sergeant. He enjoyed some polite exchanges with him in Polish, which pleased the Polish police officer, who then had Marty escorted up to the detective bureau. He was introduced to the department's commander, and after some further polite exchanges, Marty said, "I was wondering if I might be able to look into some old records. I would guess sometime around early nineteen hundred to nineteen-oh-three. It was an old murder investigation involving a Professor Szymon Szymanski from Jagiellonian University."

"Why would someone from America be interested in our fifty-year-old murders?" the commander asked with a broad smile on his face. "Do you want to learn how we solve our murders?"

Marty explained about the current Shemansky murder investigation going on in Cleveland, and how someone thought they might be tied together.

The commander summoned a young police officer and told her, "You are to assist Detective Sergeant Kowalski with anything he might need."

She nodded and took Marty to the police records room, which was unbelievable as far as size and architecture. The seventeenth-century Baroque building had been updated many times over the years, but it appeared that the record room was never modernized. Marty could see stack after stack of boxes, filing drawers, ledger books, and bound and unbound documents all arranged in an apparently well-ordered fashion. It was apparent that the records in this room went back hundreds of years, to a time well before there was a Kraków police department.

"You said it was an investigation between nineteen hundred and nineteen-aught-three that you were looking for?" the police officer said in the more cultured Polish accent that is spoken in Kraków.

"Yes, and the name is Szymanski, a Professor Szymanski from the university," Marty said, trying to emulate her accent.

Smiling at Marty's attempt to sound like her, she went over to a collection of ledgers, pulled out a couple, and started to go through them quickly. Then she stopped and said, "Yes, here it is. Thursday, the twenty-seventh of November, nineteen-aught-two—interview with Herr Doktor Professor Szymon Szymanski." She then mumbled some numbers that sounded like cataloguing information and wrote something on a piece of scrap paper. She went efficiently and knowingly over to a collection of boxes, all marked with catalogue numbers, selected one that looked quite full and heavy, and carried it out. She then took Marty to a carrel off to the side and put the box on the desk, saying, "Will this be all right for you, Detective Sergeant? Do you think you will need help with the translation?"

Marty said, "No, thank you. I think I'll be able to handle it for now."

"You may work here as long as you please, and if you need anything, I should be out in the duty room," she said pleasantly, leaving him there with the huge box of notes and files.

Marty sat down at the desk, a little overwhelmed at all the material in the old storage box—and all of it in Polish. He pulled out the first file folder and read the beautifully handwritten label: HERR DOKTOR REUBEN WICKLER, SUSPICIOUS DEATH—INVESTIGATION NOTES: FOLIO I.

He almost dropped the folder when he saw the name Reuben Wickler.

Marty stayed there almost the whole day, reading all about the drowning of Reuben Wickler, how he argued with Szymanski, how he harangued Szymanski and accused him of witchcraft and cheating on his dissertation. His anti-Semitic tirades, his distrust of everyone—it was all there, plus all the interview notes, including the ones with Szymanski and the one with Reuben's widow, as well as the police notes and their speculation that Szymanski might have thrown him off the bridge. They even mentioned his son Stanislaw Wickler, who was living in Luboml with his mother, Rena Wasser. But the kicker was the final report, indicating that the investigation be terminated by order of Chief Inspector Janiak. Marty knew when someone used his political influence to end an investigation, and this was most evident here.

* * *

It was now Monday, April 18, and Marty had just returned from Poland on Sunday. He was talking with Dave and Frank. "You wouldn't believe it," Marty said. "I walked over the bridge—well, actually, the new bridge—where the murder supposedly took place. I even went to Szymanski's house on Jakuba Street. It's a Russian-style restaurant now, but it was still interesting."

After hearing Marty's trip report, the investigation team agreed that there must have been a lot of bad blood between the Wickler (now Wicken) and Shemansky families. It wouldn't have been much of a stretch if Ed Shemansky's murder did turn out to be a revenge killing. Especially when Marty told them that he thought the investigation in Poland was terminated because of some outside influence. Also, if Wicken's family believed that Shemansky did kill their patriarch, Reuben Wickler, that would be cause for seeking some kind of retribution. Marty made arrangements to go back to Ann Arbor to meet with Ben and Clarice on Wednesday to see what else they were able to dig up on Jewish mysticism ... and if they'd run across anything on revenge killings.

* * *

"Sorry for not keeping in touch with you," Marty said when he sat down at the table in the Union. "But I think we finally have a breakthrough on the Shemansky case."

"That's great," Ben said, "I think we have some interesting information too; it may not be pertinent to the case, but it is interesting."

"Remember when you asked us in February to see what we could find out about Professor Shemansky?" Clarice said. "It seems that in his early years, he published a lot of his work in collaboration with another faculty member from Jagiellonian, a mathematician by the name of Shlomo Zilber ..."

"Yeah, yeah … that's right," Marty said. "His name came up in my research in Poland. The Szymanskis and the Zilbers lived in the same house on Jakuba Street. I was there."

"But did you know that Shlomo Zilber is my grandfather?" Clarice asked, pulling her arms close to her body as if she was cold. "He's better known now as Seymour Silver of the Polytechnic University in New York. He's emeritus, but I never knew that Ed's family and my family were that close. I asked my mom last week about them, and she told me that she actually grew up with the Shemansky kids in Poland. When she asked me to see Ed, she just said they were friends of the family."

"How old is your grandfather?" Marty asked. "Do you think he'd talk to me about Professor Szymanski?"

"Gosh, my *zaydie* must easily be ninety years old. He's in an old folks' home on Long Island. My mom visits him every week, and I go with her when I'm in town. He's such a sweet guy … and so smart. He probably doesn't even know about Ed. Yeah, I guess you can probably call him—but be gentle. He's at that age when any tragedy to a friend or family member is terribly devastating for him."

"Then you'll get me his number?" Marty asked. "I promise I'll be extremely careful and gentle, okay?"

Marty brought them up-to-date on his trip and explained why the investigation was heading toward the revenge motive.

Clarice thought for a bit and then told Marty about Exodus 21:12. "You wanted to know about revenge killings." She looked at her notes. "Well, in Exodus it says, 'He that smiteth a man, so that he die, shall be surely put to death,' but it's not clear who does the putting to death." Clarice explained that the Kabbalists discuss the revenge aspect of this passage and point out that if a person kills someone accidentally, the murderer could "seek refuge." The accused would know that a family could ask for revenge and try to have the murderer killed. "Seeking refuge by moving out of the country might be a way of saying I'm sorry; it was just an accident."

After a pause, Ben said, "You say in Kraków that you found out that the Shemanskys left Poland soon after the death of Wickler. The Kabbalists talk about 'cities of refuge,' where, if someone did kill somebody accidentally, he could seek refuge in one of those cities. I think Clarice's research is right on target."

"Are you saying that Professor Shemansky was trying to send a message to Wickler's family that his death was an accident?" Marty suggested.

"I guess it's possible," Ben said, "Shemansky might have made a deal with someone to leave Kraków if they agreed to call it an accident and end the investigation."

"I doubt if Professor Shemansky himself could have brokered that kind of a deal with the police at that time. Jewish people were subjected to a lot of discrimination then. If anything, his university might have arranged it," Marty said. "It all sounds possible, but without more evidence, it's only an opinion—but it certainly adds more credence to our theory about Ed's murder being a revenge killing."

Marty then told them about his visit to the Auschwitz and Birkenau concentration camps, where, for the first time, he fully realized the true horrors of World War II, even though he had served in the military in Europe. Both were touched by his sincerity and let him know it.

* * *

On Wednesday, April 20, Marty called the Jewish old folks' home near Great Neck and asked for Professor Seymour Silver.

"Hello, Professor Silver," Marty confirmed more than asked. "My name is Martin Kowalski—I think your granddaughter Clarice mentioned I'd be calling."

"Yah, yah ... she did tell me. Now vat's dis all about?" Seymour said.

Marty took a deep breath, and in his best newly refurbished Warsaw-accented Polish, he said, "I'm a detective with the Cleveland Police Department, and we are interested in something that happened many years ago in Kraków—the death of Professor Reuben Wickler. Would you mind talking a little with me about that incident?"

Seymour was a little surprised hearing Polish like that, but he had no trouble recognizing the coarse Warsaw accent, and he answered in his refined Kraków Polish accent, "So long ago, so long ago ... Why now, fifty-two years later, would someone be interested in that tragic death?"

"We think that a Mr. Robin Wicken, whose father's name was Wickler, might be involved in a crime, and we think that what happened over fifty years ago has something to do with it," Marty replied.

"And what kind of crime would that be?"

Marty briefly filled him in about Ed's murder, not saying who the victim was just yet.

"I don't understand how the accidental drowning of Reuben could in any way be associated with … You say that was Reuben's grandson?" Seymour asked.

"There was a rumor at the time that Professor Szymon Szymanski, whom you know, of course, might have accidentally murdered Professor Wicken. We know that wasn't the case, but could you tell me a little about the rumor?" Marty persisted.

"It was just that—a rumor. Szymon wouldn't harm anybody; in fact, he went out of his way to help Reuben, who was going completely mad," Seymour explained. "But Reuben kept harassing him unmercifully with his sick, sick accusations. Accusations of a crazy man. Does your investigation have anything to do with Szymon? I know he's there in Cleveland. Has Wickler's grandson injured him?" Seymour sounded most concerned now.

"No, no, Professor Shemansky is all right, but I regret to tell you that his grandson, Edward Shemansky, was murdered. We suspect that it might have been the result of a revenge killing, and that is why we are investigating Robin Wickler. I'm sorry to have brought you this sad news in this fashion." After a long pause, Marty said, "Professor Silver? Are you still there?"

"Oh my God," Marty heard Seymour moan. "Why didn't Irenka call me? Why didn't she tell me? Oh my God," Seymour repeated with tears in his voice. "Oh, Joseph, my poor Joseph, my son, my son … why did they harm you?"

Marty felt that Seymour might be losing it calling Ed's father his son. Clarice was right; he did have trouble with grief. "Professor Shemansky's son Joseph is fine," Marty said. "Well, I mean unharmed. Neither he nor his wife were in any way physically harmed, but you're right—it is a tragic turn of events for the Shemansky family. And I can understand how tragic it must be for you as well since you were all so close at one time."

Marty stopped, waiting to hear from Seymour, but all he could hear was a soft sobbing and "My son, my son … our beautiful son"—and then there was silence. The phone clicked to let Marty know that Seymour had hung up his phone.

Marty called the home back and asked to speak to the director. He told the director who he was and said that he had just had an emotional conversation with Dr. Silver. He called to make sure that someone would look after him. He received assurances from the director that Dr. Silver would indeed be taken care of.

Marty immediately called Clarice in Ann Arbor. "I'm sorry, but I think I might have blown it with your *zaydie*. I just talked to him, and he took the news about Ed very hard. He was crying and sobbing, and strangely enough, he kept saying something about 'my son' when he referred to Ed's father, Joe. I think he might have been a little confused. So I called the home and told the director to make sure someone would stay with him. Once again, I'm sorry, Clarice—I tried my best to be gentle."

"Oh shit!" Clarice said, "I'll call my mom and tell her what happened. Maybe she'll be able to get over there today. Did you find out anything about the old murder or whatever it was with Professor Shemansky?"

"Not really. I told him why we were interested in it, and he gave me the party line about Professor Shemansky not being able to hurt anyone. It sounded well rehearsed even after fifty-some years. What a dumb move on my part, calling your grandfather and even thinking of asking him about the old investigation. I just caused him more grief and learned nothing new. Once again, I'm so sorry."

"Yeah, you're right. We probably never should have bothered him, but I'm sure he'll be all right. Okay, I'll call my mom now and talk with you later. And stop blaming yourself so much. I know you meant no harm."

Marty went back over his notes to see where he went wrong, and why Professor Silver responded the way he did. His first impression was how sharp the old man was, and how he acted with great caution before giving any answers. In fact, he never did answer anything; he just kept asking more questions. But why, for someone who sounded like he had it all together, did he think Joseph was his son? Could he just have been using "my son" as a term of endearment for the family member of an old friend? Marty didn't think so; the two families had not maintained contact for many years. Not since Joey's wedding almost twenty-five years ago. At least that's what Clarice had told him. He couldn't recall anything in the conversation that would have precipitated Professor Silver's reaction.

Marty decided that he had to do a follow-up interview with Professor and Mrs. Shemansky. He knew it would be as difficult as his interview with Silver, so he would have to be as gentle as ever on this one.

* * *

"First of all, let me thank you for agreeing to meet with me on such short notice," Marty said in Polish to Professor and Mrs. Simon Shemansky. It was the day after he'd spoken with Seymour Silver that he was meeting with the Shemanskys in their home on 117th Street. It was a lovely old house near Case Western, in a mixed neighborhood of older turn-of-the-century homes and some postwar cracker boxes put up to ease the housing shortage.

"I had an interesting conversation with your old colleague and friend Professor Seymour Silver, and I thought it would be worthwhile to talk to you as well," Marty continued.

"You said it had something to do with Edward's murder," Simon said in his distinct Kraków accent.

Marty was feeling comfortable talking in Polish now, so he continued doing so. "Yes, sir, it does. I know you're still grieving over his death, so if you would prefer another time …"

"No, no … How can we help you?"

"I was in Poland earlier in the month, doing some research on a person of interest in Ed's case, and I came across an old investigation regarding this person's possible grandfather, a Professor Reuben Wickler, someone I'm sure you would remember," Marty said gently. "As you might expect, your name came up in my research. His accidental drowning was quite traumatic to you, it would seem, but the record showed he was angry with you at the time." Marty paused. "Is this too difficult for you, sir?"

"I'm confused," Simon said, obviously upset. "What would Reuben's death have to do with my grandson?"

"We feel that maybe—and I do mean a strong *maybe*, or otherwise I would not be bothering you with this very sensitive matter—that a person here in Cleveland, a Mr. Robin Wicken, who we have surmised is Professor Wickler's grandson, may have been involved in Edward's death. Specifically, we think that Edward's death might have been an act of revenge." Again, Marty paused waiting to see how Simon reacted.

Out of the corner of his eye, he caught Mrs. Shemansky holding her breath, terror evident in her eyes. "Mrs. Shemansky, I am deeply sorry for the pain this is causing you and your husband. I'm sure these are terrible old memories that you would rather have not been reminded of, but I assure you it's absolutely necessary if we are to pursue who was responsible for Edward's untimely death."

"You say revenge?" Simon asked. "Revenge for what?"

"Sir, we feel that it is possible Robin Wicken, in his misguided reasoning, might have tried to avenge his grandfather's death, and either accidentally or some other way harmed Edward more than he intended." Marty spoke carefully so as not to come out and say directly that Robin had killed Edward.

"What evidence do you have for your suspicions, other than this ancient case that took place long before Edward was born? How did you come to this outrageous conclusion? From what you told me, you don't even know if this 'person of interest' is Reuben's grandson. What physical evidence do you have linking the two people? I'm shocked at your obvious lack of any scientific proof, and yet you still come to this totally extraordinary linkage. What would you expect me to say?" Simon was getting angry, but this was not a problem for Marty. Anger he could deal with; sadness and grief were much harder for him.

Marty quickly brought Simon up to speed on all the evidence, including the *vav*. "We are just not sure enough about the motive, or else we would arrest him. That is why I am here today, to see if you can help corroborate his motive. If you can, then we will arrest him as soon as the proper paperwork and warrants are issued."

There was a long silence, and Marty saw that Mrs. Shemansky was quietly sobbing, shaking her head from side to side, and saying nothing.

Finally, Professor Shemansky spoke. "That bastard ... that no-good evil bastard. He has attached his dybbuk to his grandson just to continue torturing me. Why, why does he do this?"

"So you do think it's possible for Edward's death to have been an act of revenge against you?" Marty asked.

"Revenge, you say? Reuben was so full of hate. So angry ... He was crazy with rage and jealousy of me. Yes, yes ... he would do anything to make me feel great pain, including having his grandson murder my grandson. Revenge, payback—I would think so. And the *vav*, how did he do that? No, no ... I don't want to know ..." Simon's speech became more and more labored, so he just kept shaking his head from side to side and motioning "no more" with his hands.

Marty was concerned that what happened yesterday when he talked with Professor Silver was happening again with the Shemanskys. "I know that this has been much too painful for you to have gone through, but you have no idea how much it has helped our case. I apologize for all the pain I brought you today, but I hope you'll take some measure of comfort in knowing that it will be used to bring Edward's murderer to justice. Thank you." Marty stood and left the house.

* * *

What Marty didn't know, nor could he possibly understand at this point, was why Mrs. Shemansky appeared so horrified. The reason was that Irene knew that if the murder was committed for revenge against Simon, then it was all for nothing because Ed was Shlomo's grandson by blood, not Simon's. Fate had dealt her such a cruel hand to see her only grandson murdered because of Simon's doing.

Was it because she was unfaithful that God was punishing her? *No,* she thought, *it doesn't work that way.* As she sobbed and sobbed on that unfortunate Thursday late in April, her husband, Simon, was experiencing great difficulty speaking, and he was feeling some numbness in his arms and hands. He was also complaining of a headache that seemed to be worsening. Later that afternoon, she called an ambulance.

By the time he got to the hospital, he was already going through the advanced stages of a hemorrhagic stroke, and he was unconscious by the time they wheeled him into the emergency room. Professor Simon

Shemansky, at eighty-eight years of age, was dead by two o'clock the next morning.

* * *

Simon's death was about all the family could bear. Joey's sister Rebecca and Ben's Uncle Saul and Aunt Hanna came down to Cleveland to help Irene and Joey get through the pain. They notified the Silvers in New York, but Seymour himself was much too frail and depressed to travel to Cleveland for the funeral. Adele, Clarice's mother, did come in for the funeral, even though she hardly remembered the family anymore. Clarice and Ben came in from Ann Arbor; they brought Doc Coulson with them. Clarice wanted to be with her mother, and Ben wanted to support his aunt and uncle.

Simon's funeral was held on Monday, April 25. Marty was there too, but in the background. He felt somewhat responsible for Simon taking ill so suddenly. He saw Clarice, Ben, and Doc Coulson at the funeral, and he nodded to them in recognition. Later, when he had the chance, he went over and told Ben and Clarice how sorry he was for their family's loss.

It seemed strange that Irene stood throughout the graveside service in relative silence, not crying or wailing in grief. Nobody knew exactly what was on Irene Shemansky's mind that day. Was it the loss of Morris and Simon's intolerance of homosexuals? Her affair with Shlomo and the resultant pregnancy with Joey? The senseless murder of her grandson? Or was it the loss of her husband of over sixty-seven years—the good times, the sad times, and all the years in between?

* * *

Later, when Marty had time to review his interview notes, he was troubled by one word, *dibick* or *dipick*, which his ears had picked up when Professor Shemansky was talking about how Reuben would want to hurt him. In fact, that whole conversation of his was a little troubling because he kept referring to Reuben wanting to get even, how he would "do anything to make me feel great pain ... have his grandson murder my grandson." Those things were written in his notes. As if Reuben were still alive and orchestrating the whole thing. He just assumed that the old man was expressing how he felt and not being as rational as he normally would have been. It was obviously quite a shock to find that Reuben's grandson was the suspected murderer in this case, so it was not surprising that he would see Reuben's hand reaching from the grave to get even for whatever sins Reuben thought Shemansky might have inflicted on him.

Marty looked in his Polish-English dictionary for the word *dibick*. He tried various spellings, but he found nothing. They were talking in Polish at the time, so he just assumed it was a Polish word that he had never heard. He thought it might be Yiddish or Hebrew, so when he had the chance, he called Ben at his dorm. "Ben, what does the word 'dibick' mean?"

"It's a ghost or spirit of a bad person that somehow got pushed into another person to do whatever it is the dybbuk—that's D-Y-B-B-U-K—wants done," Ben explained. "That's the simple explanation, but it will work. Why?"

"Professor Shemansky said that Reuben Wickler attached his dybbuk to his grandson. It didn't make any sense to me at that time, but after what you told me, it does make sense. Thanks for your help, Ben—will talk with you soon."

After his recent meeting with Clarice and Ben, Marty now believed that Simon did tussle with Reuben on the bridge, just as the Kraków police suspected. However, Simon honestly believed that Reuben's death was accidental, which it might have been. The Shemanskys leaving Poland for another country was Simon's way of trying to tell Reuben's family that it was indeed an accident. But believing in evil spirits such as dybbuks, Simon would think that the crazed Wickler would never believe it was an accident, and that he would continue to seek revenge no matter what Shemansky did. In some sense, Marty believed that Shemansky was right, and Reuben's family pursued his desire for revenge, even if Reuben's death was an accident and they knew Shemansky sought refuge in another country. Powerful feelings like that could easily lead to a major physical response like a cerebral hemorrhage.

In any case, Marty had one more tough interview to do, and he was determined not to have this one end up badly.

SEVENTEEN: *Thou shalt not bear false witness ...*
—Exodus 20:16

Marty had arranged for an interview with Stan Wicken, through his lawyer, for Wednesday, April 27. Marty arrived at the same house that Dave was at over a month earlier, a nice house in a middle-class neighborhood. The weather had turned from a mild spring back to a blustery winter. When Marty drove up to Stan's house, the windows were closed, and there was nobody outside to see him enter. Stan and his lawyer were in the front room when Marty was shown in by the maid, but there was no sign of any of his gunsels around.

The lawyer waited for Marty to take off his coat and sit down, and then he said, "Detective Sergeant Martin Kowalski, is it?"

"Yes," Marty replied, taking out his ID to show him, but the lawyer waved it off. Marty turned to Stan and, speaking in Polish, said, "How are you, Mr. Wicken? I understand you were in the army during the First World War. Where did you serve?"

The lawyer didn't understand Polish, but before he could ask what was being said, Stan responded. "You speak my language, but you're not from around here. Where did you learn to speak Polish?"

"I grew up in Hamtramck, right in the middle of Detroit. Are you familiar with the place? I notice that both of us speak a lot like my family, who originally came from Warsaw. Is that where your family is from?" Marty asked.

Stan was smiling. He knew what Marty was trying to do, and he continued playing the game a little, much to his lawyer's dismay. "Why are you here? Your partner was here a few weeks back, and I told him—or I should say my lawyer told him—all that he needed to know, so why have you come back?" Without waiting for Marty to answer, Stan continued. "Look, we are having a talk that only you and I understand, so lay it out honestly and we'll see where we can go from here."

His accent was like Marty's, a mix of an old eastern Poland dialect interwoven with local Polish colloquialisms. Marty knew he was sincere because there was no way this conversation—without being recorded and translated—would ever hold up in court. So Marty came right out and told him what he knew about Stan's father's hatred of Professor Shemansky and the ensuing events on the bridge in Kraków back in the fall of 1902.

Stan remembered the story his mother had told him about a "Shaszemski" (Stan thought she must have mispronounced Szymanski) who might have killed his father because he was a Christian. Stan knew his mother was a simple soul, so he never pursued the story. But now, for the first time, he might get the truth about what happened, so he prodded Marty into relating everything he knew about the Reuben Wickler affair.

His lawyer finally had it with all the Polish talk and said, "Mr. Wicken, if I can't understand what you and the detective are talking about, there is no way I can advise you on how you might best respond. You understand that, right?"

"Yah, yah, yah … It's okay. We are all right—just family talk now, that's all."

After Marty brought Stan up-to-date, there was a long pause while Stan tried to digest the scene of his father going crazy—probably because his mother took him and left his father alone in Kraków—and that seemed to touch a nerve. After a while, Stan said in English, "So … what you want to ask?"

"I just would—," Marty started to say in Polish.

"In English, please, so lawyer can hear, okay?"

"Okay," Marty said. "I just would like to know if your son might have heard that story about your father and sought to get revenge for him by harming or frightening Professor Shemansky's grandson, Edward Shemansky."

The lawyer interrupted. "I don't recall my client ever having told you, or anyone else, that Mr. Robin Wicken was my client's son—"

"Enough," Stan said, cutting him off. "Robbie is my son. But you know I leave him and him mother when just baby, so he never know me. Maybe was bad thing; maybe I should have not done. I pay full for him … I cover all expenses so mother not work. I can tell you truth: his mama know nothing about my father, and I never tell him about his grandfather. That is truth. So … what will happen to Robbie?"

"Thank you, Mr. Wicken, for your honesty. I cannot say at this time what might happen to Robin, but there is good evidence that Robin killed Ed Shemansky, and if he's arrested and convicted, he can get life in prison. If the murder was premeditated, then he could even get the electric chair. I'm sorry to have to tell you this," Marty said, and he truly was sorry.

* * *

When Marty left, Stan filled the lawyer in on all the information and asked him what he thought.

"Well, if they can prove that Robbie did it as a revenge killing, then they'll want to know how he learned the story, and you're the only one in his family that seems to know it. You may be charged as an accomplice to murder if they think you put him up to it. That is all highly unlikely, but you should know this. By the way, that's why I wanted you to talk in English from the beginning." The lawyer was clearly a little miffed.

When the lawyer left, Stan sat and thought long and hard as to what he owed his son. They'd never really bonded, and he had to admit that when he finally did meet him, he was not greatly impressed. Stan had grown hard over the years, and one thing he'd learned was to take care of yourself and cover your ass at all times. And that is exactly what Stan intended to do in this case. If his son was a murderer, for whatever reasons, Stan was not going to burn with him on some trumped-up revenge charge.

* * *

Marty was now ready to reinterview Robbie, so on a rainy Friday, April 29, Robbie was picked up at the warehouse and taken to police headquarters for questioning. He was not handcuffed, nor was he told he was under arrest.

Robbie was terrified. His dad's "friends" had not contacted him since he was roughed up by those gunsels over a month ago, but he had noticed that his relationship with Abe had definitely cooled down. Abe ignored him after that meeting with Detective Gordon and treated him as if he was just another employee.

Robbie was sitting at a table in the interview room. The table had three other chairs around it, and that was all the furniture in the room. There was one door and an obvious two-way mirror on one wall. Robbie was wondering who was watching him through the mirror, but he kept his cool and controlled appearance so as not to arouse any suspicion.

After a little while, Detective Sergeant Martin Kowalski entered and introduced himself. "Would you like anything to drink, Robbie?"

"Uh … just some water, thank you," Robbie responded politely.

Marty relayed his request out the door and placed on the table a folder with a bunch of pages in it. He started to go through them. He stopped at one page and read it—apparently making sure he knew its content well—before putting it back in the folder. He closed the folder and started the interview.

"We're investigating the murder last November of Mr. Edward Shemansky. I understand you knew him and attended the last game that he played before he died, is that correct?" Marty asked.

"Well … he sorta didn't actually *play* in that game. He was second string, and he just watched, like all the rest of us in the stands," Robbie answered, trying for a little levity.

Marty ignored his attempt. "Now, was it you that drove him back to Cleveland after the game?"

"No, man—I never said that."

"That's odd," Marty said looking at his notes in the folder. "We just assumed you drove him home because we found fibers from your car on his clothes. Did he ever travel in your car?" Marty held up a sheet that looked like a lab report.

"Uh … no, uh … I don't think so." Robbie was now a little rattled as to how he should answer. He wondered if any fibers from his car were on Ed. "Uh … maybe, you know … uh … I guess it's possible. Uh … I just can't remember exactly when it was."

"So you say he was in your car," Marty persisted.

"I don't know, man; lots of people were in my car," he said, irritated and nervous about not knowing where this was going.

Marty continued down a different path, pulling out another sheet from the folder. "You knew, of course, that Ed's grandfather knew your grandfather, right?" Marty said, again catching Robbie off guard.

Robbie's eyes widened. "Huh? I never knew that. I don't even know my grandfather. Man, I don't even know my father. He left when I was a baby. All I know about that side of my family is what my mother told me, and that ain't much," he said with some conviction.

Marty got close to Robbie's face and said, "Are you telling me that you haven't seen your father at all since you were a baby?" he asked with some incredulity in his voice.

Robbie got scared on this one. Maybe they knew that his father had visited him. But the gunsel warned him about ever mentioning his father again. *I'm fucked*, he thought. *Either way, I'm dead.*

Robbie turned his face away from Marty. "Man, I told you I haven't seen my father since I was a baby," Robbie repeated.

Marty stood up, picked up his folder, and leafed through it, stopping at one point. "Now that's strange. Your apartment manager at your old flat told us your father and two other men went into your apartment and met with you on Wednesday, the seventeenth of November, just three days prior to Ed Shemansky's murder." Marty knew that Robbie had three visitors, but he lied about the manager saying it was his father. It seemed to work, and Marty was getting to him now.

"What? What are you saying, man?" Robbie was scared, but he stopped fidgeting and began pulling himself together. "My father was not there that day, you understand that? My father was not there that day, and that's the *truth*!"

"Then why did the manager think one of the men was your father?" Marty persisted. "He claimed that's why he let them into your apartment."

"I don't give a fuck what he said or what the fuck he thought—my old man was never there, and that's all I'm telling you. Can I go now? I don't like this shit." Robbie stood up now and acted as if he was going to leave.

Marty stared at Robbie with a blank expression for a couple of seconds before saying, "We found the tread prints of your car's tires at the place where you dropped Ed's body on Saturday night after the UM-OSU game. We have someone who can identify you as having waved and yelled at Ed as his team came down the tunnel before the game, and we have a witness who says he saw you and Ed leaving the stadium together. We know you killed Ed and dumped his body, hoping it wouldn't be discovered until spring. But it was discovered covered with fibers from your vehicle, and we have witnesses who claim to have seen you and Ed Shemansky together on Saturday, the twentieth of November, 1954." Marty played his hand with a bunch of unproven conjectures and hoped it would work. "It will go a lot easier for you if you confess now. Why did you do it, Robbie?"

Robbie sat down again, seemingly shocked for a few seconds. "Wow!" he finally said, "That's some fairy tale you got there. Man, I have no idea what the fuck you're talking about. That's all a bunch of shit. Why the fuck would I kill Ed Shemansky? We were friends. I don't know where you got those ideas, but you're full of it, and I ain't saying another thing." Robbie folded his arms and turned away from Marty.

Marty just stared at him, and then he pulled out his trump card, hoping he wouldn't have to play it—because if it failed, the whole game was over. "Robbie, I can understand why you're scared and why you would lie to the police. But you can avoid the death penalty by being honest with us now, or you can just continue to lie and be assured that you will be tried and convicted of first-degree murder, a capital crime in Ohio, and you'll probably get the chair. Is that clear?"

Marty continued without waiting for Robbie to answer. "Your father wanted to avenge his father's murder at the hands of Ed Shemansky's grandfather, so he enlisted you to do the job, convincing you that he would take care of you with his connections if anything went wrong. He told you why you had to murder Ed, possibly also instructing you to put the Hebrew letter *vav* on Ed's forehead, which you know stands for 'You shall not murder,' the sixth commandment. Well, things have gone wrong for you, and I don't see your father here to get you out. In fact, when we talked to your father, he admitted that he knew Ed's grandfather murdered his father. But he denies he knows you, or that you even exist." Marty watched Robbie turn around, unfold his arms, and lower his head. Marty waited to let that sink in before continuing. "Here's the deal. We don't want you as much as we want your father. Give him up, and I promise you won't get the chair. In fact, you may only get a minimal sentence and still come out a young man. Give him up, Robbie, and tell us how he convinced you to kill Ed."

For a long time, Robbie sat there looking conflicted. If he said his father had put him up to it, then he was a dead man for sure. If he denied it, then he was still a dead man. He had no choice other than to tell the truth of how Ed died accidentally, trying to score a couple of joints. He knew that he might get some jail time for a drug offense, but that would beat murder anytime.

Robbie finally took a deep breath and told Marty the whole story about taking Ed home and then deciding to get some pot. That they went to the warehouse, found nothing, and how Ed fell on the angle iron and was killed by hitting his head. How it was all just a terrible accident, and there was no murder. But he did admit to taking the body and trying to dispose of it because he was scared half to death.

Marty had Robbie write up what he told him, and when he was finished, they arrested him on an open charge of murder in the death of Edward Shemansky. They held him in the police lockup over the weekend, and on Monday, May 2, they turned Robbie's case—along with his confession and all the other evidence—over to the district attorney's office. Robbie was shocked and felt totally violated. They got him to confess, but since they didn't get his father, the mobster, they were taking it out on him in the hopes he would still tell on his father. But Robbie wouldn't do that. First of all, he honestly didn't have anything on his father to give up. Robbie also knew that if he lied about his father, it would definitely be a reason for his father to have him killed. And finally, Robbie felt that his father was the only chance he had of beating the rap. He could only pray that maybe his father would arrange for some smart lawyer to take his case. That was the least he could do for not giving him up to the police on a false charge just to save his own ass.

Robbie would think about that night after night while waiting in jail for his trial. But even sadder for Robbie was that he had no visitors at all—not his mother, his father, Abe Gorski, any of his friends, or any of the gunsels that worked for his father. That was the hardest thing for Robbie to reconcile in his mind: that he was totally alone in the universe, without a soul who cared one bit about him ... about whether he lived or died.

EIGHTEEN: *For dust thou art, and unto dust shalt thou return.*

—Genesis 3:19

At Robbie's preliminary hearing on Monday morning, May 2, 1955, he was bound over for trial on the charge of first-degree murder in the death of Mr. Edward Shemansky, a citizen of the United States and a resident of the city of Cleveland, Ohio. He could afford neither bail nor a lawyer, so the court appointed a lawyer for him, and when he was asked, "How do you plead, guilty or not guilty?" the judge instructed him that if he stood mute, the judge would enter a plea of not guilty. He also selected a lawyer from the pool for him, telling him to take the case. So Robbie stood mute, as he was instructed, and was led out of the courtroom. He was returned to jail, where he'd be confined until his trial. His court-appointed lawyer told him that he'd see him at the jail, and then he went over to do some paperwork with the court clerk.

Robbie was confused but still hopeful that his father would be sending someone top-notch to take care of him. But then he realized that if a top-notch lawyer showed up for him, people—in particular, the police—would wonder who sent him, and they would connect it back to his father. So if he was to keep his mouth shut about his father, and nobody was supposed to know who his father was, then how could his father help him? It was a real quandary for Robbie. He was not only confused, but he was scared stiff as to what might happen to him.

Later in the day, on Monday, he was taken to the inmate interview room to meet with his lawyer, whom he saw only briefly at the courthouse. "Hi, my name is James Scanlon, and I have been appointed by the court to help defend you in your upcoming jury trial. Before you start talking, I should tell you that if the charges against you are true, and even if you did confess to murder, I am not legally obligated to give the court any other evidence that you might offer me corroborating your guilt—it's called attorney-client privilege. However, I cannot allow false evidence to come into play; all I can do is make certain that you get a fair and honest trial, and that the prosecution proves your guilt as required by law. Do you understand what I am saying?" Scanlon asked.

"Uh … not really," Robbie said. "How do I know if the trial is fair and the prosecution isn't lying?"

"They have to bring enough solid evidence—eyewitness testimony, fingerprint information on weapons, that kind of stuff—to reasonably convince anybody of your guilt," Scanlon explained. "If they can't do that, then even if you are guilty, they have to let you walk. Also, if they try to introduce any evidence or other information that you feel is false, then you'll let me know, and I will register a formal objection that could require them to substantiate it more clearly."

Robbie then filled Scanlon in on the "murder," telling him it was all just an accident, but that the police think it was for revenge or something like that. Scanlon explained a little about how the prosecution had to turn over all evidentiary materials to him before the trial. He told Robbie that he would look over the evidence and get back with him. But after hearing about the confession to the potential drug deal, and Ed banging his head on some metal thing, Scanlon told him that wouldn't help him get off any easier. "Robbie, there is something in the law called felony murder. If an innocent person is killed, or simply dies from fright, during the commission of a felony—and dealing drugs is a felony offense here—then that death may be judged a felony murder, which carries the same penalty as first-degree murder."

"But it was an accident!" Robbie protested. "I had no reason to kill Ed; it was just an unlucky accident—that's all it was!"

"Let's wait till I have a chance to go over all the evidence and your confession before we decide what the best line of defense would be for you, okay?" Scanlon offered.

Robbie had tears in his eyes when Scanlon was about to leave. He was getting more discouraged by the minute. "Have you talked with anyone in my family?" Robbie asked weakly.

Scanlon shook his head and got the guard to release him. Robbie was taken back to his cell, where he sat down and cried like a baby.

* * *

The next time Robbie saw Scanlon, he felt that Scanlon was different somehow. Something in his manner had changed. Robbie couldn't figure it out, but something was definitely different in the way he was talking and giving Robbie information about the case. Robbie felt that Scanlon was not doing a good job, and he wondered why. There was no doubt that Robbie's confidence in him was sorely shaken.

"Robbie, I've looked over all their evidence—the confession, their witness list, and lab reports." Scanlon paused and looked Robbie in the eye. "I think it best that you don't take the stand in your own defense. Trying to push Shemansky's death as a drug deal gone sour may do you more harm than good, in part for the reasons I told you last time about felony murder. There's a hearing scheduled next week to set the trial date. I'm going to try to have it set no sooner than a couple of months from now—early July at best. This will give me time to work out some of the kinks and see if we can come up with a reasonable defense. In the meantime, don't talk to anybody about the case. Don't talk to the police and try to involve anyone else in the murder—that can only backfire—and don't let any of the other prisoners tell you what to do. If they knew so much about the law, they wouldn't be here themselves. You got all that?"

"Yeah, yeah, I got it," Robbie said, feeling very unhappy about his faith in Scanlon. "Are you going to ask my mother to come and visit me?"

"I think it best we avoid getting anyone in your family involved at this time. You're not on the best of terms with your mom, and you don't know for sure who your father is, right? Maybe later we can do something like that, okay?" Scanlon ended the interview.

His statement about his father puzzled Robbie, but it was just one more thing that further eroded his trust in him. He thought more about why Scanlon's attitude might have changed. Maybe his father had gotten to him, telling him not to bring his name into the case.

Over the next few weeks, Robbie saw little of his lawyer, and when he did, Scanlon had little to report. The trial was set for Monday, July 11, a week after the Fourth of July. Robbie found out that he could have been at the hearing on setting the trial date, but Scanlon had never told him that.

Robbie had turned twenty years old two months earlier, and his youthful appearance would make him most desirable to some of his older, more-seasoned jail mates. Robbie was smart enough to know what could happen, so he was ultracareful not to offend anyone, especially the guards, in case he needed them. Robbie had lots of time to think now, and that's about all he did. He hardly slept, tossing and turning most of the night and then napping most of the day. He only left his cell for meals and for the mandatory exercise period. It was beginning to get hot and humid, and the jail had no air-conditioning, which made it even harder for him to sleep at night.

By the middle of June, Robbie was a nervous wreck. He had no idea what defense Scanlon was pursuing, or what line of action he should take concerning his father. He saw Scanlon only twice in all that time, and both times were very brief. Scanlon claimed he was still working on his defense, but things were looking up. He claimed that after looking at all the evidence the prosecution had, they would end up killing their own case with it because he would question its relevance and substance. He said that there was no physical evidence linking him to the murder ... and no evidence that a murder actually occurred. Scanlon said that he planned not to say a lot initially, but he would have copious questions after the evidence was presented.

"It's going to get rough in there," Scanlon told Robbie, "but I think they're on very thin ice. They're going to claim that someone they've identified as your father made you do it. But he's not on the witness list, so I don't see how they can prove it without him. As for all the supposed other evidence—your grandfather's murder, someone claiming they heard you yell Shemansky's name at the game—it's the same thing, little substance and no definitive proof, so we'll challenge everything they bring in. They have no eyewitnesses, no one that can put you anywhere near the scene of the crime on the day Ed was killed. So they essentially have no case. We'll just let them talk it out and show that no reasonable person could convict you. Anyway, I'll see you next week. Did you get the clothes I sent you for the trial?"

"Yeah, I got them," Robbie said in a rather negative way. "Couldn't you have picked out something nicer for me?"

"No, no … let's just keep it conservative. Always looks better when you dress conservatively for a trial, okay?"

Robbie nodded and watched him leave, and then he was taken back to his cell, where he would think about his trial, feeling that he was definitely fucked.

* * *

On Monday morning, July 11, at seven o'clock, Robbie was brought to the courthouse and held in a lockup until jury selection, which was set for eight. He was dressed in his working clothes—denim trousers, a denim shirt, black shoes, and white socks. He thought it looked more like a prisoner's uniform than his own prison uniform. Scanlon said he looked more like a working-class person, and that would get the jury's sympathy. They brought him into the courtroom in shackles and sat him at the table with Scanlon. The jury pool, sitting in an area near the witness box, looked like a bunch of average people. They had all finished filling out a questionnaire, and both the prosecution and the defense had copies of their forms.

"Juror number four, are you currently working?" the prosecutor asked.

"No sir, I'm retired from Fords … you know, the plant over on Industrial. I worked there thirty years, and now I have my pension."

"Juror number three, are you opposed to the death penalty for a capital murder conviction?" he asked a middle-aged woman.

"If someone kills somebody, then the Bible tells me an eye for an eye, so I'm not against sending a killer to the electric chair."

Scanlon took notes, but he never challenged a juror, nor did he ask any questions. The judge asked the jurors if anyone knew Robbie, Scanlon, the prosecutor, or him, the judge. He then gave the jury brief instructions as to their role and duties as jurors. It seemed surprising to

Robbie that neither Scanlon nor the prosecution challenged anyone. *Maybe it's always that way in real life ... and challenges are just something you see on TV,* Robbie thought. But after hearing what some of them said about capital punishment, Robbie felt they would have no problem sending him off to die if he was found guilty. But how could he be found guilty of an accident? He just hoped and prayed that Scanlon was right, and the case would fall apart on the evidence. He hadn't slept or eaten much that weekend, and he felt dizzy and exhausted by the time jury selection ended around ten fifteen.

There was a brief recess before the trial actually started, and when Robbie was brought back into the courtroom, he noticed that there were more people there than he thought should be there. Most were from the press, but he could tell that many were friends of Ed or his family. He didn't see any of his family or friends there to support him. He felt lonely, scared, and completely defeated. He just hung his head and waited for the whole thing to be over.

Mr. Marion Fischer, the prosecutor, presented his opening arguments to the jury, first telling them that the preponderance of the evidence would show that Robin Wicken did willfully murder Edward Shemansky. He explained that his reason was to avenge his grandfather's death, which the Wicken family blamed on Edward Shemansky's grandfather. They would show that the murder weapon was a broken piece of angle iron, which was later used to mark the victim with a symbol standing for revenge. They would show that in his own confession, Robin stated that he drove Edward back to Cleveland ...

And so it continued, with the prosecution telling them who the witnesses were and what they would be telling the jury. They had it down pat and seemed completely confident that they would easily make the case for murder against Robbie.

Scanlon then made his opening arguments, telling the jury that the prosecution's case was weak, and that no eyewitnesses were on their list of witnesses because there weren't any. He also pointed out that the alleged murder weapon—the piece of angle iron—was never found, nor were there any fingerprints or other physical evidence at the purported crime scene. He finished rather weakly by telling them the judge would instruct them about the "reasonable doubt" principle, and they would then realize that no reasonable person could possibly convict Robin Wicken based on the circumstantial evidence the prosecution intends to show.

Opening arguments ended shortly before noon, so the judge ordered them to break for lunch, and Robbie was taken back to the holding cell. He didn't eat the lunch they brought for him; his stomach was tied in knots as he sat there and thought about what was going on in the courtroom. He was bothered by the fact that he was told a Judge O'Malley was supposed to be his judge, and all of a sudden, there was this Freeman person on the bench. The name rang a bell for some reason …

Then Robbie remembered reading an article in the *Cleveland Plain Dealer* over a year ago, when he first got his own subscription. It was one of those Sunday feature reports about judges. He remembered it now. Freeman was the one they said never convicted mob members. Or, if they did get a conviction, his punishments were essentially a slap on the wrist. They didn't say he was in the mob's pocket—they wouldn't dare say that—simply that he was soft on mobsters who appeared before him. *Shit, that's it!* Robbie thought. *My dad got to the judges! He got Freeman assigned to get me off. Of course, he would do it that way; then there's no way of tying him to me.*

After that enlightening monologue with himself, he relaxed a little and even ate some of his lunch.

After the lunch break, the trial resumed, and Fischer called the person who'd heard someone call Ed's name when the UM team passed through the tunnel. Scanlon had a chance to question the witness, but instead of asking him if he could positively identify Robbie as the person, he simply asked him if he had been drinking or if the crowd noise confused him, and so on, none of which seemed to help Robbie's case. When Robbie asked him about that, he said, "It's my job to throw doubt into the jurors' minds as to the trustworthiness of the witness. If I asked what you wanted me to and he then identified you, what would I do? Even if he lied, it would be harder for me to impugn him than it would be for me to show that he was an unreliable witness to begin with. Look, I know what I'm doing, okay?"

This went on for some time with all the other witnesses. Scanlon asked the police crime lab specialist, "How many other vehicles had the same tires installed as the 1953 Chevrolet Bel Air?"

"Oh, quite a number of General Motors vehicles came with those tires," the lab tech said.

"As for the carpeting and trunk matting, how many vehicles came with those same materials?" Scanlon asked.

"Again, there were a lot of them."

"Would you say that maybe there were thousands of vehicles that had the same tires, floor, and trunk mats as the 1953 Chevrolet Bel Air?" Scanlon asked.

"Probably. I don't know how many thousands, but thousands is not unreasonable."

"Thank you," Scanlon said dismissively.

"Yeah, but did they find those things in my car? Why didn't you ask them that?" Robbie said.

"Are you crazy? Then they'll know immediately that you tried to cover that up by replacing them before you sold the car," Scanlon told him.

Robbie sat quietly through much of the other testimony, only speaking when Scanlon asked him a question. Later in the afternoon, the judge decided that enough testimony had been heard that day, and he ordered that the trial be continued at nine the next morning. The judge ordered that the jury be sequestered, and he instructed them about not talking about the case, reading newspapers, and all the other protocol that goes with any high-profile murder trial.

* * *

The court was back in session Tuesday morning at nine o'clock sharp. It had been hot and humid on Monday, with scattered thundershowers, and the courtroom was stuffy and uncomfortable. But the storms had passed, and it was beginning to clear that morning. When Robbie was brought back in the courtroom, he had a shallow smile on his face, knowing the fix was in for him, or in other words, the judge was bought. He also guessed that Scanlon was in on it too, and that's why all this "reasonable doubt" shit was being raised.

Marion Fischer called Detective Sergeant Martin Kowalski to the stand, asking him first about the confession and how it was obtained.

"When I presented him with the facts that we knew about the case, and our knowledge of his family history with Professor Shemansky's family, he admitted that he killed young Edward Shemansky," Marty said. "He initially claimed it was an accident."

"Was his confession given freely?" the prosecutor asked without any objection from Scanlon.

"Yes, it was. We have his own handwritten account of the story he told us," Marty replied.

"You said *story*, Detective; how did you know it was a story?" Fischer asked.

"Oh, that's pretty standard. You see when criminals are confronted with the facts of their crime, it's not unusual for them to try and confess to a lesser crime in the hopes that their confession will actually be used to prove the lesser crime, and that the real crime will not be prosecuted," Marty explained.

"So it is your professional opinion that Mr. Wicken's confession was fabricated by him to fend off a murder conviction?"

Marty again spoke with no objections from Scanlon. "It's more than just my opinion; we checked out his story, and it didn't hold water. The only part that was true was the part about picking young Edward Shemansky up in Columbus and bringing him to Cleveland, where he was subsequently killed, and the part about how he drove the body to the farm and discarded Edward Shemansky's remains in a ditch, hoping it would never be discovered."

"You say it didn't hold water—that is, parts of Mr. Wicken's confession were invalidated by you. Would you please elaborate on that for the court, Detective Kowalski?"

"He told us that the murder was committed in a warehouse, and he actually gave us the address. When we went there, the building was completely empty—no shelves, no boxes or crates, not a piece of furniture, shelving, storage equipment, or anything was found. And the broken angle iron he claimed was Edward Shemansky's cause of death was nowhere to be found. We also found the owner of the warehouse, who told us the building had been empty for months while he was looking for someone to lease the space. Finally, Mr. Wicken said that it was a drug-related deal gone bad. That he, Robin Wicken, had taken Edward Shemansky, a skilled college football player, there to sell him drugs. No drugs were found on Edward's body or in any of his possessions. His story—that is, Mr. Wicken's story—was fabricated to make us believe that Edward died accidentally, banging his head on some piece of metal. He wanted us to charge him on a drug offense and illegally disposing of a body, but not for murder." Marty finished, still sitting upright with a military bearing that strongly suggested how professionally he had conducted the entire investigation.

Then the prosecutor switched gears and asked Marty to explain why he thought the motive was revenge. Marty related his research on the Shemansky-Wickler feud during his trip to Poland.

"The police report clearly and concisely listed the cause of death to Professor Reuben Wickler—Robin Wicken's grandfather—as an accidental drowning," Marty told the jury. He went on to explain how Reuben taunted and harassed poor Professor Shemansky. "Whose recent untimely death," he said, "even though he was eighty-eight, was in all likelihood brought about by the tragic events surrounding the murder of his grandson." Marty then clearly and succinctly described how he'd concluded that revenge was the motive. He also said they had a witness who claimed Robin Wicken's father visited him just days before the murder. They had a witness who said Robin Wicken attended Hebrew school and learned the Hebrew alphabet. They raised the issue of his taking a job where his father once worked, of moving to another place and selling his car, of living modestly and even changing his name to his grandfather's name. All of it was quite compelling.

Scanlon didn't cross-examine Marty because, as he told Robbie, "He's a highly respected cop, and it would be more harmful to try to add doubt to his testimony."

After a brief recess, Mr. Fischer went on to explain the motive further. An expert on Judaic studies from Cleveland State University was brought in to explain the meaning of the *vav* on Ed's forehead. He reported on all the various significances of *vav*, focusing on the sixth commandment: "You shall not murder." He also pointed out the time reversal explanation from Kabbalist literature, which could imply that what was done to someone in the past is now being done to someone else. Again, Scanlon didn't object or cross-examine.

The testimony of the expert witness ended a little after noon; the judge asked if the prosecution had any more witnesses. They didn't. He then asked Scanlon if he had any witnesses to examine. He didn't. "Then we'll hear closing arguments after our lunch recess at one o'clock this afternoon," the judge said, banging his gavel.

Robbie was taken to a holding cell, where lunch was brought in for him. He didn't eat; he just wanted to think about the case. He wondered why the medical examiner was not called up as a witness, even though he saw his name and title on the prosecution's witness list. In all the stuff he saw on TV, the coroner or some expert testified as to the cause of death. They never even mentioned it here. He had to ask Scanlon about that. In any event, he was anxious to see just how his old man's influence would work out for him with his fixed judge.

* * *

When Robbie was brought back into the courtroom shortly before one o'clock, just before closing arguments started, Robbie asked Scanlon why the ME wasn't called to testify.

"I explained to you earlier about felony murder. If Ed died by being scared to death watching you get drugs to deal, it could be the same as first-degree murder," Scanlon explained. "I don't want the ME to give the prosecutor any opportunity to use that argument. You understand that, don't you?"

"Yeah, sure ... Whatever you guys say is fine with me. That is, you and the judge. You guys are cool with me; whatever you want me to do I'll do, okay?" Robbie spoke like a good soldier.

After the judge gave the jury some initial instructions, closing arguments started with the prosecutor. Mr. Fischer essentially repeated his opening arguments, only this time he embellished on his earlier points, quoting extensively from the witnesses in order to show that his earlier points were indeed valid.

He finished by saying, "You have no choice other than to convict Robin Wicken, aka Wickler, of murder in the first degree. The judge's instructions are clear about the meaning of 'all reasonable doubt,' whether it is based on circumstantial evidence or otherwise. The evidence presented at trial should leave you no doubt as to the reasonable belief that Robin Wicken knowingly and wantonly killed Edward Shemansky."

Scanlon then got his chance to repeat and elaborate on his opening arguments. Only Scanlon had no testimony to back up his assertion that the witnesses were either unreliable or presented invalid information. He stressed the lack of an eyewitness, and he also tried to play up the fact that no instrument of death was found. Scanlon's conclusion was weak. "Without any eyewitnesses or any physical evidence relating directly to my client, including but not limited to the lack of a murder weapon, then, by your instructions from the judge, you must have a reasonable doubt, and if you do have reasonable doubt, then you cannot convict this young man, Mr. Robin Wicken, of murder in any degree whatsoever."

The judge then gave some final instructions clarifying the reasonable doubt mandate to the jury, and they were sent off to the jury room to deliberate. It was just after two thirty when the jury left the courtroom that afternoon, and Robbie and Scanlon were put in another room with a police guard at the door. They talked little during the wait, and Scanlon kept looking at his watch. Robbie just sat there, more or less resigned to his fate and still believing that the fix with the judge was in. Scanlon told Robbie that he would wait until five, but then he'd have to go home. He'd leave contact information in case the jury came back in before dinner.

The jury deliberated the rest of the afternoon, and at about four forty-five, when Scanlon was getting ready to leave, the word came that the members of the jury had reached their verdict.

Court was brought back in session, and the jury panel entered the courtroom and sat in the jurors' box. The judge asked the jury if they had reached a verdict. The foreman stood and answered, "We have, Your Honor," handing the written verdict to the clerk. The clerk read the verdict. "We, the jury in the above-entitled action, have found the defendant, Robin Wicken, guilty of first-degree murder this twelfth day of July, nineteen fifty-five. Ladies and gentlemen of the jury, is this your verdict?"

All the jurors replied in hushed unison, "Yes."

The judge then said, "Sentencing is scheduled for Monday, the twenty-fifth of July, at nine AM." Then he banged his gavel and left the courtroom.

The courtroom was exceptionally quiet; even the press cameras sounded muted. Yesterday's storms had cleared the sky, and there were soft breezes blowing through the open windows of the courtroom. Still in shackles, Robbie was led out and transferred back to jail. But Robbie knew this was just a sham. The bought judge would just give him a slap on the wrist, and he would be out in no time. He may even be sentenced to time already served. He'd seen that plenty of times on TV. But for some reason, he felt a little nervous about the whole thing. Supposing he was wrong, what would happen to him? *Could they really sentence me to death?* he wondered. *No way—I'm barely out of my teens. I'm not even twenty-one; they would never kill a minor.*

He couldn't sleep that night, nor did he sleep very well over the next two weeks. He tried calling his lawyer, but he could never get him, and none of his calls were returned. He realized that he just had to wait it out on his own.

* * *

On the morning of July 25, Robbie was again in court. The room was once again filled with Shemansky family members, their friends, and the press. As soon as they brought Robbie over to the table and sat him down, Scanlon said, "When the judge asks if you want to address the court, you should say yes. Then go over to the microphone at that podium, and tell the family you're sorry. Don't confess; just say you're sorry and you regret what's happened. That might make the judge go easier on you, okay?"

"I get it," Robbie said. "We gotta make it look good when he lets me off, so he won't look bad, right?"

Scanlon either didn't hear him or didn't care what he said; he just ignored Robbie.

The judge made some opening comments about the trial and the verdict, and then he asked the defendant if he wanted to address the court before sentencing. Robbie looked at Scanlon, who said, "Yes, we would, Your Honor," and then he motioned Robbie up to the podium. Robbie was not the most articulate person, and in front of all those people, he was a little awed. When he got to the podium, he was quite nervous.

"Uh … I just wanna say that … uh … I'm very sorry for the family, for Ed's family. I never meant no harm to Ed—he was always nice to me. I said to the police and everyone else that it was just an accident. I didn't mean for him to get hurt. Uh … I'm not saying now that I hurt him; I'm just saying that I regret what happened to my friend Ed. So, uh … so please forgive me. Thank you …"

"Are you finished?" the judge asked, and Robbie sat back down. The judge then said, "The crime that you have been convicted of is one of the most mindless murders I've heard in this courtroom in all the years I've been here. To murder someone in these times for something supposedly done over half a century ago is barbaric. We've fought two—no, make that three—wars since the death of your grandfather. You would have thought that kind of barbarism would not be seen again in our lifetime. But here we are, with you convicted of such a senseless act against someone who had so much promise—someone whose life would have amounted to something. Someone who loved and was loved is now gone forever. You leave me no choice but to sentence you to the maximum sentence allowed by law and recommended by the jury. Robin Wicken, I sentence you to die in the electric chair for the murder of Edward Shemansky, and may God have mercy on your soul." He banged his gavel, got up, and left.

The bailiff announced that court was no longer in session, and all were dismissed. Two guards took Robbie away before he even had a chance to ask Scanlon what was happening. It wouldn't have mattered; Scanlon was out of the courtroom before anyone else.

Robbie was taken back to his cell, and that afternoon, he was transferred to the Ohio Penitentiary in Columbus, where he was immediately placed on death row. He would stay there until all his appeals had been heard … and either he was released or executed.

Everything seemed to have happened so fast. When he finally did have time to catch his breath, he realized what had happened. All he could think of was that his father hadn't bought the judge.

So how will my father save me? Robbie thought. *What's he gonna do now? Maybe I should ask to see Kowalski and offer to give my father up for a reduced sentence, or is it too late for that?* Robbie thought. In any case, he knew that all he could do now was to simply wait and see what happened. He knew that they wouldn't execute him right away because of the mandatory appeal ruling—he'd learned from the other prisoners that a death sentence was automatically appealed, no matter what.

Robbie was thinking about his future ... or if there even was a future for him. With that thought in mind, he went over to his toilet and threw up.

NINETEEN: *A time to weep … a time to mourn …*
—Ecclesiastes 3:4

"So they convicted the Wicken kid after all," Clarice said. "I guess this whole idea of revenge came together. I just find it hard to believe that some kid our age would kill someone he doesn't know for revenge."

"It wasn't unheard of in biblical times," Doc Coulson said. "But I tend to agree with you, Clarice. I feel somewhat responsible for sending Detective Kowalski down that path. I think there is more to the story than we know or ever will know, don't you agree?"

"Yes," Ben said, "especially since Marty called me and asked what a dybbuk was. He said something to the effect that Professor Shemansky believed Professor Wickler's dybbuk took over Robin. I just never put it all together, but it seemed that Professor Shemansky agreed with Marty about the revenge motive."

"If my recollection serves me well," Doc Coulson said, "during one of my many conversations with Professor Shemansky, he told me, almost jokingly, that his success was attributed to his being taken over by a dybbuk." She paused in thought and then continued. "So many times in history people in power assumed certain mythological significance to natural events—like comets and eclipses—and they've made such tragic decisions based on their false assumptions. Myths about dybbuks and spirits have always been believed to have great influence on the living. I can see why that particular myth would be so powerful, even today, to a great scientist like Simon Shemansky."

It was then that the three of them realized that the revenge motive was totally contrived.

After awhile, Clarice said, "Did you know that my grandfather kept referring to Professor Shemansky's son, Joe, as his son? What do you think that was all about?"

"That's interesting, Clarice," Doc Coulson said. "From everything you've told us about your grandfather, he's not easily confused, even though he's in his nineties. If he repeated it more than once, then it was no slip of the tongue. He meant it. Didn't the Silvers and Shemanskys live together for a while?"

"That's right," Clarice said. "It was just last month I learned that my mom was around one when they moved into the house, but she still remembers a lot about what happened there. I asked her to tell me what she remembered about living with the Shemanskys. She told me she was eight years old when the Shemanskys left Poland seven years later."

Clarice paused to gather her thoughts and then went on. "She told me how Irene, Professor Shemansky's wife, was so thrilled when Joey was born. She remembered it even though she was only three years old. Until then, my mother said, she was the youngest in the house, and she got all the attention, but when Joey came, he got all the attention … and she was jealous. She said she still feels cheated that Joey became her father's favorite, even if he was Simon's son." Clarice was smiling about that remembrance.

"Well, I'm no mind reader," Doc Coulson said, "but my sense of history and what was going on in Europe in the so-called 'gay nineties' would have me believe that your grandfather and Irene had an affair, and it wouldn't surprise me if Joseph Shemansky should have been Joseph Silver."

"*You think?*" Clarice said incredulously.

"You're an adult now, Clarice. I know it's hard to believe that your ninety-year-old grandfather was a sexually active human being, but in all likelihood, he was."

They were all quiet for a while, thinking about all the consequences of their doubt about who Joe's father was, when it finally hit them: even if revenge was the Wicken family's motive, then Robin Wicken killed the wrong person. He wasn't Shemansky's blood-related grandson.

It was getting late, and Doc Coulson had other things to attend to. But there was little doubt that the conviction of Robin Wicken, based on the motive of revenge, was all wrong. The question in their minds, of course, was whether an innocent man was convicted. They would have to wait and see. Maybe it was time to confront Martin Kowalski and ask him what was going on, and why he was so sure that revenge was indeed the motive in the Shemansky murder case.

* * *

In late August, sometime after the end of the summer semester, the Ann Arbor team got to see Marty. Fortunately, Clarice and Ben were staying in Ann Arbor that summer, and Doc Coulson was always there for the summer classes she taught.

Marty walked into her office in the old observatory building, thinking how grand it must be to have an office in such a uniquely beautiful spot on an out-of-the-way hill in Ann Arbor. Clarice and Ben had already arrived, and they were sitting around one of the tables that Doc Coulson had cleared off for the meeting.

Marty joined them at the table saying, "Hello, everybody. I'm sorry I've kept you so long in the dark about some of the events that led up to the trial, but I'm sure you'll be able to understand my reasoning."

"Maybe we should have contacted you earlier," Ben said, "because we feel that there's a chance that you convicted the wrong guy. We think the motive you accused Robbie of was not solid and—"

Marty interrupted. "Ben, you're right about the motive being weak. I, for one, stopped believing in that motive after talking with Robin Wicken. I had to follow through with it since Professor Shemansky strongly felt revenge was the motive, but that was just one reason. After Robin's confession, I thoroughly investigated his story about Ed's death being caused by a messed-up marijuana deal."

"C'mon!" Clarice said. "Ed hadn't used any pot since high school. I can attest to that because we talked about it. Why would he want any drugs now?" she questioned.

"We knew that Ed experimented with marijuana—like a lot of affluent kids of his age—and that he hadn't used drugs in a long time," Marty told her. "But it's not unusual for kids to begin experimenting again after they enter college, especially if the drugs are easy to get. But the drug issue isn't what changed my mind about the revenge motive.

"There's something called the felony murder rule that could have made Robin guilty of murder if Ed's death occurred during an attempted felony. Especially if Ed was just a bystander and didn't know that Robin was getting drugs. Ed was dead because of a massive heart attack. Robin, thinking he murdered Ed, compounded the situation by trying to hide all the evidence, concealing his car and changing his name. I could have just as easily made a case for felony murder, and the prosecution would have gone with it."

"Then why didn't you?" Doc Coulson asked. "What was so important about the revenge motive that caused you to go with that, especially if you didn't believe it? And what about the *vav*? How do you explain that?"

"It's a little more complicated than that," Marty began. "What you didn't know before is that Robin's father is a member of an organized crime syndicate. We feel that even though he abandoned Robin as an infant, he was in some way involved in the sordid affair. Either he pushed Robin to kill Ed, or get Ed to go dirty ... or he was involved in trying to cover it up after the fact. We don't know. But we do know—I guess I should say *strongly suspect*—that Robin's dad visited with him shortly before the murder. After the murder, he helped Robin hide his identity and got him a job at his old place of employment." Marty paused to let them take it all in. "As for the *vav*, I believe Robin when he said that Ed hit his head on the metal rack. The mark was formed postmortem—after death—and could easily have been the result of a fall onto something hard after he died."

"When you say 'get Ed to go dirty,' what does that mean?" Clarice asked.

"It means he could have wanted Ed to sell drugs here at Michigan, or for Ed to get involved in a point-shaving scheme with the football team," Marty said. "We know that last one was highly improbable, but you never really know what's happening with those wise guys. We don't think that Robin was capable of murdering for revenge. He might be capable of attempting to scare Ed, and maybe that's what led to the heart attack, or he actually tried to sell Ed some dope. Either way, Robin was involved in a felony murder. We really wanted Robin's dad, but that would be hard to do. He's a seasoned criminal with access to a lot of money and slick lawyers. He also has many years of experience dealing with the system."

"So why don't you arrest him and let Robin off the hook?" Ben suggested. "It seems that would be the only reasonable thing to do."

"We have no evidence of any kind to arrest Robin's father—Stanislaw Wicken. If we did arrest him, his lawyers would have him on the street and a hassling injunction against us in no time flat. On the other hand, if Robin would give him up, then that would at least allow us to get a search warrant so we could find out more about Robin's father."

They talked about how Marty thought the sentence seemed unduly excessive, and that a felony murder conviction might have given Robin a less severe penalty, but that was up to the prosecutor and the judge; and no matter what, Marty would have little or no impact on the sentence. He said the worst thing about it all was that if Robin did give his father up, he would probably be murdered in prison. Marty explained how overcrowded the penitentiary was now, and that it would be easy for a guy like Stan Wicken to have another prisoner killed—even his own son.

"What surprises me," Doc Coulson said, "is that so much of what you just said never came out at the trial—the autopsy, the disposal of his car with evidence in it. Didn't the young man have counsel?"

"We think his court-appointed counsel was either incompetent or bought off by someone to do a generally legal but terrible job of defense. But I should tell you that the judge overseeing the trial was somehow given the job at literally the last minute. And that particular judge was thought to have been—again, without any proof—in the pocket of the mob. I guess I'm saying that poor Robin was doomed either way."

They were quiet for a while, and then Clarice told Marty about their conclusion that Joey was really Seymour Silver's son, as Professor Silver kept saying, and not Simon Shemansky's son. That meant that Ed was not Shemansky's grandson by blood, and if they murdered him for revenge, then they got the wrong guy.

"I didn't know that," Marty said. "But if you figured that out, then it wouldn't have been too hard for Stan Wicken's organization, with all their money and power, to have known it as well. If they did know that, it would just be another way for them to try to make Ed go dirty by blackmailing him about his family. That further bolsters my argument as to why we have to get Stan Wicken." Marty's eyes narrowed, and he gritted his teeth when he said that.

In the end, they all had to agree that Robin Wicken was also a victim in this thing. He was a born loser and didn't have much of a chance of making a go at life. Worse yet, the father who'd abandoned him once before was not only abandoning him again, but he was having him executed, and having the State of Ohio do it for him.

They broke up the meeting late in the afternoon, and Doc Coulson put the whole thing in perspective when she quoted from Shakespeare: "Lord, what fools these mortals be!"

* * *

In order to satisfy their natural science requirement, Clarice and Ben took the introductory astronomy sequence from Doc Coulson in 1954–1955. It was also in that summer of 1955 that Ben and Clarice got together as a couple. Their student-tutor relationship was definitely ending, and they were becoming more like partners in their learning and growing-up process. And love bloomed in that process. At first, it seemed a little awkward as they cuddled up and started making out. Clarice felt like she was cheating on Ed, in some strange way, and Ben felt that he was disrespecting their cousin's memory. But they got over it by talking it through, and once they overcame their mixed emotions, their discovering each other physically got easier and most enjoyable.

"You know, Clarice, I never thought this would happen in my wildest dreams, but I do love you and want to be with you forever," Ben told her.

"I can't think of anyone else I would want to spend my life with either," Clarice responded. So, for all practical purposes, they were engaged, even though neither of them had mentioned marriage … yet.

Ben never got enough of Doc Coulson's teaching style. In the fall of '55 Ben signed up for Doc Coulson's astronomy history course, which was listed as a science class, but everyone who took it knew that it was about the people who made the discoveries and what they were like, and not necessarily about their science. Doc Coulson started with the earliest astronomers, like the ancient Egyptians who named many of the stars. She lectured on Ptolemy, the Egyptian scholar who was thought to be a Greek because he published his works in Greek.

Her favorite story was about Tycho Brahe, a Danish nobleman who did much of his work with Johannes Kepler, a German, at Charles University in Prague, the same university that Szymon Szymanski had attended. It seemed Tycho was an excellent observer of the stars and kept meticulous records, but he, like Doc Coulson, was more interested in the romance of the stars than their science. He had a bawdy reputation ... and supposedly a very hot temper. It's recorded that he got into a duel with another nobleman, and he had a portion of his nose chopped off. Being wealthy and proud of his dueling skills, he simply had another nose made, which he pasted on his face. His artificial nose was not made to look anything like a real nose; it was fabricated like fine jewelry from gold and silver. He carried around a small container of paste, which he frequently applied to keep his obvious metal implant attached squarely on his face.

Doc Coulson relished telling her students about Tycho and his famous nose. She went on to explain that Kepler had used Tycho's observations to develop his theory of planetary motion. Had Tycho's records not been so accurate and complete, Kepler would never have gotten the elliptical orbits that changed astronomical history. But more important to Doc Coulson was why the duel was fought.

"It's not recorded, but some historians say that the duel was inspired by a difference of scientific opinion," she pointed out, "but other historians claim that the duel was over a girl! Now what do you suppose it was?"

"It was definitely over a woman—no man would lose his nose or any other part of his body over some boring science thing," a male student pointed out.

This made Doc Coulson go into her girlie mode, blushing and giggling and saying, "Let's stick to the subject here—we're talking about celestial mechanics and planetary observations."

"You asked us what we thought about Tycho's nose, not his astrological observations, and that's what I was telling you," the student said, wanting to keep the discussion alive.

"That would be astronomical observations, not astrological—he didn't do astrology, although many thought of him as an astrologer because he did dabble in the field," Doc Coulson said.

That was all it took to set the students off. All kinds of raucous comments—such as "But he did 'dabble' with the girls, didn't he?"—flew amid the laughter. Doc Coulson, as always, kept her good nature, but she did not let the situation get out of hand, even if she was laughing along with the students. And after a suitable period, she let the topic die, took over the class again, and continued on with Galileo and Kepler.

When she mentioned Kepler, Professor Szymon Szymanski came into Doc Coulson's mind. She thought about how he came up with the currently accepted theory of cosmic dynamics, which was an order of magnitude higher in complexity when compared to what Tycho Brahe and Johannes Kepler worked on. The difference between Brahe and Szymanski was that Szymanski was certain he was helping mankind with his scientific observations, whereas Brahe knew leaf chasing when he saw it. Doc Coulson thought, *Tycho may have lost his nose to chasing leaves of one form or another, but Szymanski lost his family chasing leaves of another form—so who was better off?*

* * *

Just a few days after the lecture about Tycho, Doc Coulson came into class. Visibly distraught, she had tears in her eyes when she said to her class, "They're going to tear down the observatory."

The university had a 12 5/8-inch refracting telescope in an old observatory on the hill where the women's dormitories were built. The observatory and the telescope were used mostly for teaching at that point, not for scientific research, since the university had more modern telescopes, both optical and radio, situated around the world for research purposes. "They claim it's too old and of no scientific use," Doc Coulson continued, tears streaming down her face. "They said it would be better for me. I wouldn't have to walk all that way to my office. I don't mind the walk. I like having my office in the observatory building with that telescope's giant pier supporting my office and my work, as well as keeping the telescope stable." She wiped her eyes with a Kleenex, took a couple of deep breaths, and, completely unashamed of having cried in front of her class, started the day's discussion.

The entire class was visibly shaken, and all the students felt a great sadness for Doc Coulson. They didn't know at the time—and most never would know—what other event happened that day to move Professor Coulson so deeply.

Professor Coulson had just found out that Mr. Robin Wicken had his mandatory appeal adjudicated the previous day, and he lost that appeal on all counts. Not only was Doc Coulson losing the institution of her old office, but she was also losing her strong belief in the ability of society to arrive at rational decisions in times when they really counted.

Clarice and Ben cried too when they read the newspaper article about Robbie's appeal being denied. They hugged each other for a long time that afternoon, and as sad as Ben was, he couldn't help but think of how marvelous it felt hugging Clarice like that. That's when they both realized that maybe it was also *bashert* that the two of them should be getting together officially. And so they became formally engaged.

* * *

Ben and Clarice graduated a semester early by going to summer school over the following two summers. They thought about Ed Shemansky and Robin Wicken every day, although they didn't always talk about it. When Ben went on to graduate school to start work on his teaching certificate in February of 1958, he had the opportunity to become reacquainted with Doc Coulson. Ben was working as a graduate assistant on a research project in the Radar Astronomy lab, one of the university's many research laboratories. The major work they were doing, and the reason Ben was hired, was in anticipation of future space flights. The Russian space module Sputnik had already been launched in October 1957, so space travel was now a reality as opposed to a theory.

Ben was working with a retired Air Force colonel who had an engineering background but was lacking knowledge about astronomy. Ben suggested that they visit with Doc Coulson and pose their questions to her.

When they walked into her new office in the new Physics and Astronomy Building (she had been recently moved out of the observatory), she was sitting there with her green eyeshade visor on—old term projects, papers, memorabilia, and astronomical *tchachkes* piled everywhere one could imagine.

Ben briefly explained their project of trying to use reflected radar signal information to determine the material makeup of the moon's surface. When it seemed they had gotten all they needed, Ben casually asked her about his clepsydra—his history course project—which he'd noticed still sitting on her table. He asked her if she enjoyed using it. *Dumb me!* Ben thought, when almost immediately, she went into a harangue on how she hadn't been able to get it to work properly for almost four years.

"That's interesting," Ben said. "I remember it working fine when I turned it in—I'll come back and adjust it for you, okay?" Ben caught her perceptive smile out of the corner of his eye, for she knew well that the damn thing never did work properly.

About a month after his visit with Doc Coulson, Ben was reading the *Detroit Free Press*, when, on page three, he spotted a small article with the headline OHIO MAN EXECUTED FOR MURDER OF MICHIGAN MAN. He continued reading:

> *On Tuesday, April 8, 1958, twenty-three year old Robin Wicken was executed in the Ohio Penitentiary in Columbus, Ohio, for the murder of Mr. Edward Shemansky, a University of Michigan student, on November 20, 1954.*

The article related the many appeals and requests for clemency on the part of a local rabbi and other anti-death penalty advocates, but all to no avail. There were no family members at the execution, and the Ohio State University Medical School took his body for educational purposes, as the deceased had requested. Ben called Clarice and told her, and then the two of them cried together.

Robbie's execution was the third and final murder of this story. In all three cases, it was only Clarice, Doc Coulson, and Ben who pointed out that "You shall not murder" was still one of God's commandments.

They also agreed that maybe it was that sixth commandment that had given rise to Robin's murder by the state. Maybe some members of our society thought they were unerringly capable of carrying out God's judgment that "life shall go for life."

EPILOGUE: *Sunny*

Ben Bernstein retired after a thirty-five-year career of teaching high school science and math. His wife, Clarice, also finished her career as a special education teacher. When their two kids were growing up, they'd had a dog that they named Sunny because of his sunny disposition. He was all white with just a touch of apricot on his ears—a toy poodle. Sunny never chased leaves like Ben's old dog, Stormy, but he did chase squirrels, birds, butterflies, and anything else that moved quickly on the ground or flew in the air. Ben said that he did look important when he was doing his job, even though, unlike Stormy, Sunny never caught anything. Ben also wondered if Sunny thought chasing things was doing a real job like leaf chasing. Somehow Ben didn't think so, but he was not sure why.

* * *

Over the many years that passed since Robin's execution, Ben and Clarice frequently wondered about the religious meanings of the three murders in the Shemansky and Wicken families. Clarice had continued her research on Jewish mysticism and delved deeply into the Shemansky and Wickler family histories. Her research led her to question whether any of the three murders were acceptable killings under Judeo-Christian laws. And was it possible that purposely killing somebody, whether committed by an individual or the state, was not murder? She never did actually come up with a definitive answer to those questions, even in light of all the information she was subsequently able to gather. She knew that none of the three deaths were murders in the way one normally thinks of murder. Reuben Wickler's was definitely an accident, even if there was negligence involved; Ed Shemansky's was of natural causes, even though the accused perpetrator was attempting to commit a felony at the time; and Robin's was legally carried out by the government, even if the legal circumstances were murky. Yet all three deaths were judged to be murders by legitimate representatives of their respective societies.

Ben had read somewhere that the philosophers tell us that the mysticism surrounding death is all part of every society's folklore. They also tell us that the myths about what happens to our souls after we die are a necessary part of life if we are ever to maintain our sanity in this strange and inexplicable world we live in. To Ben, it seemed that only deities and other such mythological beings were able to offer any righteousness out of all the irrationally bad things that happened to so many blameless people in this world. And as for "You shall not murder," Ben would say, "I still believe with all my heart that that commandment is God given." Ben once told Clarice, "If ever, by some mystifying circumstance, I did *murder* someone and got away with it, I know I would somehow be punished for the violence. Maybe not on me personally, but probably on our kids or our grandkids, just like with Szymon Szymanski."

Ben theorized that maybe that's why "You shall not murder" is way down at number six on the list of the Ten Commandments. Maybe God knows that murder and killing are all part of the God/human condition since God himself has told us many times in the Bible to murder—sometimes for the silliest of reasons. Maybe murder is not such a biggie. Perhaps it's not a bad sin, like placing other gods before God, but a second-tier infraction—maybe just a few minutes in the penalty box of eternity. Or maybe God realizes how ambiguous human interactions can become, so that humans are not able to judge correctly if a murder was actually committed. Maybe it's best just to leave it for God to decide at some future time. And maybe, just maybe, the Kabbalists are right in saying that understanding God is not possible for us mortals. After all, God is infinite, while we here on earth are finite. In any case, Ben reasoned, trying to speculate on what God thinks about us murdering one another makes almost as much sense as chasing leaves.

* * *

Clarice and Ben frequently looked back with great fondness on their many conversations with Doc Coulson. Those same conversations would also tell them what was truly important in this world, and what stuff was probably leaf chasing—just as Ben's dog Stormy had taught him about leaf chasing so many years earlier.

It would appear that at one time in her life, Doc Coulson stopped concerning herself, at least full-time, with demanding scientific analyses. She realized that what she—and maybe even other scientists—was doing was like Stormy chasing leaves. When she was doing her early spectroscopic analyses of the stars, she was certain in the knowledge that this was what she was meant to do, because it was vital for mankind to know all these facts and theories on the structure of the stars. However, in the final analysis, she saw that many of her colleagues failed to recognize something even more vital—that the magnificence, vastness, and beauty of celestial objects make our little world look so insignificant, which, in the grand scheme of things, we probably are.

So she stopped chasing the leaves and chewing them up into small bits for further study; she instead began looking at them for their uniqueness and infinitely wonderful presence. That's what she decided was important. And as for doing anything else with the leaves, well, that would be for others. She could simply smile and say, "Look at them talking about cosmology—isn't that cute?"

LaVergne, TN USA
27 January 2010
171168LV00005B/1/P